The *Secrets* of the
Mahjong Club

A NOVEL

J. Lawrence

This is a work of fiction. Names, places, characters and incidents are either the product of the author's imagination or are used fictitiously, and any resemblance to actual persons, living or dead, events or locales is entirely coincidental.

Though *The Secrets of the Mahjong Club* is a work of fiction and the characters are imaginary, the New York Police Department does have a 23rd Precinct, and staffed with the finest police officers to be found anywhere.

Derek Jeter is arguably the best shortstop to every play baseball, although that is painful for me to admit as I am a diehard Boston Red Sox fan and Mr. Jeter plays for the NY Yankees.

Dear Readers!

It is with great pleasure that I introduce to you Catherine, Holly, Anna, Priscilla, Lori and Susan.

These unique women can be found in almost any major metropolitan area or small tightly knit community.

You may recognize these remarkable women as your friends, neighbors and/or relatives. They are mature, multifaceted survivors who live life fearlessly. The women come in all shapes and sizes, but share a commonality in their vitality and zest for life.

As you become acquainted with these characters you will be amazed, perhaps even shocked, by the details of their private stories.

This book is dedicated to all those marvelous women and to the new adventures that they are about to embark upon.

J. Lawrence

Catherine

Catherine looked out onto Central Park from the balcony of her luxury Fifth Avenue apartment. Being on the fifteenth floor, she had a commanding view of both the park and the New York skyline.

As she looked down at the park, she noticed a white horse drawn carriage pull up to the curb just outside the Plaza Hotel. The driver was wearing a black top hat and had adorned the carriage with a garland of flowers. The smiling couple climbed aboard and cuddled in the back seat covering themselves with a well worn green blanket. There was a chill in the late September air, but it wasn't cold enough to warrant a blanket. Rarely did native New Yorkers opt for a hansom cab ride, so she was certain that they were tourists. She guessed that the couple wanted the complete experience.

Beyond the carriage, Central Park stretched out in hues of rich red and burnished orange. It was a striking change from the previous seasons. Throughout the spring and summer, the park looked like a sea of green from her apartment. She adored the change of seasons and Mother Nature's varying color palette.

As she leaned over the railing on her balcony, she could see people riding their bikes on the meandering trails that zigzagged through the park. On the sidewalk local artists sold their paintings alongside the portrait artists. A policeman, decked in blue, looked as if he was whistling a tune as he strolled along his beat. Glancing to her left, she could see two young boys flying their kites that twisted and turned in the autumn breeze.

Fall was always Catherine's favorite time of year in New York. The days were still warm, yet the nights cooled down enough for her to open her windows and snuggle under her puffy quilt. In her opinion, it was the perfect time of year to go for long walks, stop at the Plaza for high tea, hijack a park bench to read a book, or merely engage in some serious people watching. Sometimes she would walk for blocks, window shopping as she went. As a confirmed "fashionista" she could spend hours going from one window display to the next.

With the arrival of the cooler weather, street vendors sold hot, roasted chestnuts in small white paper bags. She found it difficult to resist the aroma of the roasting chestnuts and often bought a bag even when she wasn't hungry. Cat wasn't the only one who found the chestnut carts alluring. They seemed to be a favorite treat with children, as well. It delighted her to watch the children's faces as they peeled off the cracked brown shell, to get at the sweet golden nut beneath.

Catherine shuddered, not from the cold, but at the thought of moving away from her beloved New York. She had lived here almost ten years, all of it in this very same apartment.

She had furnished it mainly with English antiques from her soon-to-be ex-husband's vintage furniture store. She appreciated the culture of the city, and always took advantage of the museums, art galleries and theatre productions. She enjoyed the corner hot dog stands as much as she liked fine dining. She was one of the first of her friends to try every new ethnic restaurant that sprung up throughout the city. She relished hearing the foreign languages spoken by the eclectic populace of the city.

Almost everyone she knew was surprised to learn that Catherine was an avid sports fan. She would always have a place in her heart for the Cleveland Indians, but c'mon? The Yankees? She had seen Derek Jeter in Bloomingdales one Saturday afternoon. She actually got up the nerve to approach him to say "Hi". He responded with a "Hi" back and she wasn't sure, but she thought she just floated home.

It made her sad to think that it was easier to divorce her husband than to leave this apartment and the city that had become her home.

She moved to New York from Ohio to accept a position as Director of North American Sales for Gucci. Catherine's parents still lived in Ohio. Her father was a retired police detective, who had called it quits after thirty years on the police force. He took a bullet in his leg responding to a bank robbery, and now taught Criminal Justice at the local junior college. Her mother had grown up on dairy farm outside the city of Cleveland. She was nineteen when she married Catherine's father and had bypassed college to become a homemaker. When she wasn't cooking dinner for her family, or baking her legendary deep dish apple pies, she volunteered at the local library.

Catherine had two older brothers, John and Matthew. They were classic mid-western guys, big and brawny. They both played on the offensive line for the varsity foot ball team, and let everyone know that Catherine was their baby sister. It was no secret that her brothers made it difficult for anyone who wanted to date her. While they adored their baby sister, and protected her from every real or perceived danger, they tussled with her at every opportunity.

When she moved to the city, Catherine's family and friends warned her about the surly nature of New Yorkers and the burgeoning crime problem, but she found neither to be true. In her experience, New Yorkers were friendlier than people in Cleveland. She felt safe traveling the city even at night, but of course, she was a sensible woman. Cleveland was no doubt a fine city, and it would always have a special place in her heart, but it couldn't compete with the glitz and excitement of New York. And the food! At first, Catherine couldn't believe the endless choices, and that most eateries were open nearly around the clock.

Catherine turned from the balcony and made her way to the kitchen. She brewed a strong cup of black coffee not because she was chilly, but felt she needed to fortify herself when she left her set of keys on the counter for Jack and finally left the condo for the last time. She added a healthy shot of anisette, a taste she had acquired while working in Italy.

Jack was her husband. A transplanted British man who Catherine had met while shopping for antiques in SoHo. He owned a small shop and had a wonderful eclectic arrangement of heavy, solid walnut desks, period pieces and paintings. He had the usual hunting scenes, which she would have expected, but also some unusual oils by lesser known artists. She had gone to Jack's shop intent on purchasing a painting for her new apartment. One particular piece had caught her eye. It was a colorful scene of gardens bursting with carrots, celery and lettuce, surrounded by a neat, trim white picket fence, presumably to keep the rabbits out, with mists rising from mossy, green fields. In the background turbaned women were working in their gardens, their faces lined from the sun, with hands calloused and soiled from physical labor. The style was reminiscent of the Dutch masters. Her favorite was Johannes Vermeer, and she was looking for something similar to his "Girl with a Pearl Earring." As she browsed through the shop, she decided that Jack charged too much for his pieces, but she was feeling self-indulgent. Besides, she had a wonderful new job, with an ample salary and an apartment with a doorman. She took out her credit card and Jack rang up her purchase.

While Jack wrapped her painting, she looked at him appraisingly. He was slight of build in sharp contrast to her Dad and brothers. He had an unruly shock of auburn hair, which matched his tweed sports coat, complete with brown leather elbow patches. He was tall, but not overly so. He spoke with a refined British accent, which Catherine found endearing. But what Catherine noticed the most were his piercing, green eyes, emerald really. She found them even more enchanting than the blue eyes which ran in her family. He looked up and caught her staring at him and smiled.

Their romance started with a dinner invitation. She remembered exactly what he said all those years ago.

"You know, if you're new here, perhaps you would let me take you to dinner this Saturday evening and show you the neighborhood."

Looking back over the past ten years, Catherine thought that accepting his invitation was the dumbest thing she had ever done.

Jack took her to *Roberto's*, a trendy Italian bistro in the Village. While Catherine knew virtually no one in the city, except for her doorman, Jack seemed to know everyone.

Giacamo, the maitre-d', greeted Jack warmly, holding both of his hands adding "Where have you been my friend? Roberto's been asking for you". Looking to Catherine, he responded with a warm, genuine smile, "Welcome to

Roberto's. We have arranged a special table for you this evening."

As he led them across the room, Jack stopped often to either shake hands with people seated at their tables, or waved across the room at others. Giacamo guided them to a quiet table set in an alcove against the wall with an elevated view of the restaurant. He removed the *"Reserved"* placard and slid the table over so that Catherine could slide in easily. Before he left, he lit the candle in the small crystal lamp that sat in the middle of the table, and told them to enjoy their meal. As soon as they were seated, a waiter appeared with a bottle of red wine. "Compliments of Roberto, sir". He uncorked the wine and poured a small amount in Jack's glass for his approval. "Excellent!" Jack responded." So the waiter filled the two glasses, with just the right amount to allow the rich bouquet to breath.

"It seems you know everyone here" Catherine said looking at him over her wine glass. The red wine was indeed good. She didn't know a great deal about wine, as beer was the drink of choice in her house, but this red was smooth, with no bitter aftertaste.

"Ah, it's just that I've becoming here for years. I was one of Roberto's regulars when he was just starting out, and it was a good place for me to network. I had just opened my antique store, and really needed to drum up some business. The rent in that place isn't cheap, and I didn't have the money I should have had to even open it".

"It's truly a lovely store, and you seem to have a knack for choosing unique pieces."

"Well thank you" he said as he reached over and kissed her hand lightly. Catherine could feel the blush flow warm into her cheeks.

The rest of dinner seemed to drift by. Roberto sent over dish after dish, each one better than the last. While they ate, Jack asked Catherine everything about her life. How did she decide to move to New York? The new job. The new apartment. Her family. The men in her life. Catherine, normally reserved, couldn't help but open up looking into his inquisitive emerald eyes. No doubt the wine helped loosen her up. She couldn't remember any man being so interesting or so interested in her, except of course to get her in the sack. There were plenty of them. But Jack seemed different.

After the dinner plates were cleared, Roberto came to their table carrying a silver platter. He set the platter down and gave them each a tiny white porcelain cup filled with steaming black espresso. Despite their protests he presented two large cannolis dusted with confectionary sugar and cocoa powder. The shells were golden brown, and overflowed with sweet ricotta cheese. "I made the cannolis myself. I was a baker in Roma before I came to America".

"Then I cannot refuse" Catherine said while dipping her tiny fork into the crusty shell and placing a small piece in her mouth. "Heavenly! I've never had better!"

"Grazie. You honor me. Now please enjoy the rest of your meal and if need anything else, you only need to ask." Catherine suddenly smiled at the thought of her brothers. Their idea of dining out was to go to *Mack's All-You-Can Eat* dinner buffet, and gorge themselves on fried chicken, ham, mashed potatoes and rolls for $10.99. As an added bonus, dessert and drinks were included. And here she was in the big city, with a charming (and sexy?) man in the fabled Village, dining on Italian delicacies.

Jack finally asked the waiter to bring the bill, explaining to Catherine that at *Roberto's*, as in Italy, at least at the non-tourist restaurants, the waiter would never bring the check unless it was requested. He pulled out a silver money clip and peeled off two crisp one-hundred dollar bills. She couldn't help but think that her father and brothers always kept their money in old, brown leather wallets. Jack didn't need change, and the waiter thanked him profusely for the generous tip.

He hailed a cab and gave the directions to her apartment on Fifth Ave. It had started to drizzle when they arrived at her place. The doorman ("I have a doorman!" she thought) came to the cab and opened the door. They both slid out and walked into her lobby. The doorman discretely turned his back, facing the street. Not knowing what to expect, she thanked Jack for the most wonderful night, and the delicious dinner. He reached over and taking her right hand, he brought it to his lips and once again, gave it a chaste kiss. This was definitely not was she was expecting! She assumed he would want to come up to her apartment (that wasn't going to happen), or at least, give her a kiss on the lips.

He asked to see her again, and she said yes. They made a date for the next Saturday night. She went up to her apartment, and didn't even bother to check her mail voice messages. She stripped off her clothes and without even taking the time to hang them up, climbed into her bed. She didn't want any distractions while she re-played the evening with Jack in her mind. She smiled as she drifted off to sleep wondering what it would be like to kiss him.

The sound of a jet passing overhead jolted Catherine out of her reverie. She raised the cup of anisette sweetened coffee to her mouth and gingerly took a sip. Normally she would have an almond biscotti to go along with her coffee, but her stomach was in knots and she wasn't in the mood to eat.

She thought back about her whirlwind romance with Jack. It was too fast she knew now. As they say, "hindsight is twenty-twenty." He moved in with her, a month after they started dating. She didn't dare tell her parents. She loved him, didn't she, he'd ask. They were meant to be together, weren't they? They would save money by living together, although with a generous salary, money wasn't an issue for her. So she ignored her nagging doubts, as women often do with men, and acquiesced. He continued to sell antiques from his shop.

He proposed three months after he moved in with her. It wasn't the kind of proposal she had fantasized about as a little girl. He didn't get down on one knee exclaiming his undying love and passion for her, but instead said it made sense for them to get married. That way he could be included on her health plan. To make matters even less romantic, they had been riding on a bus going by a Staples Office when he suggested it. It seemed more like a business proposition than a marriage proposal.

She insisted that he call her father and ask for her hand, and strongly advised him to take a different approach than just wanting to be on her health plan. Jack was reluctant to do so. Although he had never met her father, he was actually afraid of him based on Cat's description. In the end, he relented and made the call.

Jack had wanted to just go to the court house to get married, but she told him that that would break her mother's heart. To appease her parents, they had a small wedding with family and close friends at an inn in Cleveland. Jack's parents were deceased, and his maternal aunt Mildred, was the only one who could make it from across the pond. Catherine's two brothers attended, looking uncomfortable in their seldom worn suits. Her friends from high school and college also came. Catherine was afraid that when Jack found out one of the male guests was her former boyfriend, he would blow up and ruin the wedding. A few whispered words and a strong grip on Jack's elbow from one of her brothers, made him re-think any outburst.

Catherine wanted to honeymoon in Tuscany, but Jack said he couldn't take the time off, so they settled for three days in the Adirondacks. Catherine noticed immediately that the man who wooed her so passionately, changed into a man with a much cooler demeanor. She expected to spend more time in bed with her new husband, but Jack was more interested in visiting the local antique stores.

Initially they were happy. She had a demanding job and traveled to Italy often, while he expanded his antique store, buying more furniture and paintings with their joint money. They would always spend Sunday mornings in bed, reading the Times and eating lox and bagels from Zabar's. They would make love, and while it was nice, he appeared less and less interested in it. He didn't like it when she would suggest that they make love, so she learned just to wait for him to be in the mood. One night they went to a party where they both had too much to drink. When they got home she was feeling dizzy with desire. As they sat on the sofa together she reached over and placed her hand on him. He was instantly hard. She unzipped his pants and hiked up her skirt. He was shocked to see that she was wearing sheer, crotchless panties. Contemplating the rush of ecstasy, she mounted him from the top. She was expecting a mind-blowing, bed rattling orgasm, but was sorely disappointed. In the morning, he was unusually quiet, and when she asked him what was wrong, he replied that she "really helped herself" the previous evening. She never initiated sex again.

When they did have sex, maybe once a month, it was too quick, with not enough foreplay to satisfy her. She dismissed it thinking that the honeymoon phase of their relationship was over and this was the reality of married life. She wanted to experiment and had even bought a book on the Art of the Kama Sutra. She felt guilty about wanting more and found herself having erotic fantasies. He teased her about being a nymphomaniac which didn't help matters. She thought about old boyfriends, and whether or not it would have been the same with them.

One of them, Tommy, was a big (in more ways than one) German boy that played on the football team when she was a cheerleader. He was her first love, and she lost her virginity on the playing fields after a party when their team won the Regional Championship. She had just turned sixteen. It was the first time she ever saw an erect dick (besides the peeking at her brothers), and remembered being amazed at the one-eyed monster, as Tommy liked to call it. She was mesmerized by his penis. The feel of it in her hand, the way it tilted to the right. The texture of his balls. She helped Tommy put on a condom, and laid down on the grass, wet with evening dew, as he mounted her and put it in. She gasped as he entered her, but then fell into a smooth rhythm as his penis glided against every steaming inch of her vagina. While that was the first time, it certainly was not the last. Tommy could not get enough of her, and she felt the same way about him. They met many times for fast, frenzied sex, usually on the same playing fields.

When the weather was uncooperative for their furtive meetings on the field, the backseat of his Chevy Caprice accommodated them quite nicely. Their relationship, and their sexual interludes, ended when Ohio University recruited him to play half-back for the Buckeyes. There were others, but one thing rang true, you always remember your first. Now she wondered if her Tommy had lost interest in having sex with his wife (if he was married) as her husband had. Somehow, she doubted it.

Catherine looked around her kitchen. A six-burner Viking stove stood across from her, its stainless steel gleaming. An espresso machine from Italy (Jacks' idea, not hers) stood alongside the Cuisanart blender and all the other expensive modern kitchen gadgets Jack felt they just couldn't live without. She found it amusing since Jack couldn't even boil water.

Ultimately it was money, the money she earned that destroyed the marriage. Money meant very little to her. She didn't have it growing up, and didn't let it define her now. She invested in an expensive wardrobe only because of her position at Gucci. The shoes, the handbags, held no more appeal to her than the clothes and boots she wore growing up. What she loved best, was wearing an old pair of jeans and one of Jack's faded blue denim shirts.

Jack was the clothes horse. He never seemed satisfied with what he had. He always needed something new; an Armani leather coat, a Hugo Boss suit, or a pair of Ferragamo shoes. He bought a Jaguar sports car, which they rarely used since they both lived and worked in the city. Catherine didn't care. She shared the money she earned freely. Her salary was almost ten times what he made, and she encouraged him to buy what he wanted. As his business began to flounder, it seemed he wanted more and more and she always said yes to appease him.

The marriage started to disintegrate when he began to resent the fact that her salary was supporting their lifestyle. At a restaurant, he'd quip, "Well I guess I should thank you for this meal". She would tell him repeatedly that as husband and wife the money she earned was their money. . .not just her money. He never refused her gifts, or stopped buying things they didn't need, but neither did it temper his resentment. It only inflamed it. But it got worse and he started drinking. First too much wine at dinner, then he began to drink at home. Not long after that, she dropped into the antique store unannounced and found him asleep at his desk, passed out from overindulging in Pinot Noir.

He became verbally abusive. He never hit her because he knew her brothers would hunt him down and kill him. However, he regularly accused her of infidelity and not loving him. In reality, he was developing a large black hole in his soul that all the love in the world could not fill. He would go from crying and pleading with her not to leave him, to accusing her of having sex with other men. He accused her of sleeping with every man she encountered... her boss, the kid who delivered the groceries, and even Roberto. He was consumed by a jealous rage. He'd called her vile names. He criticized the way she dressed, and insisted on knowing where she had been and with whom she had spoken.

He eventually lost his store due to his drinking problem, and the brusque manner in which he treated his customers. He confined himself to the condo (when the apartments were converted to condos and came up for sale, Catherine bought it), and fell into a deep depression. He refused help, would not consider couples counseling or seeing a doctor for a medical check-up. Catherine finally reached a breaking point and confided in her longtime friend Anna, who advised her to see a lawyer.

Jack had drained her emotionally. The divorce was perfunctory because she no longer cared about him. She did not have a pre-nuptial agreement (she could hear her father saying "I told you so"), and since New York was a joint property state, she was going to take a bath, but she didn't care. She gave up the condo which she so dearly loved, all the expensive appliances she never wanted, the Jag she never drove, and the membership in the country club she never frequented. She didn't even play golf, for God's sake.

The movers packed up her personal belongings this morning and they were on their way to Florida. Catherine rented a house in Greenbrier Golf Estates, primarily because her closest friend Anna lived there. She needed Anna's emotional support in order to start over. She had to get away from Jack and the sad memories of New York.

Gucci gave her six months paid leave. Catherine was very valuable to them in both the way she developed the North American sales market, but also as a cherished colleague. While it was easier to get to Italy from New York, Florida had three major airports, so it would only be a minor inconvenience.

The doorman buzzed her unit and advised her that her car was ready. Looking around the apartment for the last time, Catherine placed her keys in the wicker basket that had held them for the past ten years, and walked out the door.

She was ready to start her new life.

Friday Night/ Anna's House

"Bend your knee to your rightful King or you will feel the steel of my sword upon your neck!"

"Oh for God's sake Freddy put down that umbrella before you break the TV! Honestly, you've reverted to being a child since you began watching *"Game of Thrones!"*

"Ah, I was born in the wrong century M'Lady. I should have been born back then and I would have been a gallant knight, swinging a mighty sword, fighting wars on my trusty white stallion and wooing young maidens".

"Jesus Freddy, you don't even ride a horse, you can't stand the sight of blood, and I doubt you'd win any fair maiden with that belly hanging over your belt."

"Ah you wound me with your sharp tongue woman. Nevertheless, I am bound by honor to protect your maidenhood. And besides, I carry a very large sword down in my pants."

"My maidenhood hasn't been protected for a good many years, and why must you men always brag about your dick size? Now will you please put down the umbrella and go change? We're supposed to be at the Greenbrier Golf Club in a half hour."

Freddy put down the umbrella but not until he took one last thrust into the cushions on the couch, and then padded off to the bedroom to change. Anna looked at him fondly. He was her second husband, and by far the better of the two. Her first husband was a scoundrel who thought fidelity was a mutual fund. She tolerated his indiscretions, even accepted them, until she caught him screwing the babysitter.

Anna had been in New York for a long weekend. She had hired Louise, their usual babysitter, to watch the children while she was away. She flew home a day early since she felt like she was getting the flu. She didn't know if she was more upset that he was screwing an 18 year old, or that he was doing it in their bed. Either way, she walked out carrying the same luggage she had walked in with. That was over eighteen years ago and she never looked back.

Six months later she met Freddy at a party given by a mutual friend. They talked from the moment they were introduced until the party came to a close. They connected instantly. He was handsome and charming, but reserved and not flirtatious. They shared many of the same interests. They both enjoyed cooking elegant meals, reading the latest bestsellers and spending quiet nights at home. Freddy fit her as comfortable as an old pair of slippers. She was no slouch in the kitchen, but when Freddy cooked, it was always something special. He had cooked dinner tonight. Before sitting down to eat he poured them each a glass of Chianti Classico. He began the meal with fresh buffalo mozzarella and Roma tomatoes, sliced and drizzled with extra virgin olive oil imported from Italy and a balsamic reduction from Morocco. He used fresh basil from his herb garden as a garnish. Freddy was from a little town named San Polo Dei Cavalieri in the mountains surrounding Rome, and would only buy the best olive oil from Italy. Andrea Bocelli played softly in the background as they ate. As Anna was finishing the appetizer, Freddy put veal cutlets, pounded and lightly breaded, in a pan with capers and just a pinch of salt and pepper. He topped them off with just a drop of freshly squeezed lemon juice. When the veal was done, he placed it on a bed of angel hair pasta, taking care to spoon some of the gravy over everything.

Anna loved the way he set the dining table. He always used a red and white checkered tablecloth and a charming pair of candlesticks. After they had finished eating, he cleared the dishes, refusing her offer to help. Next, he poured espresso into two handmade delicate porcelain cups they had received as a wedding gift from Freddy's aunt in Italy. Along with the espresso, he served panna cotta with fresh strawberries.

Anna knew how fortunate she was to have Freddy in her life, and she never took him for granted. She believed Freddy felt the same about her. Their mutual admiration and respect was the foundation of their marriage. Anna felt a little guilty about her good fortune as she thought about her friend Catherine. Catherine had called to tell

Anna that she had left Jack. Anna immediately invited Catherine to come to Florida. Catherine accepted the invitation in a New York minute and was already driving down to Florida from New York. Anna never liked Catherine's husband. Jack had always seemed aloof and pretentious. As far Anna was concerned, if Freddy wanted to be a knight, he could run a lance through that asshole if he wanted.

Freddy stepped out of the bedroom wearing a pair of tan khaki slacks and his favorite white polo shirt. Unlike most men who didn't have a lick of fashion sense, Freddy always looked quite polished. "Ok I'm ready" he said. They got into their navy blue Beemer, put the top down, no rain tonight, and drove the whopping two miles to the Greenbrier Country Club. Tonight was Friday night and that meant once they arrived at the Club, Anna went to play Mahjong with the ladies, while Freddy played poker with the guys. Gambling for money was not allowed at the club, but the rule was never enforced. After all, playing for money was what made the games fun, right? They walked into the main lobby and headed to the bar.

The bar was crowded and noisy. It seemed everyone was out celebrating the end of the work week. Anna spied her friends in the corner, including that birdbrain Ashley, who she could see was filling the air with her endless chatter. Anna headed to over to her friends, but not before giving Freddy a peck on the lips and whispering in his ear "Don't get too tired dear. I have plans for you tonight." Freddy smiled. "Don't worry. I'll be ready for my tiger. See you after the game."

"Hello ladies." Anna said as she walked over and joined her friends.

"Anna! I want you at my table tonight" her friend Susan stately firmly, as she shot a hostile glance toward Ashley. Roger, Ashley's husband, was almost twenty years older than her. He had recently retired from his executive position at Verizon. He was well educated and clearly had been a successful businessman. Too bad he went for tits, (fake tits at that) over brains, Anna thought. Ashley and Roger moved to Florida to escape the harsh winters of Chicago. They joined the club shortly after purchasing their sprawling, 5000 sq. foot house in Greenbrier Gold Estates. Roger was a good golfer, but he was a terrible poker player. So he, and his money, were always welcome at the Friday night poker game. Roger was a regular guy who liked to watch sports and drink beer, so he fit right in with the guys at the club. Not so for Ashley. She pranced around in skimpy shorts and halter tops, and spent most of her time and her husband's money shopping. She was a terrible gossip, name-dropper and social climber. As far as anyone could tell, her only goal in life was to find a rich, older man to marry. She achieved her objective with Roger. Luckily, Ashley had no interest in playing Mahjong, so the ladies didn't have to tell her that she was not welcome to join their group. Ashley preferred to hang out at the bar and flirt with the guys, which was something else that didn't endear her to the ladies.

"Honestly, I don't know why you're all so interested in playing that silly game. I've had so many exciting adventures, usually with men" she winked and said in a low voice so that Roger wouldn't hear her, "that I'm not ready to slow down yet."

"That and the game is too complex for you." Anna retorted, while the other ladies chuckled. Ashley may have been twenty years younger than the rest of them, but looked better only because of the thousands of dollars Roger paid to a plastic surgeon for a tummy tuck, facial lift, and of course, the fake tits. But in the brain department, there wasn't anyone home, and the plastic surgeon couldn't help her with that.

"Yeah yeah." Ashley snickered. "You're a wild bunch" she said over her shoulder as she turned and headed back to the bar.

"I hope she chokes on an olive." Lori said. "And even though I know the Heimlich maneuver I'd be hard pressed to administer it to her."

"Ashley Fake Tits isn't the only woman who has had some adventures with men," Anna said, as the rest of the ladies raised their eyebrows.

"Really Anna? Care to share?" Holly asked.

Out of the whole group, while Susan was firmly anchored as the most timid and meekest, Holly was the polar opposite. She had a mouth on her that would make even the crudest longshoreman wince. She was five foot, eight inches tall, had blondish frosted hair, was very sexual and made no apologies for her behavior. Before retiring she had worked for years in the wholesale plumbing industry, a profession dominated by men. She used to brag with a big smile that she laid more pipe than any five guys.

Holly was in her early sixties. She had married and buried two husbands. She always kidded that the money they left her helped with the grieving process. She was attractive, in a mature way, but vigorously battled the aging process. She swam laps, took Zumba classes, biked and hit the gym every week. She was actively looking for husband Number Three. She tried *Match.com* and *eHarmony* with little success. "The last one they sent over tried to finger-fuck me in my pool. I wanted to tell him shit, I can do that myself. It was his dick I was interested in!"

The problem with most of the men, she complained, was that she was just too hard driving for their taste. That and her vulgar mouth. They were intimidated by her wealth, the car she drove, a bright red Porsche, and the jewelry she wore. Holly said the older guys wanted a younger girl, and the younger guys, while initially interested in an older woman, rarely hung around after a few months. But, she had to admit, those few months could get kind of wild. Holly had her own pool, and not just once the neighbors had complained of her skinny dipping and more with young men in the middle of the night.

"Really Holly!" Susan whispered. "The words that come out of your mouth!"

Susan was the meekest of the group. Also married twice, she was sixty- nine, and quite attractive. Her current husband Tony was a golf pro at the club, and he was also sixty nine. They had moved to Florida from Pennsylvania. They had sold their investment property in Pennsylvania, and relocated to Florida to retire. Besides being timid, Susan was the very definition of a "Nervous Nelly". She worried incessantly about global warming, nuclear war and whether every little dimple or blemish on her skin was cancerous. The other ladies knew she was taking anti-anxiety medication, but they didn't think it was very effective.

"All I know is, tonight, I'm going to be winning and the rest of you can just pay up and kiss my ass," Lori laughed. Lori was another member of the Mahjong group. She was sixty four, had beautiful short silver hair, and had retired from her job as hospital administrator in Manhattan. She had started her career as a nurse and climbed her way to the top of a very male dominated profession with her sheer determination and competence. She had forgotten more about medicine than most doctors knew. She attended every seminar offered in order to stay current with the latest developments in her field. Because she was considered an expert, she was always answering the ladies medical questions, which she did happily. Her friends were her family, and she loved each and every one of them, as different as they were.

Out of concern for Susan, Lori suggested that a little green pill might help her to relax and alleviate her anxiety. Lori had a steady boyfriend for almost twenty years after her own marriage ended. Art, her boyfriend, was a retired restaurateur from New York City, but most people felt he really made his living by being a bookie. He had boyish quality about him, always seeking attention from whoever was in the room. He claimed to have sung with the likes of Jay Black and Frankie Valli, but hearing him sing at parties, one doubted that too. Lori adored him, and he was good to her and that was all that mattered to the ladies.

About fifty women played Mahjong in groups of five. Other women brought their books and held their book club at the same time. In the past, the ladies would play more or less in the same group, but recently some of the new members had suggested rotating the players in an attempt to boost community spirit. Anna and her friends didn't really give a damn about the community spirit, and took their game far more seriously than most of the others.

"So what do you think about starting our own Mahjong club? We all agree that we don't want to break up our group, which is what they are planning to do here.

We can meet once a week, and rotate it from house to house." Anna suggested.

"No men allowed." Susan quickly replied.

"Not even a couple of half-naked pool boys to get our drinks?" Holly begged.

"I'm in. With or without cabana boys." Lori said.

"No men. I agree with Susan." Anna said. "This will be *The Mahjong Club*. Admit it, we are the best players, and our most competitive games are with ourselves. Whenever someone joins our table, it's never the same. And when I have to play with other people, it drives me crazy. They're more interested in what they're wearing, than the tiles they're playing. No men, we can rotate it, so everyone knows when it is, so the house will be a man-free zone."

"Okay, but there's one problem. We only have four. We need a fifth." Susan pointed out. Priscilla can't commit as she travels so much, but offered to be the alternate or bettor if we wanted, but we'll still need a steady fifth player.

"Actually, that may not be a problem. You all know my friend Catherine from New York. Well she's finally booted out that mooch of a husband, and is renting a house here. She's an excellent player and could use a diversion and some shoulders to cry on." Anna said.

"I love Catherine!" Lori said.

"She'd be great. When is she getting down here?" Holly agreed.

"She should be here Saturday late morning. How about all of you coming over for drinks and appetizers Saturday night around seven o'clock? Anna asked. "Knowing Freddy, he'll cook up a small feast for Cat. They always got along famously."

"Perfect! Have Freddy make eggplant rollatine and I'm so there!" Susan drooled.

"Okay. So it's agreed. Saturday night we'll welcome Catherine to Greenbrier, and Wednesday night we'll have the first meeting of The Mahjong Club at my house. Now let's play, before anyone else bothers us" Anna said.

Catherine

Catherine drove down to Florida in the new Subaru
Forester she bought before leaving New York. She
splurged (for her) and bought the L.L. Bean Edition with
the roof racks. She chose the forest green color, and
already had nicknamed her new car the Green Lantern,
after the comic book hero she followed as a child. She felt it
was a practical car, like her, and with the rising gas prices,
got 34 mpg.

She drove south on Interstate 95, deciding to keep her
sightseeing to a minimum. At night she stayed at a Holiday
Inn Express since she was a priority member. She liked
that they were located close to the highway, and were
comfortable for the money. In the morning, they served a
decent breakfast, but usually she just had coffee and a
bagel, maybe some fresh fruit, while she read the
complimentary USA Today.

At lunchtime, or thereabout, she liked to stop at a Cracker
Barrel restaurant where she would get the *Uncle Hershel*
breakfast special, which came with two eggs cooked
anyway you chose, for her over easy, and country ham. She
usually preferred the city ham which was sweeter, but
since she was moving to the South, she figured she should
try to eat native, so went with the saltier country ham. It
also came with grits, cheesy potatoes and cinnamon
apples. She loved the sourdough bread toast with

blackberry jam, and all of it, washed down with three cups of black coffee. After eating she would shop in their Country Store and get snacks for the ride, most of the time choosing their caramel popcorn with walnuts. A bottle of water and she was good to go.

She was blessed with good driving weather, and she could feel the stress drain from her body with each passing mile. She enjoyed talking to people whenever she stopped. Her father always said "Catherine, you'd talk to a rock if it'd listen." At one rest area, a truck driver gave her a low wolf whistle, which rather than offend her, was music to her ears. She waggled her finger at him, and blew him a kiss upon driving out, her smile lasting for miles. She knew one thing; she was not like Jack and refused to wallow in any kind of self-pity. She would mourn the passing of her marriage and move on. She was too young to wall herself up, and besides, she liked the company of men, in and out of the bedroom. The thought of her taking a lover gave her a tingling she hadn't felt in quite awhile.

Catherine pulled into Anna's driveway on Saturday morning, feeling far more refreshed than she would have guessed. The moving truck with all of her belongings, hell, her life, wouldn't arrive until Monday morning, so she'd be spending the weekend with Anna and Freddy.

She hadn't even had a chance to shut off the car or open her door when Freddy came bounding out of the house. "Hey! Welcome to Florida Cat!" A nickname he had given her years ago. He opened her door and was giving her a big hug and kiss on her cheek when Anna came bouncing out of the house as well. "Cat! You look fantastic! Leave your bags and c'mon in and get a cup of coffee. I just brewed it fresh."

"Bingo!" Catherine squealed as she walked in the front door. Bingo was their dog but really was more human than canine. Bingo jumped into her arms and licked her cheeks and chin. "You know Anna, why didn't you recommend I just get a dog instead of a husband?"

"Ah Honey, giving a nod to Freddy, there's still a few good ones out there. In fact, I have my eye on one for you to meet."

"Oh Jesus, Anna! I barely got the stink of Jack off me. I think I'll stick with Bingo."

"Ok" Freddy said. "I think I'll let you ladies catch up. Art called and wanted to play golf so I think I'll take that sonofabitchs money."

"Bye honey." Don't forget to be back for the party."

"Party, Anna?" Cat questioned with an eyebrow raised.

"Oh it's nothing. Just some friends, old and new are coming over to welcome you to Florida.""Oh you're too much!" Cat laughed and hugged her friend. She could feel the stress of the divorce and the trip down begin to bleed off already. "Coffee sounds great!"

Saturday night was the type of magical evening that lured people to Florida. The warm winters, and miles of sandy, white beaches, were an added bonus. The sky was clear of clouds, and brilliant red streaks sparkled throughout an azure canvas. The moon was visible even in daylight. It hung in the sky, wireless, while a gentle warm breeze swayed the fronds of the ever erect palm trees.

Most of Anna's guests were crowded around the picnic table that was located outside on the brick veranda. The large distressed oak table looked more like a banquet table one would find in a twelfth-century medieval stone castle. It was overflowing with various cheeses, toasted brie covered in paper thin almond slices, baby mozzarella balls in olive oil, sliced aged white cheddar cheese from Grafton Farms in Vermont and the more traditional Colby. Alongside the cheeses were sliced imported Genoa salami, hunks of mortadella and sopreassata , grilled Italian sweet and hot sausages with fennel, hand-rolled meatballs, and platters of grilled green and red peppers with onions. Loaves of warm scali bread rested in a wicker basket alongside a bread knife. A tureen of homemade Italian minestrone soup, made fresh earlier that day, was kept warm on a heated server.

Bottles of both red and white wine were located nearby on a small table. Since this was a special occasion, Anna had set out her Waterford wine goblets for her guests. Two ice chests were on another table; one was full to the brim with cold beer, another with soft drinks and bottled water.

Freddy was manning the grill preparing bacon-wrapped scallops, and lamb chops that had been marinated overnight. Of course, the men gathered around Freddy by the grill talking about their usual subject, golf.

"Jesus, Art, how the fuck did you miss that putt?" Freddy asked, turning over the lamb.

"Hey, all I know is he put twenty bucks in my pocket". Tony grinned.

"I should charge you the twenty bucks I lost for dinner. Jesus, what was it all of four feet?" Freddy asked.

"Yeah like you pros never missed a putt. Fuck you guys!" Art cursed.

With that, they all had a good laugh.

Anna looked over and said "I swear they only play golf so they have something to bitch about."

"Better than him bitching at home" Susan said ever sensitive to Tony's' moods. Turning to Catherine, Susan said "I'm so glad you came down here. This change is just what you needed. It was time to get out of that big city. Do a little boating. Get a tan."

"Maybe I can find a big strong guy to rub suntan lotion over my shoulders, Susan" Catherine replied.

"I'm sure he'll rub something. It just may not be your shoulders." Holly said. "I know I wouldn't mind a nice set of strong hands massaging my body. It's been too long for me, that I know".

"What's it been a week, now?" Anna kidded. "Honest to God Holly, you should have been born a man with your libido. "

"Hey! There is nothing wrong with a woman enjoying sex the same way men do. It's about time we women were completely open about our sexual desires. Fuck them if they can't handle it."

Just then, Priscilla walked out onto the veranda. Both the men and the woman stopped mid-conversation to look at her. Priscilla was stunning. Tall, practically five feet 10 inches; she carried herself regally, almost like a princess. She had shoulder length blond hair, the color of summer corn, cut fashionably. Her eyes were green, almost like Jack's, Catherine thought. She was slim, but strong from her daily routine of tennis and swimming. She was bronze from the time she spent in the sun, and had perfect white teeth. She could have been the bane of every woman at the party, but she wasn't. In addition to being their good friend, she was also gay, thus no threat to any of the women.

Priscilla was a very successful political consultant. She was often sought to help in high profile election races around the country. Her job took her took her to Washington D.C. often, and she ran in the inner circle there. It was rumored that she had an off and on sexual liaison with a prominent female senator, but the ladies were too polite to ask if the rumor was true.

"Now that's a waste of a perfectly good piece of ass." Freddy said.

"You couldn't handle that." Tony said, sneaking a look. That's all he needed was to have Susan catch him looking at another woman. She was insecure as it was.

"If I screwed her" Art said to the group, "she'd never want another woman or a man again."

"Shit, Art. You probably DID screw her and that's what drove her to the other side." Freddy roared.

The lamb was cooked a perfect medium-rare, the only way Freddy would serve it. He yelled out to everyone that it was ready, and people grabbed their plates and sat down at the two picnic tables set end to end to accommodate everyone.

"Here's to our good friend Cat. We're all so glad you've finally decided to come down here and live with your friends and people who love you." Anna toasted.

"And dump that asshole." Holly had to add.

With a rousing chorus of "here here" everyone dug into the feast that Anna and Freddy had prepared yet again. Anna and Freddy were always looking for a reason to host a party, and Cat's arrival was the perfect excuse.

"So what's the plan, Cat?" Priscilla asked, putting a lamb chop on her plate.

"Nothing for awhile". She replied. "I'm going to set up house, get into a routine, and maybe have you teach me to play tennis and brush up on my Mahjong game. It's been quite some time since I played and I know how cutthroat you girls can be. " Cat said playfully. "I've taken some time off from work and want to kick back and relax for a bit. I was burning the candle at both ends and feeling the effects. Travelling back and forth to Italy really took a lot out of me.

"I'd be glad to teach you a few things" Priscilla laughed.

"I bet you would!" Cat laughed back.

"Cat. The rest of us girls have decided to start our own Mahjong club, and would love for you to join us. Priscilla travels frequently, so she offered to be an alternate when one of us can't make it. What do you say? Would you like to join us?" Anna asked.

"Will it be rowdy with lots of drinking?" Cat asked.

"Hell ya, but no men." Holly said dejectedly.

"Right now, no men works for me. All I need is a fresh supply of batteries to keep me happy in bed." Cat laughed.

"Great. Then it's settled. We have an official Mahjong club! The best one ever put together!" Anna said.

Anna looked out over the table. Surrounded by friends, true friends, all eating and laughing, she realized that she was truly blessed. Freddy was accepting compliments on his culinary expertise, Holly was telling bawdy jokes, Cat and Priscilla were locked in a conversation about politics, Art and Tony were talking about the best golf courses they had played, and Lori was telling Susan that the spot on her neck was nothing more than a pimple. How dare Ashley Fake Tits make fun of her friends? She didn't know them, and certainly didn't know what secrets lay in their hearts. She had her share of adventures, before Freddy of course, but those were her secrets, tucked away in the deep recesses of her mind. She wondered what her friends would think if she ever revealed some of her escapades to them? Would they be shocked? She mused about what secrets they might have. In her experience, men tended to boast about their sexual conquests and all the women they had taken to their beds. On the other hand, women placed those same experiences into a locked, jeweled box, to be opened in silence, alone, taken out, looked at and remembered, not always with a fond smile, but sometimes with an ache, and then, placed back into the box and locked away.

The night drifted away, as nights do, and one by one people left and the party ended. Cat thanked everyone for coming and for making her feel so welcome. Anna reminded the ladies not to forget their first Mahjong game on Wednesday night, back here at her place. She also took the time to remind the men that it was ladies only, and they should make other plans.

"Bye Honey. What are you going to do tonight?" Anna said.

"I'm going to grab a burger and a beer with Tony, and then we're heading over to the Cineplex to see the new James Bond movie", he said.

"Okay, but remember, it's girls night here, so don't come back until after eleven." Anna said.

"Jesus. Should I sit in the car if I'm early? " he said.

"If you want, honey. Or you can sit in the garage." Anna said with a smile.

"Right. Okay honey. Have fun and kick some butt. Is Priscilla coming?" Freddy asked.

"You never mind about Priscilla. Have fun at the movies. If it gets out early, maybe you can go to Panera for dessert and coffee. Bye dear."

As Freddy looked out the bay window in the living room he saw Tony pull into the driveway. "Here's Tony now. Love you." He said.

"Love you too." Anna said as he went out the door. Freddy was a confirmed homebody, he'd probably be back by 11:01, Anna thought.

Just as Freddy left, Anna heard the kitchen door open. "I'm here!" Susan yelled. Susan didn't like to drive at night, so Tony had dropped her off. Susan worried about everything. She thought once it got dark people paid less attention to their driving and were more likely to cause an accident.

"Hi Susan!" Anna said with a smile. Tony and Susan lived about a half a mile away. They could easily have walked to Anna's house. It was a lovely evening for a stroll, but Susan was afraid she might get hit by a car.

Anna had made a pitcher of martinis and poured herself a drink. She usually drank wine, but tonight was in the mood for something different.

"Come on in and pour yourself a glass of wine or have a martini." Anna knew full well that Susan would be helping herself to a glass of Chardonnay whether or not she offered. Susan discovered that a few glasses of wine helped her relax. Sometimes she had a few too many, but only when she was with her friends.

"Pour me one, too." Lori said breezing in the front door. "Anna, something smells wonderful. Have you been cooking?

"Oh, Freddy made eggplant rollatine and sausage and peppers."

"Smells great!" Lori and Susan chimed together.

"What smells great?" Priscilla asked walking in.

"It's not your ass." Holly said walking in behind her.

"Holly!" Susan said exasperated. "Must you always be so crude?"

"Well I figure I balance us out since you make Mary Poppins look like a slut" Holly said.

"Yeah well you might be surprised. I'm not as virginal as you think" Susan said.

"Two husbands. So that's what? Two times?" Holly asked.

"Like I said, you'd be surprised." Susan said.

"Really? Susan you are full of surprises." Anna said.

"Now where's that good scotch? Oh, here it is." Holly rummaged through the liquor cabinet and found the scotch nestled behind the bottle of Jack Daniels. Holly had developed a taste for Johnny Walker Blue label, much to Anna's chagrin. It was expensive and Holly wasn't shy about helping herself. Holly poured herself a generous amount and then added very little ice.

Holly never enjoyed wine. Her friends were always encouraging her to try a white burgundy, Pinot Noir, or Barolo. They said after one sip of a Barolo she would become a wine aficionado. She thought her aversion to wine might be related to getting sick on Boone's Farm when she was a teenager. Scotch would remain her drink of choice.

"Ok ladies. Get your cocktails and head into the dining room. I have the Mahjong tiles ready. Are you ready for the very first Ladies Mahjong Club game and meeting?"

The girls settled into their chairs around the dining room table. "No cabana boys?" Holly asked, looking under the table.

"You wish." Anna said. "It's just the girls. No men. And while I'm at it, let's create one very important rule."

"And that would be?" Lori asked.

"Whatever we say here stays here. Just like Vegas. That way, we can all speak freely without worrying about things being repeated. With the alcohol freely flowing, who knows what we'll tell each other. After all, trust it one of the most important things in our friendship." Anna said.

"Oh great! Our own secret club!" Priscilla squealed!

"Let's all go to Vegas sometime! Just us girls." Holly said.

"Okay! But for now, mix up those tiles! I'm feeling lucky!" Lori said.

The tiles were set in the middle of the dining room table. Anna had taken the leaf out to make the table smaller and the gathering more intimate. She spread a rich burgundy colored cover on the table to protect its finish. It was the perfect backdrop for the white and red tiles.

Anna, Holly, Catherine and Lori sat around the table. It was Susan's turn to be the roving bettor and this week Priscilla was the alternate.

Anna walked to the entertainment center and put on an Elvis CD. She swung her hips as she sashayed back to the table and thought, "Who could resist The King?" She couldn't understand the younger generation's fascination with rap music or Justin Beiber, for that matter.

The tiles swirled around in a circle, clacking as they bumped into each other, and the ladies made their choices.

"This is so exciting!" Susan said. "Our very first game of The Mahjong Club!"

"The virgin game." Anna agreed.

"Well, Anna, since you brought up virginity, let's explore the topic a little." Holly quipped.

"So when did you lose your virginity, Lori?" asked Holly.

"Jesus, Holly! Must everything revolve around sex with you?" Susan asked.

"Everything does revolve around sex, honey. It's not just me. Open your baby blue eyes. Don't you and Tony fuck?" Holly said. "Or would you prefer if I put it more delicately?

46

Do you and Tony make love? Although fucking and making love are two very different things. Wouldn't you agree?

"My sex life is none of your business, lady." Susan said.

"I'm not even sure I want to hear about it. It's probably incredibly boring. Let me set the stage: the lights are always out, it's always the missionary position and there are never, ever any sex toys. Am I close?" Holly asked sarcastically.

"You'll never know. But it may surprise you!"

"Alright Susan!" Cat chimed in.

"So Lori? Holly persisted. When did you lose your virginity?"

"I'll tell only if everyone else does, and it does not leave this house." Lori said. "After all, there aren't any virgins at this table."

"Well, we did make a pact that everything stays here, so that's not a problem. Ladies? Do we all agree to share that first time?" Anna asked.

One by one, amidst laughter and memories, they all agreed.

"Ok, but I'm last." Susan conceded reluctantly.

"Well Lori? How about it? Let's hear the juicy details." Holly asked.

Lori pulled the last of her tiles from the table, and carefully arranged them in order. The corners of her mouth turned up into small smile as she thought back upon her first sexual experience.

"Wow. It was a long time ago. I grew up in a suburb outside of New York City. As you may recall, my mother was a devout Roman Catholic almost to the point of being obsessive. Ever since I was a little girl she preached about the evils of sex and of boys. I think my father just tolerated her religious fanaticism. She had a Victorian attitude about sex and it definitely escalated as she got older. She always preached about the horrors of hell and reminded me that it was essential to be a virgin up until the time I married. My mother had been a virgin when she married my father and she expected me to follow her example. She believed that sex was for procreation only. I'm sure my father couldn't have disagreed more, but in those days sex wasn't openly discussed, as it is today. Hardly anyone talked about it, and it wasn't depicted on TV or at the movies. Do you remember the *Dick Van Dyke show*? Even though Rob and Laura Petrie were a married couple they slept in separate twin beds. But in fairness to my mother, all my friends were raised in a similar fashion, but perhaps, a bit less restrictive fashion. I don't remember anyone having sex in high school. Of course the boys would brag they did, but no one believed them. One girl left school abruptly, fueling rumors that she was pregnant, but again, they were just rumors. "

So I remained chaste throughout high school, and focused on academics. I was always interested in medicine, so I thought pursuing a nursing degree made sense.

At the time, it never occurred to me that I could attend medical school and become a doctor. I did my student nursing at the Cleveland Clinic. It was all such heady stuff for a young girl. I loved everything about the hospital; the frenetic pace, the blaring emergency announcements that emanated from the loudspeakers; and the sight of the hospital staff running to respond to Code Blues. One day, I was checking the blood pressure of a middle aged man who was being admitted for a minor procedure to repair a hernia. I was alone in the room with him, when he started to have a seizure. He was on the way to convulsing himself off the bed, and taking the monitors he was hooked up to with him. I did my best to hold him down as I yelled for a nurse, a real nurse. A doctor who was passing by the room came in and helped me get this gentleman back into the bed. After extensive testing, it turned out the guy was epileptic, so we stayed with him until he stabilized.

The doctor complimented me on my fast response and clear thinking. I remember looking up at him; he was so much taller than me. I kept looking at his handsome, angular face, but didn't hear a word he was saying. I thought he was gorgeous. He had curly brown hair that fell loosely over his forehead into his eyes. I remember, even to this day, how I wanted to reach over and brush those curls out of his eyes. He looked as if he hadn't shaved and the dark stubble on his face gave him a rugged, masculine look.

He said he was on his way to the cafeteria when he heard me yelling for help. He decided that we could both use a respite from the sterile, institutional atmosphere of the hospital. So instead of going to the cafeteria we left through the automatic doors and went to the café across the street. He praised me again on a job well done, and asked me if he could take me out sometime. I think I just nodded my head like one of those toy dogs people put on car windows. He was so polite, opening doors for me, holding out my chair and buying me a cup of coffee. I didn't even drink coffee, but there was no way I was going to tell him that. I added several teaspoons of sugar to my cup and an ample dose of cream.

He asked me so many personal questions. He wanted to know how I became interested in nursing, where I was from, and what I did for entertainment. He seemed interested in me. I never had that sort of attention before, especially not from a handsome doctor. I felt like the whole experience was surreal. Things like this never happened to me. He glanced at his Rolex and realized he was due back at the hospital. When he stood up to leave, I was tempted to grab his sleeve and ask him not to leave. . I never got the opportunity to ask him any questions about his life. But before he left, he asked me whether I would like to go to his favorite pizza place some night.

We agreed to meet Friday night at *Mario's* for pizza and beer after he completed his rounds at the hospital. The week seemed unbearably long. Friday night finally came and I wanted to be fashionably late, to make myself seem intriguing. Instead I was thirty minutes early. So much for being a mystery woman! Michael, that was his name, walked into *Mario's* wearing a crisp white shirt with the sleeves rolled up. His lean forearms were tanned a golden brown. His shirt was tucked into a pair of Armani jeans which outlined the contours of his body. I couldn't help but notice his amazing ass. We ordered a pepperoni pizza and two pitchers of beer. He made me laugh until my sides hurt. He told me funny stories of the different people in the hospital, and how the patients would go crazy if they ever knew half the things that went on.

After we polished off the last piece of pizza he suggested getting dessert at *Dolci*, a nearby Italian bakery. It was still early, and I wasn't ready for the evening to end, so I agreed. When we walked into Dolci, I was overwhelmed with the variety of pastry displayed in the glass cases: biscotti, amaretti, cannoli, cantuccini, panna cotta, pizelle and sfogliatelle. Michael's favorite was the latter. He explained to her that it was a crunchy, shell shaped pastry filled with ricotta cheese and candied fruit. He ordered two sfogliatelle and two cups of espresso.

Fully satisfied, we walked down the street for awhile and came to Michael's apartment building. He asked me if I wanted to come up for a drink. You know, it's funny, but somehow I knew I was going to sleep with him before I even got to the pizza place. Or at least I knew I wanted to. That night I wore my sexiest bra and panties courtesy of *Victoria's Secret*.

I had even taken the precaution to tell my parents I would be spending the weekend out of town with a friend. Anyway, we went up to Michael's apartment. I was a little disappointed that it was a third floor walk up. I thought his place would be one of those apartments you might see in *House Beautiful*, clean and modern, with fine art on the walls. Instead it resembled a fraternity house with an empty pizza box on the counter, and dirty dishes in the sink.

He took a bottle of Prosecco out of the refrigerator and poured us each a glass. He had dimmed the lights before joining me on the sofa. The bubbles tickled my nose as we sat on the couch drinking and talking. It didn't take him long to reach over and kiss me. I've been kissed before, but not like this. When he slipped his tongue into my mouth, I melted. He took the Prosecco from my hand and he led me into the bedroom.

I didn't protest as he caressed my breasts and ass. His breath was warm on my neck, as he kissed and nibbled the side of my throat, I could feel myself getting excited. I ran my fingers through his hair and pulled him down on the bed. He didn't waste any time. He had my slacks off in an instant, and when he pulled my panties down, he placed his mouth and tongue on me. His tongue made me crazy as he licked me, but when he put his fingers inside me at the same time, I exploded. Well let me tell you, that was my first orgasm, and it was unforgettable. He opened the drawer of the night table, removed a condom from an open box of Trojans. He tore open the gold foil, and rolled the rubber down his dick. I wanted to help, to watch it go on, but he had it done in a moment's time. He rolled on top of me and used his knees to spread my legs apart, not too gently, but urgently. I reached down and grabbed his dick to put him inside me. While I never had sex before, I masturbated and played sports, so he entered me easily. Plus I was deliciously wet! God was I wet! When he started to thrust his dick in and out of me, it sounded like it was someone else's voice moaning, but it came from my lips. Before long, much too early for my liking I could feel his long lean body stiffen, and he grunted into the pillow when he came. I think the whole sex act lasted no more than five minutes.

"Wow! Then what happened?" Anna asked.

"Not much." He got up and went into the bathroom. I stretched out in the bed, inhaling the smells of our lovemaking, and wondering how long it would take him to do it again. To my surprise, he came out of the bathroom wearing pajamas. He told me that he was sorry, but he had an early shift the following morning and really needed to get some sleep. He said couldn't sleep well with someone else in his bed. What could I do? I said I understood, and went into the bathroom to put my clothes back on. I would have liked to take a shower, but I could tell he really wanted me to leave so he could get to sleep.

So I dressed and called my roommate, who worked at the hospital as well, to let her know I would be coming home, which is what I did.

"Did you see him again?" Susan wanted to know.

"Oh yeah. Our paths crossed a few times in the hospital, but the girlfriend with whom I spent the night, told me his nickname in the hospital was Dr. One Time. I guess he got off on seducing the new nurses. I felt so used I wanted to stick a catheter up his ass."

"Wow! What a great story Lori." Cat said.

"He pissed me off so much, I think I would have told everyone he couldn't get it up and preferred young boys, but I didn't want to jeopardize my job by maligning a highly respected doctor." Lori added.

"Okay who's next?" Lori asked. "You heard my sorry tale."

"Okay. I'll go next Anna said. But it's not as exciting."

"Let's hear it." Priscilla said, crowding in closer to the table.

"Alright, but let me re-fill my wine. Anyone else for more wine?

A chorus of me, me and me bellowed out.

After she refreshed her martini and filled everyone's glass with wine, and poured more scotch for Holly, Anna began.

"Well as you know, I grew up in the country in western Massachusetts, and was quite a tomboy as a girl. My dad owned a small construction company and my mom managed the finances for him. Peter was my younger brother. A lot of the fathers in our community hunted, the boys too. But, I never went hunting. It seemed too cruel. However, often times I would go fishing with my father. I even put the worm on my own hook. My family went camping a lot and my mother was fairly accomplished at campfire cooking. Anyway, when I was in eleventh grade, a boy named Dan moved to our town from Boston. He was in the 11th grade too. It was rumored that his father had been transferred to our town to manage the power plant. There was something magnetic about Dan. He wasn't particularly handsome, nor was he tall. He didn't have the physique of an athlete, but he certainly was cute. He was definitely different from the other boys in our high school. Initially, I thought he was conceited, but learned from other friends that he was painfully shy. When I tried to start a conversation with him, he responded with one word answers. I was determined to get him to open up to me, so I devised a plan.

I invited him to a Friday night football game as my date, but he never made a move on me. Nothing. We studied together, and again, he never even tried to kiss me. Now I wasn't a raving beauty, but I was pleasant looking. I was so drawn to him that I couldn't concentrate when he was nearby. I had never felt this way before. Ever. I wanted him to kiss me, and gave him enough signals to that effect, but he never tried. I decided I had to take a more aggressive approach. One week, I told him that a group of us were going camping up at the lake and suggested that he should come along. He agreed and said he'd pick me up, but I told him I would drive. I had asked to borrow my father's car to make certain I was in control.

When Saturday rolled around, I picked him up in my father's station wagon with the wood sides. Remember those? They called them woodies. Something I hoped to give Dan.

"God Anna! You too!" Susan exclaimed.

"Susan! Shush! Anyway, I picked up Dan, and we loaded the sleeping bags and food in the car and headed north to the lake. When we arrived, the other kids were noticeably absent. I feigned ignorance, but of course I never invited them. I was surprised that Dan didn't seem upset that we were alone. We unpacked the car and selected a campsite. Then we started up a trail. We hiked until our legs ached, then swam in the lake under a cloudless sky. When he tried to dunk my head under water, I wrapped my arms and legs around him and kissed him on the lips. He didn't pull away, but he didn't kiss me back either. I was confused, and aroused. We swam until the sun set, then dried off and started back to our campsite. I made a campfire and put some hot dogs on to cook. He was such a city boy. It was fun to see him react to this new experience. We ate hot dogs and drank coke, and finally crawled into our sleeping bags. We talked for awhile about school and our parents. The evening sky was clear so I was able to point out all the stars and constellations to him.

It got cold once the fire died down. Dan had an expensive L.L. Bean sleeping bag that promised to keep the occupant warm even in Arctic temperatures. I had quite the opposite; an old, inexpensive, flimsy sleeping bag from Sears's. We were lying side by side in our sleeping bags. We were so close I could feel his breath on my cheek. Dan seemed toasty ensconced in his down- filled LL Bean, but I was freezing. I told him I was cold, and he asked me if I wanted to pack up and drive home. I couldn't believe he even thought of leaving. I told him I wanted to stay and suggested that we zipper our sleeping bags together. Dan didn't even know you could do that, so I rousted him from his bag, opened the two of them and zippered them together. Dan crawled in first, then me. I immediately snuggled next to him, putting my head on his shoulder. Now finally, he began to kiss me. Slowly at first, then more passionately. I could feel his erection against my upper thigh, so I placed my hand on him. It wasn't the first dick I ever touched. It felt hard yet silky at the same time. There was no doubt in my mind that I wanted to have sex with Dan. I was still a virgin, but preserving my virginity wasn't a priority. Most of my girlfriends were already having sex.

Dan kept kissing me, but ventured no further. I assumed that if this was going to be the big night, I would have to make it happen. I undid Dan's belt and I was shocked that he wasn't wearing any underwear. I pulled my jeans off and rolled down my panties. I placed Dan's hands on my breasts. His hands were soft and without calluses, unlike most of the boys I knew. I guided his hands down past my stomach and he explored me gently, like I was made of fine china."

"No chance of that." Holly added.

"Hush Holly. Anyway, I rolled under him, pulling him on top of me. He surprised me by pulling out a rubber, but I had to help him put it on. I think he'd been carrying it around for months. I was afraid he'd either drop it or break it and ruin our big night.

I had assumed that I knew what it would feel like to have sex, but I was wrong. His dick felt hot inside me, and was much thicker and longer than I expected. He went in deeper than my fingers ever did. I could feel his balls slapping against my ass, and that excited me even more. I put my hands on his ass and pulled him deeper and deeper into me. He was gentle, but also out of control, which I loved. He lasted a lot longer than I heard some boys lasted. When he finally came, his whole body shuddered against me, and I could feel his hot cum exploding inside of me. Dan fucked me two more times that night. He was a quick study, or maybe I was a great teacher. "Impressive story honey." Cat said. "Whatever happened to Dan?"

"Well we dated through high school. We had a lot in common - we both loved camping and screwing. After graduation we went our separate ways. Dan was accepted at the University of Arizona and left for Tucson that September. I was clear across the country at the University of Rhode Island. Unlike your doctor Lori, he was a sweetheart. Very romantic."But I never saw him again after that. We vowed we'd keep in touch, but knew that wouldn't happen."

"Wow! This is getting good. We're really doing some sharing here .Okay, who's next? How about you Holly?" Anna asked.

"This ought to be good." Susan said.

"Do blowjobs count?" Holly asked.

"No. Not unless it was when you lost your flower." Anna said.

"Ok then. I lost my virginity when I was 14. "Holly said.

"What!" Priscilla said not too quietly.

"Let me finish. I was fourteen when I lost my virginity. As you know, I grew up in Maine. Not on the coast, but inland where most of the tourist people don't go. It isn't as charming as people think. There were long cold winters, and most people had to eke out a hardscrabble living. Nearly everyone was in the same boat, which was poor. We had more than our share of alcoholics, and domestic abuse was just swept under the rug. A lot of the families either drove truck or were in the logging business. No one shopped at Wegman's. In fact our family ate what either my father or me and my brothers shot. They would take a deer out of season, so that we always would have fresh meat. It wasn't uncommon for girls to hunt. Our vegetables all came from our garden, and we canned whatever we had extra to save for the winter.

We heated our house with wood, which is not as romantic as people think. There was always dirt and wood chips on the floor, and the smell of smoke always filled the house. Like most of our neighbors, we didn't have any other form of heat, so keeping the damn woodstove going was a crucial chore the kids were responsible for. If it went out, the pipes could freeze and burst. And that meant our asses getting whacked.

All of us kids had hand-me-down clothes, and we were none too proud not to go to the Salvation Army for them. Dad worked driving truck, when he could find the work. My brothers usually skipped school and worked for the lumber mill up in Machias. I was the only girl, so Dad had me cooking, cleaning, mending and taking care of the house. My mom died when I was three, breast cancer, so I really never knew her, but grew up knowing my role in the family was to take her place doing the woman's household chores. My dad kept a picture of my mom on the mantle and always said I looked like her.

It didn't matter to my father whether I went to school or not, but even back then I knew that unless I did get an education, the same fate that befell most of the girls up there, which was to get knocked up and continue that circle of poverty, would be my destiny. So I went to school, was a good student, and when I finished my chores at home, would secretly read books I borrowed from the school library. I say secretly because if my father caught me, he'd say I was just wasting my time and give me some other chores to do. More likely something one of my brothers was supposed to do.

One weekend, my father came home after a week on the road, and brought my Uncle Harry, who was my father's younger brother by about five years. They sat in the parlor by the wood stove and drank themselves drunk while complaining about the government, minorities, gays and anything else their small minds could think of. My brothers had all gone away hunting for the weekend.

I pretty much stayed out of their way, but responded when my father wanted me to get him or his brother another beer. I was uncomfortable with the way my uncle was looking at me, especially my breasts. I was large for a girl my age, maybe I took after my mother, but I don't know. Talking about my mother was a subject guaranteed to put my father in a black mood, and he was mean enough without it.

I excused myself, saying I was going to bed. My father made sure I put on more wood, and got them each another beer before I headed up to sleep. My bedroom was on the second floor and was unheated. To this day, I hate to be cold. I covered myself with as many blankets as I could find and went to sleep. At some point during the night, Uncle Harry came into my bedroom. I only woke up when he crawled into my bed naked and drunk. He told me to be quiet, that my father would blame only me for this, and proceeded to roughly pull off my flannel nightgown. I tried to protest and stop him, but he was too strong for me. He forced my legs apart, and thrust himself inside of me. I thought he would split me in two. The pain was immense, and when I went to cry out, he covered my mouth with his hard, dirty hand. He squeezed my breasts so roughly, I can almost feel his hands on me now. He tried to kiss me, but every time he'd try to take his hand off my mouth, I'd start to yell. So he just took his tongue and slobbered all over my neck.

At that point, I didn't care if my father came in. I wanted to be dead. He finally came in me, rolled off me, and threatened that if I ever told anyone, he'd just say it was me who came to his bed. With that, he pulled up his pants and left.

I went into the bathroom. Blood was seeping down from my vagina, and it was almost too sore to wash, but I gritted my teeth and did it. I had to get the stink of him off of me. My breasts were already swollen and bruising from where he grabbed me, and I began to throw up in the toilet. I stayed there the rest of the night as it had a lock on the door and I couldn't even fathom going back to bed and possibly being raped again.

When it was just daylight, I packed my backpack with a few items and left, never to return. I guess I was blessed I never got pregnant. Before you ask, I never returned home or have had any contact with my family since. They're dead to me. I changed my name, and the rest I'd prefer not to talk about."

"Jesus Holly. I had no idea." Anna said softly.

"Well it's not the kind of story that you tell people. But it's over, and I'm not that girl anymore. Ok Priscilla, you're next."

"Let's take a break from the game and go outside. It's cool on the patio and I'm getting hungry." Anna said. "Beside, Freddy will be so annoyed if we don't eat the feast he made for us. Bring your drinks outside, and Cat, please help me carry the food to the table."

"Don't forget the eggplant rollatine." Susan said.

"Susan you eat constantly! How do you stay so thin?
"Priscilla asked.

"Tony says it's nervous energy. He thinks my metabolism is always in high gear because I worry so much. I don't know if that's the reason. Maybe it's all the sex Tony and I have," she said with an impish smile, "or maybe I'm just blessed with good genes. "

The ladies moved the party outside and sat down at the round, glass-topped patio table. The pink Chinese lanterns that Anna had hung around the patio, before her guests arrived, cast a rosy glow over the festivities. Anna generally used her gold trimmed Lenox china when entertaining guests, but because this was intended to be a casual affair she set the table with colorful paper plates and matching napkins. However, she couldn't bring herself to use plastic cutlery, so her sterling silver flatware adorned the table.

Lori had won the first two games of Mahjong and was bragging about it to the other women.

"Ok ok." Anna said. "Let's eat since we still have more games to play."

Cat brought out Italian rolls that had been warmed in the oven, and then helped Anna arrange the food on a granite topped cart adjacent to the table. Anna pulled back the aluminum foil that covered the platter of sausage and peppers and stirred them with a large wooden spoon.

Next, she uncovered the casserole of fresh eggplant rollatine. She assembled a large Caesar salad with crisp romaine and homemade dressing. As soon as the ladies finished their salads, they began to scoop the sausage and peppers into sliced sandwich rolls. Susan helped herself to a large portion of the rollatine. Neither she nor Tony were great cooks so they took advantage of the many two-for-one dinner specials offered at local restaurants. Susan considered a home cooked meal a special treat, especially one prepared by Freddy or Anna.

"Ok Priscilla. It's your turn. " Who was the lucky lady who took your virginity?" Lori asked.

"Oh no!" Cat corrected. "We're talking male anatomy okay, unless you've been deprived of one? You know, being a lesbian an all."

"Actually I was deflowered by a man. I wasn't always gay you know. Well, maybe I was. But I had straight sex too."

"This gets better and better!" Holly piped in.

"Well, as you know, I grew up in San Diego. I was a bona fide California girl; just like the song by the Beach Boys. I loved the beach and living on the coast. I couldn't imagine a better place to live; it felt like paradise. My friends and I surfed whenever we had the time, made campfires on the sand, celebrated the sunsets, the whole nine yards. My parents were permissive, in fact I know they smoked weed, but I pretended that I was oblivious to that fact. Despite that lifestyle, I was fairly conservative. I had boyfriends, but there wasn't anyone special in my life. In fact, when I was young, maybe fourteen or fifteen, I knew I was attracted to girls. One day I told my mother how I felt. She tried to reassure me by saying that I was going through an adolescent phase, and in fact, she went through the same phase when she was my age. So I pushed the issue to the back of my mind. But when I went to the beach with my friends, it wasn't the boys that I checked out, but the girls in their itty-bitty bikinis.

When I was seventeen, my friends and I often camped out on the beach. We would make a little bonfire with driftwood that we collected. Someone would bring beer, someone else would bring a bottle of wine, and there was always a joint passed around. Because we were all from affluent families, and never caused any real trouble, the cops didn't bother us. Anyway, when the campfire died out, people would pair up. It was pretty liberal back then, and people often hooked up with people they weren't dating. The summer before I left for college, I went to one of those beach parties. Everyone paired off with someone, leaving me and this guy Skip alone. He was the classic California beach boy. He had broad shoulders, a golden tan, shaggy blonde hair and the bluest eyes. He looked like he could have been a Calvin Klein model. I knew some of my girl friends found him utterly irresistible and secretly wished that they were dating him. But he was a little reserved like me.

That night we talked for hours about leaving home and going off to college. Not far from us several couples were having sex. We could hear their soft murmurs and muffled moans. It was a little embarrassing to be in such close proximity to their intimacy. After awhile, we stopped talking and he just looked at me. It was fairly obvious he wanted to have sex, so we started kissing and caressing each other. He pulled off his bathing suit, and to this day, I don't know what possessed me, but I went down on him. I was surprised, nicely surprised actually, by how hard his dick was, and how it felt in my mouth. He put his hands on my head, and began to push his dick in and out. I had my hands on his naked thighs and just went with the flow. I felt his dick jerk, and heard him moan at the same time as his grip on my head tightened, and he came in my mouth. I didn't even gag, just swallowed. It was actually sweet. No words were spoken all this time, and he pulled up his bathing suit and we snuggled together on a blanket and fell asleep in each other's arms."

"Hey! No fair! A blowjob isn't sex!" Holly crying foul.

"Yeah? Ask Bill Clinton that question", Susan responded.

"Okay. Okay!" Priscilla agreed. "That was my first sexual encounter. Now I'll tell you perverts want you really want to hear. I was a freshman in college when I lost my virginity. I went to college at Berkeley. Good school and liberal enough to appease my broadminded parents. I majored in political science, and minored in math. I loved political science which was easy for me to master, but I had difficulty with math. During my junior year I took advanced statistics. The professor was young, maybe in his mid-thirties, and very amiable. His name was Grant Winthrop. Everything about him was cool. He wore jeans to class, had really funky black glasses and drove a red Volkswagen Beetle. Believe it or not, sometimes he took his sandals off and stood at the podium barefoot.

He was a great professor, and he connected well with his students. Everyone loved his class. He welcomed challenging questions and encouraged lively class discussions. Anyway, one day he asked me if I could stay after class because he wanted to talk to me. We left the lecture hall and he steered me through a linoleum maze of hallways to his office. He unlocked the door and invited me to sit on the sofa. He sat in the black leather chair behind his desk, and took off his glasses. I thought he was going to tell me that I was failing. However, once we were seated, he told me that he sensed I was struggling with some of the concepts we were covering in class. He offered to give me extra help, and I gladly accepted. I wanted to get a good grade in his class in order to maintain my grade point average. He suggested we meet on Saturday morning when we were both free. I didn't think his offer was inappropriate. Lots of students met with their professors outside of class.

On Friday night I went to a fraternity party on campus. I had a great time but stayed too late and drank too much. I paid the price on Saturday morning. I woke up with crushing headache and bloodshot eyes. I took a hot shower and swallowed a couple of aspirins before I left my dorm. Then, I headed directly to Dunkin' Donuts. I bought each of us a cup of coffee and a corn muffin then ambled over to the math building. I sipped my coffee as I walked and the caffeine definitely eased the pounding in my head.

I arrived at his office and knocked on the door. I could hear his voice and realized he was just ending a phone conversation. I distinctly heard him say, "Love you, honey. See you this afternoon."

He opened the door wearing a tie-dyed shirt and well worn jeans. Again, he was barefoot. When I handed him the coffee and muffin, he gave me a big hug. I was a little taken aback, but didn't give it too much thought. Everyone was touchy feely back then. Unlike our previous meeting, this time he didn't sit behind his desk, but instead suggested we sit on the sofa. He put his coffee cup on the end table and opened up the text book we were using that semester. We reviewed the two chapters we had covered in class, until I finally felt that I understood the material.

I thanked him for his help, and we started walking toward the door of his office. I really wasn't surprised when he took me into his arms and kissed me. We can sense those things, can't we? It was more comical than romantic. His glasses slipped off his nose and fell on our lips, so I removed them. We walked back to the sofa and sprawled out. I wasn't physically attracted to him, but liked him as a person and admired his intellect. While I considered him to be "an older man", I also thought it was time to lose my virginity. For some reason I assumed he was an experienced lover and probably had done this sort of thing with other students. Well, it turned out he wasn't. He bumbled his way out of his clothes and seemed to be more embarrassed than I was. When he took off his shirt, he wasn't as muscular as the boys I dated, but again, I guess that was to be expected, being a professor and older and all. He had on this crazy pair of paisley boxer shorts, which I helped him take off. He was hard, but still probably only five inches fully erect. Much to my surprise, he wasn't circumcised. It was the first dick I had seen, not counting pictures, that wasn't circumcised, so this was totally different.

It's funny the things we recall in retrospect. I remember that the sofa was too small to accommodate the two of us. It was more the size of a loveseat. My neck was cramped into an awkward position as it rested on the wooden arm. I reached down and guided him into me. I felt a little discomfort at first, but then again, I was tense. He kept telling me how pretty I was while he was screwing me. My head kept banging against the arm of the sofa. The entire time I was thinking, "Is this it?" I was disappointed. I expected some fireworks, at least inside my vagina, but he came with a whimper and then it was over. After we got dressed, he became quite nervous. He apologized profusely for his behavior and promised that it wouldn't happen again. I imagine he envisioned his entire life and the reputation he had earned crumbling; losing his wife, his kids and his job. To allay his fears, I assured him that it would remain our little secret. He never knew it was my first time, or how anticlimactic it was for me. He was far more rattled by the experience than I was. I kissed him on the cheek, thanked him for his help, and left his office. He was an excellent teacher, in statistics that is, and I don't regret the experience. We never met outside of class again. That tryst confirmed my suspicion that I was attracted to women, however it wasn't until later that I had my first sexual experience with a girl. That encounter, blew my drawers off!"

Tell us that one!" Holly wanted.

"No way. I'm still in touch with her, and besides, that wasn't the agreement." Priscilla replied back. "Now, who's next? Cat?"

"My story is pretty dull compared to you all." Cat said, and went on to tell them about Tommy, the football player that took her virginity on the high school playing field, the night their team won the Regional Finals. I remember thinking Wow! I like this! And I liked it better every time we screwed. I liked everything about sex! The way I felt when he put his hands on my breasts, when he used his fingers to explore between my legs, and those long make out sessions we had. In the beginning we used condoms, but then I went to a free clinic and got a prescription for birth control pills. I thought that going to the clinic was very mature and responsible on my part. We had sex anytime and anywhere we could. It was such a rush to feel him come inside me, and both of us enjoyed oral sex as well. I liked the way he tasted, and when he went down on me, I'd end up pulling his hair because he drove me so crazy with his mouth and tongue. I think the only position we didn't try was anal. No thanks. When the weather was crappy, we'd drive out to the country with a six pack of beer and I would pull down his pants, suck him until he got hard, then sit on him. God one time while I was going up and down on his dick, I hit the horn with my ass and before I could get off of it, half the lights came on in the houses around us. We laughed like hell as we sped out of there!

Back then, sex was fun. It was pure pleasure. Tommy and I didn't have any guilt or hang-ups about it. He was the perfect guy for me to learn about sex with. A few times while he was away at college, we would meet in a cheap hotel room for the night, but somehow we just moved on and it was never the same. That's my story, ladies."

"And now ladies, the moment we've all been waiting for! How our little Susan got her first dick!" Holly announced loudly.

"Jesus Holly! Why don't you yell it louder, so the whole damn neighborhood can hear you?!" Susan said. "Okay. I was older than you experienced ladies when I lost my virginity. I was a senior in college and my story is truly boring. I wasn't a wild girl, by any stretch of the imagination, but I did like boys. My mother always said I was boy crazy. In high school usually dated the nerdy guys. You know the type I mean. They didn't play sports and they weren't very popular, but they were very smart. They are the ones that now are probably making millions, while the jocks are likely to be working at Wal-Mart changing tires. Like every other girl in high school, I was attracted to the jocks, but they weren't attracted to me

I focused on my studies, and graduated near the top of my class. I applied to, and was accepted at several Ivy League schools, but ultimately decided on Amherst College, a small, but very elite, school in Massachusetts.

At Amherst, my life remained much the same. I dated, fooled around a little, but kept waiting for the right guy. And waited. And waited. I wasn't willing to have my first experience with just anyone. I dated one guy for awhile and I thought he had potential. We didn't have sex but I would jerk him off. He wanted to fuck me, but I knew he wasn't the *one,* so I never let him. He pressed me for a blowjob, but I put that in the same category as sex, so I wouldn't. He gradually got bored with me and my refusals, and found someone else to have sex with.

During senior year, I felt like I was the only virgin on campus. When the Fall semester started, there were lots of fraternity parties. We called them "mixers." One Saturday night in September, Delta Upsilon, the jock fraternity, was having a mixer. I never felt comfortable at mixers, but some friends convinced me to go. Anyway, it was far better than staying in my room studying. I saw a couple of my former boyfriends with other girls; girls from Mount Holyoke and Smith College. There were so many pretty girls at Amherst I never understood why the guys went off campus to find dates. Anyway, I wasn't going to let that spoil the evening; the music was playing, the fraternity was on tap, and there was plenty of beer.

I took my usual spot against the wall, watching everyone drinking and dancing, when I noticed a boy looking at me from across the room. I recognized him as the star running back of the football team, and the best rugby player at the college. He was devastatingly handsome. His name was George, and his nickname was Handsome George or Gorgeous George, depending on who you asked. He came from a tough part of South Boston, and was raised in a low income housing project. He was big and strong, with striking, chiseled features. George was *the* big man on campus, and he was looking at me. I assumed I must have dropped something on my blouse, or maybe a button was undone.

George continued to look at me and then gave me a wide smile. Not a predatory one, but a warm friendly smile. He walked across the dance floor and introduced himself. He didn't need to since I knew who he was. He asked me my name and then asked me to dance. I was awe-struck and it took me a few seconds to reply with a weak sounding "sure". Johnny River's *"Poor Side Of Town"* was playing on the juke box as he pulled me onto the dance floor. The floor was slippery with spilled beer. I could see everyone watching us and probably wondering who the hell I was. That song ended, and another song began. I think it was something by the Four Tops, or maybe The Temptations. Anyway, we continued to dance. Mid-way through the song, George reached down and cupped my chin, lifting my face up. He smiled and lowered his face to kiss me. I leaned into him and kissed him back. Maybe the music kept playing, maybe the music stopped, but George and I ended up in a corner locked together in one long kiss. I knew I wanted him. He was going to be my first. I suggested that we go up to his room which was very atypical for me. The bedrooms were located on the third floor of DU, so we didn't need to go far. He looked at me surprised, but softly took my hand in his, and led me across the dance floor. He said he had to find his roommate first to tell him he needed to find somewhere else to sleep that night."

"Why Susan! You little slut!" Lori yelled.

"See. I told you girls. You don't know *everything* about me. Now let me finish. George brought me to his room. He put a tie on the doorknob, which I found out later, was a signal he was in there with a girl.

I went right to his bed, and took off my blouse,"

"Jesus, Susan!" Cat said. "You wild woman!"

"Oh, Hush. He came over and started to undo his belt but I stopped his hand and told him I wanted to undress him. I took off his belt, and undid the top button of his jeans, and carefully unzipped him. I pulled down his underwear, briefs if you must know, and kissed the top of his penis."

"God, Susan!" Priscilla said.

"Then I stood up and unbuttoned his shirt. He wasn't wearing a T-Shirt, so I opened his shirt and kissed and licked his nipples. I assumed if I liked that, men must like it too. George's chest rose and fell, but he never made a sound. I had him lay down on the bed and took his whole dick in my mouth. It was big and strong, like him. It barely fit into my mouth. He ran his fingers through my hair, and caressed my cheek. With one hand, I slid out of my clothes, and sat on his legs, bending over to kiss him. I slipped my tongue inside his mouth and he hungrily sucked on it. I rubbed his big dick back and forth across me until I thought I was wet enough, and then slowly lowered myself on him. Oh God! It felt so good. I slowly moved up and down on him, savoring every movement. I placed my hand behind me, and softly stroked his balls. We stayed in that position for what seemed to be a long time. Somehow, we both came at the same time. You want to talk about a sweet release?

After we both reached orgasm, I stayed lying on his chest, with him still inside me. He stroked my hair and held me tight, and we stayed in that position all night. In the morning, we made love again, this time with him on top, but it was just as sweet and fulfilling. George took me out for breakfast at the Lord Jeff Inn, a historic old tavern next to the college in Amherst. We held hands the whole time, which made it difficult to eat, but neither one of us wanted to let go.

The semester flew by. Suddenly it was December. On Christmas Eve, George gave me a beautiful, but small, diamond ring that belonged to his mother. She had died several years earlier and left the ring for George to give to his future bride. He brought me home to meet his dad and brother Robb. On Valentine's Day, we were married in a quiet ceremony up at the Thornbird Hill Inn in Vermont. We stayed there for three nights as our honeymoon. Those were the happiest three nights of my life.

We were married for two wonderful years before God took my George from me. He had a heart attack in his sleep. I woke up to find him gone. We were never blessed with children, but I always have George deep in my heart. I say "Good morning George" everyday, silently because of Tony's feelings and "Good night" every evening. I know when I die, I will be reunited with George, not Tony."

"I had no idea." Anna said.

"Me neither." Lori said.

"Wow! What a story." Holly said.

"You poor thing." Priscilla added.

"But at least you had the kind of love that most people never find." Cat added. "George sounded like a wonderful guy and you had some special years before you lost him."

"That's true." Susan said agreeing with Cat. "In a way, I feel bad for Tony. He is really a sweet man in his own right, and always worries and takes good care of me. But he knows he can never fill the emptiness left in my heart when George passed. I told him all about George when we started getting serious. I felt I owed it to him. He accepted it the best he could, I guess, but it can't be easy on him knowing what he knows. We never talk about it anymore, but I can see some sadness and some jealousy in him, especially on Christmas Eve. We do love each other, and we just move on, I guess. Speaking of Tony, I think the guys will be here soon, so there's no sense starting another game. Are you all going to the Greenbrier Club Saturday night? They're having a band with a singer who sounds just like Smoky Robinson."

"Freddy already mentioned it, and he wants to go, so it'll be fun. Cat, you can come with us. They'll be lots of available men there!" Anna said.

"Sounds good. So is this singer as good looking as Smoky Robinson? I always found him so sexy!" Cat said. "I think I have a secret fantasy of being with a black man."

"Oh yeah, he is. Last year when he played, I got up and danced with him while he was singing. He's hot!" Holly said.

"Holly, did you…?" Susan asked.

"No, but I damn well wanted to. I never slept with a black man, but hear they're great in bed." Holly answered.

"You just want that big black dick." Lori said.

"That'd be nice. Did I ever tell you about the smallest dick I ever had?" Holly said.

"No. Keep that story for the next meeting of the Mahjong Club." Anna said. "And it's at your house next week, right?"

"Yeah. That's fine. I have no guy to bounce out, so I just need to grab some wine." Holly said.

"So, I suppose Ashley Fake Tits will be at the Greenbrier Club Saturday night? "Anna asked.

"Does she ever miss an opportunity to show them off?" Lori asked.

"It's funny, because her husband Roger seems like such a nice guy. He's bright, attractive, and wealthy, what the hell is he doing with that bimbo?" Susan asked.

"It's the wealthy part, Susan. Ashley Fake Tits honed in on him for that no doubt. Men can be such little boys when it comes to their dicks." Anna said.

"How much you want to bet she gives a great blowjob? Priscilla asked.

"Hey. I give a great blowjob and I still can't land my third husband."Holly said.

"God, Holly. Men need more than that." Susan said.

"Maybe so. But I never knew a man who didn't like a good, sloppy blowjob." Holly said to Susan.

"Okay girls, let's clean it up. The boys will be home any minute, and they don't need to know all of our secrets, now do they?" Anna said.

"Jesus. Art would die if he knew some of the stuff I did when I was young and foolish." Lori said.

"I want to hear all about *that* story at the next Mahjong game!" Cat said.

"OK. Then I want to hear one of yours. This could be fun. Next week, we'll share some sexual adventures we had when we were in our twenties. Same rules apply. Everyone tells a story, Susan you can't be the last to tell your story every time, and we agreed everything said remains our secret. Kind of like the secret sexual lives of the Ladies of the Mahjong Club." Lori said.

"We are definitely not getting a lot of Mahjong games in ladies. Is that a problem? Anna asked.

"No, I don't think so." Susan said. "Sharing these past experiences is more therapeutic than going to a shrink.""And cheaper," Holly added.

With that, the ladies could hear a car door open and close, and Tony complaining to Freddy about how you can't even get a decent hamburger anymore.

"For Christ's sakes! How hard is it to cook a fucking hamburger medium-rare?" Tony bellowed.

"Aw hell Tony!" It was a fucking hamburger for Christ's sake. Forget about it" Freddy said.

"Hi boys!" Anna said, kissing Freddy on the cheek as he walked in the door. "Good time?"

"It was fun. I wish I was James Bond." Freddy said to his wife.

"You are honey." Anna said back to her husband. "Every time you come to bed."

"Okay. On that note, I'm out of here." Priscilla said.

"Exciting night ladies?" Tony asked with just a drip of sarcasm.

"Oh you know how boring we girls are." Susan said. Giving a little wink to the others. "Just the usual. Playing Mahjong and exchanging recipes."

"Yeah you're a wild bunch. Well good night. I'm heading up to bed. See everyone Saturday night at the Greenbrier Club." Freddy said to a chorus of "good nights."

Saturday Night – The Greenbrier Club

"About time!" Anna said to Lori as she pulled up a chair. Priscilla and Karen, her on and off again partner, were already sitting down, as were Holly, Susan, Tony, and Cat. The music had started, and waiters were circling the room with trays of appetizers. The Club had also set up an impressive buffet on a long catering table. There was an abundance of shrimp surrounding an ice sculpture, Swedish meatballs, dainty club sandwiches, the usual crudités, and the mandatory hamburgers and hot dogs. The Greenbrier Club wasn't known for splurging on lavish buffets, mainly because the members always griped it cost too much. For people who lived in an affluent golfing community, they were a cheap lot.

The band had set up in front of the outside terrace, and was playing popular Motown songs of the 60's. Jonny "Flower" Walker, was singing "Baby, I Need Your Lovin'" in his sensual baritone voice. He announced to crowd his nickname was "Flower", because at the end of every show, he would present one of the ladies in the audience with a white rose and a kiss. It was rumored that sometimes, the lucky lady would get more than the kiss.

Some people were dancing, but most had just arrived, fashionably late of course, and were either sidled up to the bar, or grabbing the few remaining shrimp. They may have been a frugal crowd, but they were smart enough to eat the most expensive item on the buffet first.

The sun was still a flaming ball of orange, but was just now beginning to set in the distant horizon. An employee of the club was walking around lighting the Tiki torches, and the smaller oil filled glass globes on each table. Some of the more adventurous members, and the drunk ones, were on the dance floor showing off what they thought were some nifty dance moves. Because it was Florida, most of the men were dressed in shorts, white if they were really dressing up, complete with the floral Tommy Bahamas silk shirts. The ladies wore loose, colorful dresses, with sandals. Most of the men agreed they preferred the casual dress lifestyle Florida offered, compared to the North, where dressing up meant a suit or sports coat and tie, with dress shoes.

The Greenbrier Club's membership came with home ownership in the Greenbrier Gold Estates. It had an Olympic sized pool, a weight/ exercise room, complete with the latest gym equipment and flat screen televisions to watch while you were either lifting weights or walking on a treadmill. That room was usually empty. Zumba held the most appeal to the female members of the club and the classes were held in adjacent room. The women were well aware that if they did not sign up early the class might be full. Another room was dedicated to arts and crafts. Wreath making and floral arranging classes were held there. When a local floral shop offered a class in the

Japanese art of Ikebana, there was standing room only. Guest lecturers often appeared at the club, and there was a conference room that accommodated the small groups that assembled to listen to them. The banquet hall also served as a meeting room for the members when a controversial vote was pending. Outside, alongside the pool, a large brick veranda with a mini bar, served as the gathering place for most of the smaller parties. It was here everyone was gathered tonight.

"Lori, why are you always the last to arrive?" Anna asked.

"It's not because of me, it's Art. Honest to God, that man is worse than any woman I know. He spends more time in the bathroom grooming himself than I do. He's in the car now, no doubt checking himself out in the rearview mirror one last time before he comes in."

"Oh shit! Don't look now, but A.F.T. is heading our way." Susan said.

"Who the hell is A.F.T.?" Lori asked.

"Oh, c'mon. Think about it for a minute. "A "is for Ashley, "F" is for fake and "T" is for tits." Susan explained.

"Okay, okay, you two" Anna interjected. "Let's be a little more discreet, shall we? She's within ear shot.

"Hi ladies!" Ashley chirped, as she pulled up a chair. She was wearing a low cut silk blouse revealing most of her ample breasts and a short black skirt that left nothing to the imagination. "What a great night! Don't you girls dance? Priscilla I love your dress. Is that a Lilly Pulitzer? Hi Tony! You look handsome tonight! You too, Freddy! So Cat, what do you think of our little club?" She prattled on and on, not giving anyone else a chance to respond. "I asked Roger to dance with me, but he said he's not in the mood! He can be such a bore. I hope I don't get that way when I get older!"

Art came out onto the veranda looking stylish as usual. He was wearing a cream colored Ferragamo sports coat over a light blue silk Polo shirt, navy blue slacks with a white belt, and brown Gucci loafers without socks. His silver hair was slicked back, and his face had a flushed glow from having been freshly washed and shaved.

"Art will dance with me!" Ashley said.

"Over my fucking dead body." Lori said under her breath.

"Maybe later, Ashley. First, I must attend to my Princess." Art said as he picked up Lori's hand and kissed it with a flourish.

"Ok, but I'm going to hold you to it!" Ashley said as she left the ladies, seeing someone she thought was far more interesting at the bar.

"Why don't you dance with her Priscilla?" Cat asked.

"Sorry honey, she prefers the swinging dick. But then again, you all do!"

"Ah Priscilla, you know you just kill all the guys here being gay. They all would love a roll in the hay with you." Tony said.

"Would you like one too, Tony?" Susan asked her husband. Would you like a tumble?"

"No not me dear! I'm exhausted from trying to keep up with you!" Tony answered.

"Wow, was that the right thing to say!" Lori said.

"I didn't live this long by being stupid." Tony said.

"Sorry ladies, but the only person who is going to get a roll in the hay with me tonight is Karen." Priscilla said.

All eyes turned to Karen. The two of them couldn't have been more different. Priscilla was a gregarious extrovert while Karen displayed all the qualities of a self- conscious introvert. Karen was tall, yet shorter than Priscilla. She had short, natural red hair, a cute upturned nose, and full lips, the kind of lips men drool over. She wore a sheer red lip gloss that accentuated her glorious mouth. Her pale yellow pant suit was the perfect choice for the balmy evening. All the women were envious of the large diamond studs that sparkled on her earlobes. She was elegant and demure in every way.

 Karen was an attorney who specialized in immigration law, a burgeoning business, especially in Florida. She graduated from Tulane Law School, but left New Orleans after having lived through several hurricanes. She and Priscilla had been together for years, but not in a committed relationship that anyone could tell. But they were obviously very close and loved each other as deeply as any heterosexual couple. Every guy in the room, fantasized about the two of them having sex.

"I hope that white rose ends up in my fingers. It's been awhile and ol' Jonny Flowers might have more than he can handle tonight!" Cat said.

"Yikes! Art said turning to Cat. "Been awhile, huh?"

"Long enough." Cat replied. "I had a new bed delivered today, one of those Tempur-pedic foam mattresses, and I want to give it a trial run. I have up to 30 days to return it, so I might as well see if it can handle the workload."

By now, the band was slowing it down, and people began to dance. Holly noticed that Ashley Fake Tits was already up there grinding her hips into some guy who had to be at least ten years younger than her. His hands had drifted down her hips and were resting on her ass, and she sure as hell made no effort to remove them. Roger was at the bar watching them, his face frozen in a thin smile. His embarrassment was obvious. It certainly wasn't the first time. Most of the crowd, assumed that she was unfaithful to him. No one could understand why he tolerated it.

Art and Lori danced, moving together with the rhythm of a couple that had been together for many years. Susan dragged Tony up to the dance floor. Tony was athletic and a great golfer, but he was out of his element on the dance floor. He moved around stiffly, and couldn't keep up with beat. He glanced at the band and silently willed that the song end, so he could return to the table and put an end to his misery. Holly went to the bar and coaxed one of the unattached men to dance with her. As she did so, his friends hooted and whistled. Priscilla and Karen stayed seated. They didn't want to draw any attention to themselves. While they were both comfortable with their sexuality, they never flaunted it in the predominately conservative club.

Years ago, while Priscilla and Karen were enjoying a lovely dinner at the club with Anna and Freddy, a drunken member staggered over to their table and made a inappropriate comment about "lesbos." Outraged, Freddy immediately rose from the table. He grabbed the guy by his neck, dragged him over to the pool and tossed him in. The story circulated around Greenbrier like wildfire, and no one ever dared to make a similar mistake. Freddy may have been in his sixties, but you wouldn't want to fuck with him.

People began to leave the club at about 11:30. Karen went back with Priscilla presumably for a roll in the hay, while Susan and Tony left to go to bed without the roll in the hay. Art was still at the bar, his usual spot, telling jokes. Roger led Ashley Fake Tits out firmly by the elbow. She had too much to drink and was protesting loudly. Holly had one scotch too many, and accepted a ride home from an older gentleman, leaving her Porsche in the Club's parking lot for the night.

"Well, I didn't get the white rose." Cat said.

"And Jonny Flowers didn't get the fuck of his life." Anna said laughing. "Maybe, next year."

"Why don't we go to the *River Café* tomorrow for Sunday brunch?" Lori suggested.

"Great idea." Anna agreed. "I love their Coconut French toast."

"Wow. It's been awhile. I forgot all about that place. They always had the best Eggs Benedict. You can order it with fresh crab instead of Canadian bacon, you know." Cat said.

"Okay. Then it's settled. The boys are playing golf, so it'll be just the girls. I'll swing by and pick you all up, say 9:30?"

"Perfect. That way I can sleep in." Cat said.

"Not me." Lori said. Art likes a little lovin' in the morning. But he doesn't take long." She said with a smile. "A little "Oh Art! Oh Art!" and he shoots like a Fourth of July rocket!"

"I wouldn't mind that once in a while". Anna said. "Sometimes Freddy takes so long, I think I should bring a book to bed."

"Anna! Really!" Cat said.

"Alright. Enough!" We can save that for our Mahjong Club. "What's the topic? Some sexual adventure we had when we were in our twenties," Anna asked.

"I'll have to think on that one." Cat said. "So many to choose from."

"Maybe Susan will surprise us again. That was some story about how she lost her virginity." Lori said.

"And poor Holly! That might explain a few things." Anna said. "You know, under that crass, tough exterior, she really is a sweet girl. Working in the construction business with all those men couldn't have been easy. I'm sure she had to set a lot of those guys straight. Maybe they each reminded her of her uncle in some way. What an asshole, to molest a young girl. His niece, no less. His brother's daughter!"

"Well let me tell you. Nobody gets Holly in bed unless she wants him to now. I'm sure that rape, that's what it was, hardened her heart. I'm not sure if she'll allow any man to get close to her. She was married twice, and I knew both husbands. They were significantly older than Holly, and seemed more interested in companionship than sexual intimacy." Lori said.

"Ok ladies. Don't forget....Mahjong at Holly's house on Wednesday night. I'll call her tomorrow to remind her. I'll invite her to brunch, but considering the amount of scotch she drank, I doubt that she'll come." Anna said.

"Better just let her sleep." Cat said.

"Ok ladies. See you bright and early. Good night." Anna said. "And don't forget to bring a story about a sexual escapade in your twenties Wednesday night," she whispered.

Wednesday Night – Holly's Story

Wednesday night arrived and brought with it a cool rain. Looking out the bay window in her living room Holly could see a gray mist drifting languidly over the 15th hole of the golf course. The cranes that usually gathered around the fairway, had tucked their heads into their white feathers to keep themselves dry. Past the fairway was a pond with a family of ducks paddling around, clearly oblivious to the rain. Next to the pond, a golfer had traded his golf clubs for a fishing rod, hoping that the drizzling rain might make the fish bite. Holly thought, with all the fertilizer the golf club put on the course, who the hell would even *want* to catch a fish there. You certainly couldn't eat it. Unless you wanted to emit a fluorescent green glow, that is.

Since the girls weren't due to arrive for at least another hour, Holly sat back on the new sofa recently delivered by Paradise Home & Patio and closed her eyes. She sank into the down- filled tufted cushions and once again admired the botanical Waverly print she had selected for the upholstery. She thought about her life's journey. It certainly wasn't a pretty picture.

She had grown up in the abject poverty of rural Maine, and had run away from home as a teenager. The morning after he uncle raped her, just before the sun was about to rise and illuminate her shame, and while her father and uncle were still asleep, she slipped out of her house and hitched a ride to Portland. She bought a ticket to Boston at the Greyhound Bus station with her meager savings. After a four hour ride, the bus arrived at Boston's South Station terminal, its final destination, and the passengers were asked to disembark. Holly stepped gingerly onto the grimy pavement of the terminal parking lot, and felt a surge of panic. After several minutes of deep breathing she regained her composure and decided that she did not regret her decision to leave home. Even though she was from the backwoods of Maine, she knew enough to resist the advances of the men who lingered around the dingy Greyhound station. She was sophisticated enough to deduce that these men were probably pimps looking to take advantage of girls like her. She walked up Atlantic Avenue from the bus station and spied a van handing out blankets to a group of homeless men sleeping on the street. The van was from the Pine Street Inn, and the volunteers were conducting their mobile street outreach program. She approached the van a bit warily and asked where she could find shelter for the night. The volunteer workers offered her a sandwich, which she consumed immediately, and drove her to a shelter that housed runaways and prostitutes trying to leave their pimps. She spent the night at the shelter feeling lonely and scared. She didn't have a job, so the next day she panhandled on the same street where the hookers worked.

She was an easy target for the denizens of the seedy underbelly of the city. She had no skills so finding a job was next to impossible. She spent the first few weeks alone and afraid, scavenging for food and shelter. If it weren't for the kindly old couple who picked her up off the street she could have died. Despite Holly's protests, the couple, Wendell and Alice, took her to their home. She was sick, chilled to the bone, and probably suffering from hypothermia. Her speech was slurred and she just couldn't get warm. Alice and Wendell had come into Boston to do some shopping and found her lying on the sidewalk. She refused to go to the hospital, because she was afraid that they would call her father and make her return to Maine. She had eaten very little during the last few days, so she put aside what little pride she had left and graciously accepted their offer. Holly was so weak, that Wendell had to pick her up and carry her to their car.

Alice called their family doctor, one who still made house calls, and asked if he would be willing to treat her. The doctor said that he could be at their home within the hour. When he saw the condition she was in, he suggested that she be hospitalized. Holly refused vehemently. He gave her medication and told her to eat as much chicken soup as she could hold down. With that, he left. She huddled under a pile of blankets in the guest bedroom and Alice came in to check her breathing every so often. Alice and Wendell had lost their only child in a car accident several years earlier. Although the accident was nothing more than that, an accident, it was as if they sought redemption for not being able to save their child by saving Holly.

Holly recovered, but was painfully thin, so Alice fed her calorie-laden home cooked meals. When she got stronger, Wendell took her for long walks along the Charles River. Soon she was strong enough to jog. Wendell's jogging days had long passed, so Holly ran by herself. She found running to be cathartic.

With their financial help she enrolled at Bunker Hill Community college. She majored in accounting and marketing. After graduating with honors from Bunker Hill she transferred to Boston University. After college, she was offered a job at a national plumbing supply company, and with Draconian determination, rose to become the president of sales.

She had long moved out from Alice and Wendell's home, but called them every week. They became the aunt and uncle she never had. When she received her first bonus check of fifty thousand dollars for landing a multi-million dollar contract, she endorsed the check and mailed it to Alice. They called her upon receiving it, insisting that they could never keep such a gift, but Holly was adamant. "You saved my life" she said. "What's a life worth? Surely a lot more than that check", she told them. When they died, she felt hollow. The pain of losing them almost consumed her. Wendell predeceased Alice. He died from a massive heart attack while strolling along the Charles. Alice passed away exactly six months after him, most likely from a broken heart. Holly resolved to never allow herself to feel the devastating pain of loss again.

She traveled around the country for her company. She met many men and slept with some of them. Eventually, she married an older, retired man who had worked in the same business. She didn't love him, and she wasn't afraid to admit the truth to herself. Their marriage was comfortable, and she believed that he was not looking for a deep emotional commitment. When he died, he left her a sizable fortune, but not a broken heart. She traveled more, met more men, and slept with some of them as well. But no matter how passionate the sex was, she never allowed herself to fall in love. One of her many lovers opined that she had a constructed a brick wall around her heart. She didn't disagree.

A few years after her first husband died, she married again. This time her groom was a man even older than her first husband. He was kind and generous to her, and asked little in return. He loved nothing more than sitting in front of the fireplace reading a good mystery with his golden retriever by his side. He passed away on their third anniversary, sitting by the fire in his favorite chair. He left everything he owned to Holly, adding to her already sizeable fortune.

She sold their five bedroom house in Pembroke, MA, moved around some assets, and bought a spacious home with a large pool in Greenbrier Gold Estates. There she found and developed the closest group of friends she ever had. With the support of her friends, the pain and heartache she had experienced in her life began to fade away. She could be herself with them, and while they all teased her and each other, they accepted her for who she was, and for who she wasn't.

She was rattled by Anna yelling "Hey! Anyone home in here!"

"Come in. Come in!" Holly said, snapping out of her reverie.

The group piled into the kitchen. Susan brought in a bottle of pinot noir, Cat had made baked brie, and Lori contributed salsa and chips. Holly was not known for her culinary expertise, although her kitchen was one most women would die to have. The irony was that she only used the microwave oven and the Keurig coffee machine. However, she did have a complete list of every restaurant in the area that delivered.

Cat took out the Mahjong tiles and began to turn them face down before mixing them up. Anna set out the snacks along the smoky grey granite counter. Holly put out the mini lobster salad sandwiches, a tray of fruit, and the gourmet cupcakes that she had ordered from her favorite caterer. Susan opened the pinot noir and poured it into the wine goblets that lined the countertop, while Holly fixed herself a scotch.

"And why are you so dressed up Priscilla?" Lori asked.

"I can't stay. I'm meeting a client later for a drink who wants to hire me as a political consultant. He's eyeing the Congressional seat." Priscilla said.

"Ah. One lying, no good thieving bastard replacing another lying, thieving no good bastard. I get it." Holly said.

"It pays the bills honey. Besides, I might need the extra money if we do go to Vegas." Priscilla said.

"Well since you're leaving early, let's start our game of Mahjong now, and Priscilla, you can go first telling your tale of a sexual adventure in your twenties." Holly said.

"Here we go again." Susan said.

"Yeah, and you can go second, since you went last, Susan." Cat said.

"Ok. Ok. I will." Susan said.

"Priscilla? We're ready for your tale. Make it a good one!" Holly said.

"Next, you'll want to give a prize for the best story!" Susan added.

Priscilla's Story

"Ok. Here goes." Priscilla started. I had graduated from Georgetown University and started to hunt for a job. After pounding the pavement for weeks with no success, I called my former academic advisor at Georgetown for suggestions.   As luck would have it, he had connections with the White House staff. He made a few phone calls and wrote a glowing recommendation for me. I'll never be able to thank him enough for helping me land one of the coveted jobs working as a Congressional aide on Capitol Hill."

"For whom?" Lori asked.

"Sorry, that's going to remain confidential." Priscilla said. "So I'm in Washington, the epicenter of political power, feeling a bit overwhelmed by the magnitude of it all. Of course *every* damn old Senator hit on me. I think they must think they're serving the public by bonking the aides."

"Bonking?" Cat asked. "Is that a D.C. term?"

"Screwing. Fucking. Whatever term you want to call it. It all amounts to the same thing when you get right down to it." Priscilla said. I worked for a few senators, as most of the aides did, one of whom was a female senator, who shall remain nameless. I had heard the rumors that I was involved sexually with a female senator, and I won't confirm or deny it was her. One night we worked very late editing a bill she was drafting. As we left the office, she offered to take me out for a dinner and a drink. I was famished because I hadn't eaten all day. She called her car service and we waited a few minutes before the shiny, black limousine pulled up to the curb. She directed the driver to local restaurant that was popular with the politicos. Even at that late hour, there was a line of people waiting to get in. But of course, the wealthy and powerful of D.C. don't have to wait. We were ushered in ahead of everyone else. The people waiting in line were clearly annoyed. The senator asked to be seated at her usual table, and the hostess escorted us to a cozy banquette in the back, the kind that allowed for quiet conversations. After such a long day, it was heavenly to sink into the soft, buttery, black leather seats. The sommelier arrived with a wine list that was as lengthy as Holly's dildo.

"Hey! Who told you about my dildo?" Holly protested.

I wasn't very knowledgeable about wine, but I knew the bottle of Barolo she ordered was expensive. After studying the menu, we both ordered filet mignon, cooked medium rare. It was served with a creamy béarnaise sauce, shitake mushrooms and turnip gratinée. The waiter filled our wine glasses, and as the Barolo took effect, we both relaxed and discussed the importance of her proposed legislation. After the dinner plates were cleared, we ordered coffee, but passed on dessert. As we were about to leave, it occurred to me that the waiter never presented us with the check. I assumed the dinner was compliments of the restaurant or, maybe just charged to her office, but I don't know for sure.

We walked outside, past the line of people still waiting to be seated, and climbed into the waiting limousine. Her driver asked for my address, but he drove to her place first. She got out of the car and dismissed him saying his services were no longer needed. I sat for minute, confused and not quite sure what to do. I got out of the car and thought perhaps that it was an ethical violation for her driver to take me home. I was ready to hail a cab when she said to me 'C'mon dear.' Not knowing what to think or do, I followed her. Remember, this is a *Senator* we're talking about.

We entered the foyer of her building and stepped into a private elevator, and she pushed the *PH* button for the penthouse. The elevator door opened up directly into her apartment. Oops, I meant, *Penthouse*. One entire wall in the living room was glass, and the view was stunning. The apartment overlooked the Washington Monument. She walked over to a glossy ebony bar, and poured two drinks. She offered one to me with her fine-boned hand and perfectly manicured nails.

'Why am I here, Madam Senator?'

She smiled and said 'I know your gay honey. And that's okay. I like being with a woman from time to time. We're much better lovers than men, don't you think? They assume we're satisfied when they climb on top of us and poke us with their "manhood." Men can be so obtuse, and it's difficult to redirect them without fracturing their fragile egos. I'd like you to spend the night with me. You're a beautiful young woman and I want you. I always find it's better not to beat around the bush, no pun intended.'

Well, I was completely shocked and intimidated. I certainly admired this woman, but again, she was a senator; a little out of my league. I knew she had a husband, but I didn't know the state of her marriage, nor was I really concerned.

I stepped back and looked at her; that is, physically. She was probably in her fifties, but quite striking. She was petite and in good shape. Her daily workouts at the Senate gym definitely paid off. She always dressed impeccably. I'm positive she had at least a dozen St. John suits and a shoe collection that could rival Imelda Marcos. She wore Manolo Blahnik pumps with 3 inch heels. I can only assume they made her feel more powerful. She wore simple, but exquisite jewelry. Her short brown hair was cut in a flattering bob style.

As I was looking at her, she walked up to me, brushed the hair from the nape of my neck, and placed a soft, warm kiss there. A shiver ran up my spine. That one kiss was enough to get my juices flowing. I turned my head and kissed her on the mouth. She opened my mouth with her tongue and slipped it in. It tasted sweet and velvety. We French kissed gently, not like the guys who want to ram their tongue in your mouth. She explored my body with her hands, as I leaned against the bar. I was afraid I was going to topple over. Smiling, she pulled her face back a few inches from mine and said 'This is your first time with a woman, isn't it?' I could only nod in agreement, it seemed as if I lost my voice. . "I can smell you, and you smell delicious."

"You really want to hear this?" Priscilla asked the group of ladies, who were now taking shallow breaths.

"Hell yeah!" Holly whispered.

"Okay. So my Senator takes me by the hand and leads me into her *boudoir*. In case you didn't know, people who live in penthouses, have boudoirs not bedrooms." The other women detected a note of sarcasm in Priscilla's voice. "I have never seen such a luxurious bedroom. The room had a large bay window that overlooked the city. Most people I know prefer the bedroom to have shades so the sun won't wake them in the morning. Obviously she wasn't one of those people, since there were no window treatments, and the room was illuminated by the city lights.

 She guided me to the king-sized bed, turned around, and asked me to help her out of her clothes. She was wearing a simple black suit and cream colored silk blouse. A single strand of elegant pearls adorned her slender neck.

She took off her suit jacket and I unbuttoned her blouse, leaving the pearls resting upon her neck. As her blouse fell to the floor, I noticed her perfectly uniform tan. Clearly she had sunbathed in the nude. Her breasts were pert and the large nipples protruded through her lacy bra. I placed my left hand on her breast, squeezing gently. She moaned and pressed backwards against me. I undid the gold clasp that held the strand of pearls together, and placed them on top of her black suit, which was lying on the floor. She turned around to face me, and kissed my cheeks, my nose and finally my mouth. I hungrily sought her tongue as we fell backwards onto the bed. I pulled down her white silk panties and tossed them onto the floor. I kissed her feet, slowly working my way up her legs. I kissed and nibbled the inside of her knees, then the inside of her thighs. By the time I reached her vagina, she was glistening with excitement and anticipation. I deftly parted her vaginal lips with my fingers, exposing her sweetness. I placed my lips on her, allowing my tongue to gently explore her. Abandoning her self control, she moaned as she squeezed her thighs together, and came into my mouth.

For a long moment, neither one of us moved. I kissed her pubic hair, which smelled faintly of "Tresor", her signature scent. I took French 101 in college, and learned only the basics, but enough to know that "Tresor" translates to "treasure". It was the perfect word to describe her pussy. She reached down and pulled me up to her, kissing my mouth. She had me stand and removed my clothes by herself. She lowered herself to my exposed nipple, and taking it into her mouth, bit it playfully. I felt a rush flow through me. She pulled down the duvet and we held each other, softly, with a lovers' patience. We explored each others' body, with curiosity. She put her hand in between my legs and began to stroke my clitoris, first using only her finger tips, and then she put her fingers all the way inside me. I came once, burying my head into her shoulder, and the second time, crying out into her breasts. We stayed like that through the night, entwined in each other's arms.

In the morning, she rose first and made coffee. The aroma drifted into the bedroom as I languished in the decadently, soft sheets. I could hear the water running in the shower. Yet again, I didn't know what to do. I put on the robe she had left for me and padded down the carpeted hallway to the kitchen. I poured myself a mug of coffee and waited for her to finish her shower. She had put out a plate of croissants along with butter and jam. I wasn't hungry, but I ate one anyway because they looked so appetizing. I heard the water shut off in the bathroom and moments later she walked into the kitchen, dressed, but with her hair wrapped in towel. She walked over to me and kissed the top of my head, adding that she had left fresh towels for me in the bathroom.

I was relieved that she had not adopted an air of professional detachment in the morning, but treated me with affection. After I took my shower, she called her car service to drive me home. It was Saturday and one of the rare weekends that I didn't have to go into the office. I could work at home on my laptop.

She said that she had enjoyed the evening, and that I made a wonderful dinner companion. She never swore me to secrecy, or appeared uncomfortable with spending the night with me.

Her driver buzzed the penthouse shortly after she had called him. As I left her apartment she blew me a kiss. I took the elevator down to the lobby and hopped into the limo. I smiled to myself on the way home. My evening with the senator dispelled any lingering doubts I had about being gay. We saw each other from time to time, and once I accompanied her on a political junket to Hawaii. She served three terms and decided not to run for re-election, despite the fact she would have won handily. She was tired of the partisan politics in the Senate, and the enmity that came along with it. She remembered when governing the people was more gentile, and when the people in elected office put their constituency before their own political aspirations.

I don't see her anymore, but we always exchange Christmas cards.

"Hellava story, Priscilla." Lori said. "Can I ask you one question though?"

"Shoot" Priscilla replied.

"Are you attracted to men at all? Or are you only attracted to women?"

"I like men." Priscilla said. "For awhile I dated both sexes, but men never really did it for me. I find that women are better lovers. They're not in such a hurry to get to the grand finale. They can kiss and caress for hours. Men want to get to it after a few kisses. Besides that, it's the attraction. I find a woman's body beautiful. It's a work of art, whereas a man's body is more functional, like a Jeep Wrangler."

"Well put Priscilla." Susan agreed. "Tony's' body is like a Jeep, except the four-wheel drive isn't working anymore, and it stalls out now and then!"

Okay, Cat. How about you? What fun story do you have about a sexual escapade you had while you were in your twenties? One that you'll remember when you're sitting in that rocking chair in the old folk's home." Anna asked.

"Well, what comes to mind is one of my favorite memories. When I was twenty-three a few girlfriends and I drove to Columbus for the *King Richard's Faire.* Remember that? It's a Renaissance fair that recreates a sixteenth century English village. My girlfriends had been previously, but it was my first time. The fair was held on acres of grassy fields. At the entrance we bought our tickets from a young woman dressed as a wench. We proceeded past the ticket booth to a knight, dressed in full armor, who took our tickets. Inside, there was a whirlwind of activity. In one area we saw men swallowing flaming swords, jesters, mimes, magicians, jugglers and beggars. A short distance away we noticed acrobats, and minstrels. There seemed to be dancing and cavorting everywhere. All of the actors were dressed in historically accurate costumes and spoke in Old English. It was a little overwhelming at first. We walked to a booth to try our hand at knife throwing, but none of us was very good. We didn't fare any better shooting a crossbow. At least none of us got hurt while horseback riding. We passed vendors selling oils, pottery and handmade clothing. One blacksmith was hammering a sword, and another crafting armor. A leather maker was positioning silver rivets on a brown leather vest.

We strolled through the fair at a leisurely pace and chatted with the "townspeople". It felt as if we have stepped back in time to another century.

The morning flew by and by early afternoon we were hungry. We headed to the marketplace to buy lunch. Each of us ordered a bowl of rich, creamy clam chowder that was served in bread bowls. The chowder didn't fill me up, so I bought a turkey leg that had been roasting on an open spit. I guess my eyes were bigger than my stomach. The turkey was delicious, but I couldn't eat the whole thing. As we were about to leave our table a member of the royal court announced, that the jousting would be starting soon on the King's Field. The girls and I grabbed a couple of cups of ale and headed over.

The jousting court was set up in an open field. A roped off area surrounded the field. There weren't any bleachers for the spectators. A raised viewing booth, with brightly colored banners, was erected for the King, his Queen and some of his knights. Once the King and Queen were seated, blaring trumpets announced the arrival of the knights who would be jousting.

Ten knights, riding massive horses, galloped across the open field and took their places before the King. The King proclaimed the start of the "King's Tournament "and offered one hundred gold pieces to the victor. I was mesmerized. Time and time again the knights charged at one another, breaking lances and sometimes unhorsing the rider. If this was staged, I couldn't tell. The last two knights remaining faced one another. The White Knight, riding a white horse with a golden soaring eagle on his shield, faced off against the Blue Knight, riding a large chestnut horse with a stone tower on his shield.

They took their places at the end of the jousting line and spurred their horses into action. Clouds of dust flew into the air as the horses raced towards each other. Initially, the Blue Knight attempted to place his lance on the White Knight's shield, but at the last moment, the White Knight shifted in his saddle, and deflected the blow. They raced to the end of the line, and as they turned the corner, hurled themselves once again toward each other. This time, the White Knight struck first. His lance snapped with a loud crack, and threw the Blue Knight backwards onto the ground.

The crowd went wild, applauding and cheering for the White Night. I commented that it was interesting that the White Knight was the winner. Get it? The White Knight? How obvious. The White Knight rode his horse to the King's Throne to receive his prize of gold. As he did so, the sound of thundering hooves filled the air. A knight dressed in black was riding toward us upon a large black horse. He carried a shield that was emblazoned with the figure of a fire-spewing dragon. The crowd gasped at the unexpected turn of events. The Black Knight rode up to the King and apologized for his late entrance.

Turning to the White Knight he said "Can you really be the champion of the King's Tournament without vanquishing *every* opponent? I stand undefeated before you." The White Knight responded, "I accept your challenge Sir, and I will see you fall as the others have." With that, the White Knight turned his horse back once again to the starting point on the jousting line. The Black Night bowed low in his saddle to the King and Queen and moved his horse to the opposite end of the jousting field. I know this is hard to believe, but it's the absolute truth. My three girlfriends will swear to it under oath.

The Black Knight rode slowly along the ropes that held back the crowd. He stopped in front of me and whispered "M'Lady, I ask for your favor in this match." He pulled out a sweet yellow flower from inside his sleeve and handed it to me. I was in a state of shock, but I managed to reply, "Ride true my Knight, and may your lance win the day." I know. Corny corny corny. But it was the first thing that popped into my head. He rode off and took his place at the end of the line. As soon as he got there, each of them put their heels into their horse's flanks and charged down the line. When they passed each other, there was a loud crash, of horses and men, of lances shattered and the whinny of the steeds. When the dust cleared, the Black Knight rode tall while the White Knight lay defeated in the dirt. The crowd was completely silent. This was not the ending they expected. Except for me, of course. I was clapping and cheering. I guess I've always rooted for the underdog.

The Black Knight rode to the King's throne to collect his prize of one hundred gold coins which the King threw down to him in a brown leather pouch. The King asked him to remove his helmet and to state his name "I am Sir Alec" he replied as he removed his helmet. He was a young man, with lustrous, jet black hair that fell to his shoulders, an aquiline nose and piercing blue eyes.

"And which King do you serve, Sir Alec?" The King asked.

"I serve no King, M'Lord. I ride with no one other than my horse."

"Congratulations, Brave Knight" the King said.

With that, Sir Alec cantered back along the viewing field, and rode up to me.

"Come, My Princess. Join me to celebrate my victory in my mid-day meal."

He offered me his hand and helped me swing up on the saddle behind him. I looked down at my girlfriends who were frozen in place with shock. I thought 'this could be fun' so I wrapped my arms around his waist and rode off with him. We rode out of the fairgrounds, across green fields and along a narrow stream. He finally stopped, hopped off and helped me down from the saddle. Attached to the saddle was a bedroll which he spread out on the grass like a blanket. He opened a brown leather bag and handed me a wineskin and cooked sausages, bread and cheeses.

Now understand, I'm still in shock. It was like a wonderful dream and I didn't want to wake up. We sat on the blanket, eating sausages and cheese, breaking off hunks of bread and taking turns sipping wine from the wineskin. We barely spoke. He never said whether Alec was his real name, and I really didn't want to know. He was more intent on eating, which he did ravenously. I guess jousting must be strenuous work.

"Is this when you make love to the Fair Maiden, my Prince?" I couldn't believe I asked him. He smiled, paused, and then drew me close to him. Under his wool shirt, I could feel his hard chest and muscled arms. I undid his pants, which were held together with string lacing. He helped me out of my jeans and I pulled my t-shirt over my head. He undid the clasp of my bra, and threw it on the ground.

He was magnificent! He had a small mat of curly black hair on his chest, and soft black hair surrounding a long, thick penis. I think I licked my lips unconsciously. He slid me under him, but I told him to wait. I laid him down on his back, and I took him in my mouth. I slowly slid my tongue up and down his shaft and he gasped when I took one of his testicles into my mouth. I lay down beside him, and pulled him on top of me. He slid inside me easily, filling me up. He was rock-hard. Harder I murmured, as he slid in and out of me. He obliged and began to furiously bang himself into me. Harder I said, more desperately, and I arched my body to meet his thrusts. We were in perfect rhythm. It was fierce and forceful; pure, unleashed passion. He pulled my hair roughly, and I bit down on his shoulder hard enough to leave a bruise. I felt myself release all over him, and he came deep inside me shortly after.

He fell back on the blanket beside me, panting and out of breath. His body glistened with perspiration, and emitted a strong, musky odor. I stayed on my back, gazing up into the trees and listening to the rippling of a nearby stream. He caught his breath and pulled himself up, resting on an elbow. He began to say something, but I placed my finger over his mouth and asked him not to talk. I told him, I didn't want to know his real name, or where he came from or what kind of ice cream he liked. I wanted him to remain my Black Knight, forever, unsullied by the truth.

He smiled and nodded in agreement, so we dressed in silence. He put me on the back of his horse, and I wrapped my arms around him for one last time, as he rode me back to the fairgrounds.

"And Ashley Big Tits thinks *we* have boring lives!" Anna said. "Wow!"

The ladies took that opportunity to get up and replenish their glasses and get a bite to eat.

"Seriously. I get tired of younger people, not just Ashley Fake Tits, assuming that just because we're older professional women we haven't had colorful, exciting life experiences." Anna said.

"It's just like when kids look at their parents and think they've never had sex, or ran wild as kids." Cat said.

"This conversation has been good for me. I mean all of us sharing our experiences. I used to think I was the only one who occasionally, you know, had sex when I was single. " Susan said.

"I agree, Susan. So share with us. What was one of your little escapades when you were in your twenties?"

"One time comes to mind. I was living in Cambridge and working at a large insurance company. My job was boring and I was boring so it was a good fit, for awhile anyway. I was living alone in a small one bedroom apartment near

Harvard Square since George had passed away the previous year.

My office was within walking distance so I didn't have to deal with commuter traffic. I loved walking down Massachusetts Avenue especially in the summer. There was always a flurry of activity in Harvard Square; students rushing to class, people sitting at outdoor cafes reading the newspaper, a throng of MBTA riders exiting from the Red Line on the subway. The atmosphere in Harvard Square, or the "Square" as some referred to it, had an almost European ambiance.

I had a fairly regular routine. I left my apartment the same time every morning and took the same route to work. At the end of the day I walked the same path in reverse. On my way home, I often passed the *Café Pamplona,* the oldest and most iconic coffee house in Cambridge. It was a favorite spot with Harvard students and was often quite crowded. As I watched them drink their overpriced lattes and cappuccino's I couldn't help but think that their lives seemed so carefree. They smoked gauloises seemingly mesmerized by the drifting tendrils of smoke believing that were worldly and sophisticated. I guess we all did at that age.

I'll admit I always dressed ultra conservatively, but after George died my style became almost frumpy. I didn't have the energy or desire to spend time assembling a fashionable wardrobe. I usually left work around three o'clock. My walk home took about thirty minutes, if I didn't stop to treat myself to a frozen yogurt or to do some errands. Because I was a creature of habit, I always passed the *Café Pamplona*. One day a young man whistled at me as I walked by. It wasn't meant as a compliment. He was making fun of me. I wasn't the kind of girl men whistled at, and I could hear his friends laugh.

Each day as I passed their corner, he became emboldened and would say things to me like "Your skirt is too long. Why don't you shorten it and show us your pretty legs." Or "Hey baby, want to have a good time?" I always ignored him and his friends, and I didn't complain to the owner of the café. I needed to learn how to deal with men. Some of the men at work were no different, but at least they were older men. These were boys.

As I walked by, several weeks after the first offensive wolf whistle, the same young man says "So how about it honey. You want to have a good time?" I stopped in my tracts, looked at him, and I walked up to him and his shit-eating grin began to fade. I looked him up and down, like he was a piece of meat, taking my cue from men who sometimes look that way at us. After taking a good long look I said "Well, you're on the scrawny side, don't have much of an ass and with those feet, you probably have a small dick, but what the hell! Let's go. I live up the street. Unless of course, you want to bring me back to your dorm room."

Ladies, you could have heard the proverbial pin drop. Then one by one, his friends starting hooting and hollering for him to take me up on my challenge. This kid wanted to crawl inside his coffee cup and die. I had called his bluff in the most public way and gave him no way out. While he was trying to come up with a response, I added "Unless of course you really do have a small dick or can't get it up and don't want your friends to find out about it. You're not *gay* now, are you?"

He jumped to his feet and said let's go, with as much false bravado as he could muster. As we walked down I reached over and took his hand. He was so startled I thought he was going to jump into the oncoming traffic. I was enjoying making him as uncomfortable as he made me, and who knows how many other women.

When we arrived at the front door of my apartment building, I said "I'm done with you. I hope you've learned your lesson. Women don't enjoy the kind of attention you and your friends dole out. There is a huge difference between paying a woman a compliment with courtesy and respect, and your immature and cowardly behavior. Now, go on your way, and make sure you don't let it happen again."

He stood motionless in front of me, and hung his head sheepishly.

"I'm sorry he said. I guess I feel insecure because my friends have had sex with so many girls, and I, well…" He trailed off.

"So you think that invading someone's personal space with verbal assaults is a way to attract women?"

I was pensive for a moment then asked "Are you a virgin?"

"Yup, I suppose I am." He uttered as his face flushed with embarrassment.

"Well today's your lucky day, sport. I'm feeling magnanimous.".

I opened the front door of my building and led him up the stairs to my apartment. I unlocked the door, and almost had to pull him inside. I wasn't in the mood to make small talk, so I took him directly to the bedroom. He asked me if I would pull down the shades. Shy little guy. It took me only minutes to undress, pull back the duvet, and crawl into bed. I watched him as he turned away from me while he got undressed. I was already in bed naked, waiting for him.

He crawled into bed with me, and immediately went for my breasts. Men and their tits. I slowed him down, and stroked his dick until he finally got an erection. He might have been a wise ass out in public, but he was like a timid pussy cat in bed.

He awkwardly crawled on top of me, and was bumbling around so badly, he was trying to put his penis in my ass, instead of where it belonged. I told him he had the wrong place, and even in the darkened room, I could see his face turn red.

I asked him if he had a condom. He grabbed his wallet from his pants and pulled out a condom that must have been in there for years. The foil wrapper was ripped and the rubber sheath was desiccated. While I hadn't been sexually active in the recent past, I was eternally optimistic about the prospect of having a fling. As they say, 'hope springs eternal.' I reached over and pulled open the top drawer of my nightstand. Next to my vibrator was a box of lubricated, ribbed condoms. I opened the package and slipped it on his penis. He slid easily inside me. He wasn't all that big and lost some of his erection once he had the condom on. His penis kept slipping out of me, so I'd have to put it back in. I was beginning to think this more effort than it was worth. I had been looking forward to an afternoon of fucking, but he didn't last long. Once we got going it didn't take him long to reach orgasm. He muttered "Oh God" a couple of times and then it was over. All in all, a very disappointing performance. But beneath the false bravado, he was a sweet kid. I found out that he was a sophomore at Harvard, studying history, and wanted to be a teacher, but that day, I was the teacher.

We lay in bed for a time just talking. Before long, the kid had another hard-on, and this time was able to enter me by himself. When he was done, which didn't take long, I gave him a kiss on the tip of his nose and told him to get dressed. He was funny. He wanted to know if he could come back. I told him no, but the next time he made fun of me, I'd tell his friends he couldn't get it up. I never had to do that, because he stopped going to the Café Pamplona. Lord knows what tall tales he regaled his friends with."

"Well done, Susan!" Holly said. "You may be the original cougar!"

"Hardly. I don't think being twenty-six qualifies as being a cougar. But I bet he'll never forget me, and that does make me happy." Susan said.

"God. I need a drink!" Holly said. "I had no idea I was in with such a bunch of wild women!"

"That's the whole point." Cat said. "Ashley Fake Tits thinks she's the only one who's ever had fun. Just look at the stories *we* have! We don't boast or carry them around like some animal pelt the way men do. You know, when I think of my ex-husband Jack, I should have just told him some of my sex stories instead of divorcing him. He was so jealous, his head might have exploded, and think how much I would have saved in the divorce proceedings."

"Oh God! I could never tell Freddy about my past." Anna said. "Men are too territorial. He'd dwell on it. We had the *"Don't ask, Don't tell"* policy long before the military implemented it."

"Yet men always talk freely about sex." Susan said. "They might exaggerate about their experiences, and they are certainly boastful. But you have to give them credit, they are far more open about the subject than we are."

"Yeah but I'll stand by my statement. Women have been conditioned *not* to be open. Think about it. If a girl sleeps around and she's considered a slut. Sorry Holly, I'm not talking about you. But when a guy does the same thing he's a stud. There's always been a double standard for the sexes and I don't foresee that changing. And I'm not even going to discuss how women are treated in the Middle East." Anna said.

"No, I agree with you Anna." Holly said. "I just never cared what people thought, nor would I ever let any man control or abuse me again. I use men for sex just like they use women and it drives them nuts. Face it. Women enjoy sex, and I think it's great that at least in here, in our little Mahjong Club, we can talk freely about it. I think we set a good example for all women."

"Here here! Let's hear it for The Mahjong Club. Now we need to plan a trip to Vegas, and really go wild! After all, we should be making some new stories!" Priscilla said.

"Oh God!" Susan said exasperated. "The six of us in Vegas. I'm not sure Tony will let me go."

"Let you go? Why do you need his permission Susan?" Holly asked.

"You don't understand. You're not married." Susan said.

"Marriage has nothing to do with it Susan." Anna said.

"Alright. Enough of that. We can discuss the pros and cons of marriage some other time. Vegas it is. Let's play another game before we have another story. Whose turn is it for the next tale?" Cat asked. "Mix up those tiles really good. I had terrible picks the last game.

"I believe you go next Anna." Holly said.

"My turn, huh?" Anna said. "Okay. I have my story picked out. Not quite as good as the other ones, but it certainly is different. When I was twenty-seven I think, I worked for Women's' Wear Daily. I had just been promoted to Junior Editor of Fashion Accessories. In fact, that's how Cat and I met. She was promoting Gucci's new spring fashion line and I was covering it. After a few business meetings and a several glasses of wine and we became fast friends."

"Anyway, I was responsible for covering not only the big fashion houses such as Gucci and Ferragamo, but smaller, lesser known designers in the city. I was assigned to interview a bright, young star on the fashion scene. Her name was Bianca. Like Cher she used only her first name. I suppose she thought it was a unique marketing strategy.

Bianca had a small shop in Spanish Harlem, on 103rd street called *Elegante*. We had arranged to meet at her shop at

8:00 pm one mid-week night. Frankie, my photographer, came with me to take pictures of her designs.

When we arrived the door was locked, but the lights were on inside. We knocked on the glass pane a few times, and Bianca sailed out from the back room to let us in. The store was small and crammed with merchandise. There were racks of colorful blouses and scarves designed and sewn by Bianca. I was very impressed. Most young designers had dreams of making it big, but didn't have the talent to achieve their goals. Bianca was the exception. She had grown up in Puerto Rico and had an appreciation for multi-hued, diaphanous fabrics. She was inspired by the exotic designs that her grandmother had worn. She blended the tropical colors of her native island into a dazzling, but not overpowering, motif. She used only the finest silk. I was tempted to try on one of the vast array of scarves. With her permission, I chose a hot pink one with swirls of silver threads. It was as light as a feather, and draped beautifully over my shoulders. Bianca insisted that I keep the scarf, and I still have it to this day. The magazine frowned upon us accepting gifts from designers, lest it influence our reviews of their work. However, Frankie promised to keep my secret so I accepted the gift. I gave Bianca a sparkling review, and the demand for her creations grew. Her scarves rivaled those by Hermes, in terms of popularity and status. However, her financial success and brand recognition couldn't keep her in New York. She confessed that creating her product line made her homesick for her native island.

"Frankie wrapped up the photos, we said good night to Bianca and left the shop. Frankie offered to walk me to my car, but I declined. It was a beautiful night, people were out in the street, and I felt like stretching my legs with a little stroll before heading back to my apartment. I walked quite awhile, just enjoying the night air. I was so lost in thought that I hadn't noticed that I had drifted out of the residential area, and the streets were now deserted. The area housed auto repair shops, liquor stores, boarded up store fronts and a few seedy bars.

The street was not well lit and I was starting to feel uneasy. I thought I heard footsteps behind me so I decided to cross the street. The rest is a bit of a blur. As I passed by an alley a man jumped out and grabbed me by my coat. He swung me around slamming me into the brick wall inside the alley. He knocked me to the ground, pulled my purse off of my shoulder, and took out my cash and credit cards. Just when I thought things couldn't get worse, he bent down, slapped me across the face and began to unzip his pants. I started to crawl away, but I was still dazed from hitting my head on the wall. He forced me onto my back, holding me down with his legs. I could smell the alcohol on his breath as he tried to pull up my skirt. The next thing I know, a young Latino guy, pulled my assailant off me, whacked him a couple of times in the face, and threw him on the ground. My guardian angel was definitely watching over me that night. The guy was a cop! He had just gotten off duty and was on his way home when he glanced down the alley and saw us struggling.

He rolled the perpetrator onto his belly, put his foot on his back to keep him immobilized, and cuffed him. To me, he was the Latin version of Superman. As he pulled the guy to his feet, he commented that he needed to call his precinct to report the incident. I was sitting on the ground and trembling. My head was throbbing and I couldn't think clearly. Finally, a police car pulled up and the officers put my assailant in the back of the car. They were none too gentle with him. It wasn't like in the movies where they place their hand over his head as he's getting in the car saying "Easy now." They bounced this guy's head off the car's roof, and then unceremoniously dumped him head first in the back seat. The officer who had rescued me, the one who was off-duty, came back to me. He asked me if I was hurt and offered to call an ambulance. I told him that wasn't necessary and that I just wanted to go home. He said I needed to make a statement, but could go to the 23rd Precinct the next day.

I was visibly shaken and clearly in no condition to drive. I asked him to call me a cab, but he said it might be difficult this time of night and in this part of town. He showed me his shield and ID card, identifying him as a New York police officer, and told me his name was Alejandro . He said all his friends called him Al.

He offered to drive me home and I gladly accepted the ride. He helped me into the passenger seat and fastened my seat belt because my hands were not steady. I think he was surprised when I told him I lived on the upper West Side.

In my mind's eye I can still see the quizzical look on his face when he asked 'Whatever brought you to Spanish Harlem?'

I told him about my job and Bianca's story. I was still shaking like a leaf in his car. He put the heat on for me, but the chill was visceral. As I thought about the events of the evening, and how lucky I had been, couldn't stop shaking. He reached over and covered my hands with his, and I held on tightly.

We pulled up to my apartment building, and he got out of the car to open my door. Seeing us approach, my doorman pushed the door open and bid us a good evening. I didn't want to be alone. I still was afraid, even though I was home. I asked him if he would see me to my apartment. He said of course, pulled out a placard that identified him as a member of the NYPD, stuck it on his windshield, and parked his car at the curb.

Alejandro walked me to the elevator, and pushed the button for my floor. I was still leaning against him when the elevator doors opened. He walked me to my apartment door but I didn't want to go in. I know I was being paranoid, but I felt like my attacker was inside waiting for me. He reassured me that the perp, that's what he called him a perp, was safely locked up and couldn't harm me. Nevertheless, I pleaded with him to come inside and check my apartment. I'm sure he thought I was being unreasonable, but he humored me, by opening all the closets, looking under the bed and checking the guest bedroom.

I put on a pot of coffee and begged him to stay just a little while longer. As we sat at the table drinking our coffee, I noticed just how young he was. I guessed in his early twenties. Definitely younger than me. He was Spanish, or more accurately of Spanish descent. He had olive skin, and had short cropped black hair. He wasn't brawny, more of lean muscle. He looked a little bit like a young Andy Garcia. I told him he was very brave to confront my assailant, when he could have just as easily driven right by. He laughed, one of those full body laughs, throwing his head back. He told me that he grew up in Spanish Harlem, and his mother and sisters still lived there. He became a cop because he was tired of the gangs and street punks taking over the neighborhood from the decent, hard-working people who lived there. His father had owned a *bodega*, a small store, and when he died, his mother and sisters took it over. They had been robbed several times when he was young. He considered exacting vigilante justice, but instead he decided to become a cop and enforce the law legally.

By this time, I had stopped shaking, but started to weep softly. While his training at the police academy was extensive, nothing there had prepared him to comfort a victim of attempted rape. He slid his chair next to mine and put his arm around me. Sobbing in his shoulder, he told me I was safe, and when I asked him to stay, he agreed. He could feel his shirt getting wet from my tears. He stroked my hair and told me to cry and let it all out. He gently told me that this was a very normal reaction to what I had experienced, and it would be better for me later if I cried it out now. He held me tight and when I turned my face up to him, he brushed the tears off my check with his thumb. While I still held his gaze, he slowly lowered his mouth and kissed me softly on the lips. I responded to his kiss by holding him close to me, as if I should let go he would vanish as if he was never there at all.

We kissed and held each other tightly due to my need to feel safe and his growing physical passion for me. I stood up from the table and clasping his hand firmly, led him into the bedroom. I took off my clothes and asked him to do the same. I slid into my bed and watched Alejandro as he began to remove his clothes. He watched me as he undressed in front of me without a hint of shyness.

Alejandro slid in next to me, I only had a small double bed, and I wrapped my arms around him. He felt so warm, and I finally felt safe. I ran my hands over his body, brushing his hard erection. His sexual passion was aroused and my sense of needing to be with someone took over. We hungrily sought each other's body, his hard and lean. He wasn't tall, my size, but I gasped when he entered me. He made love slowly, softly. As he slid in and out of me, I kissed his shoulders and neck. His mouth was sweet, and when he softly bit on my ear, I came. He thrust in me a few more times, more passionate now, and came himself. I held him tightly all night.

After our tragic start, we actually dated for a while, but gradually drifted apart. He was my hero, and you know what girls, we ladies need heroes!"

"Here's to the NYPD! The boys in blue! *Serve* and Protect!" Susan laughed.

Lori

"Lori! You're up! What fun story do you have for us?" Holly asked.

"Ah, my turn huh? Ok here goes." Lori answered. "When I was twenty-five, oh so long ago, I was working the evening shift at the South Shore Hospital in Weymouth, MA. I had just started a rotation in Intensive Care, which was agonizingly intense. Most of our patients were recovering from serious surgery, and others were terminal and merely being given palliative care. When you're twenty-five with your entire life stretched out ahead of you, the concept of death is difficult to comprehend.

Watching patients die was stressful enough, but I was always on alert to make sure none of the recovering patients didn't have a seizure or go into cardiac arrest. I had to pay very close attention to each patient. I never knew when the next crisis would erupt. Taking an unscheduled coffee break could cost a patient his life.

It was obvious to the more seasoned nurses that I was under a great deal of stress. They recommended that I take an exercise class or find a hobby to relieve my anxiety. One day, in the nurse's lounge, I overheard a pediatric nurse saying she was close to getting her pilots' license. That caught my attention since I was always interested in flying. I introduced myself and she told me there was a small airport about twenty minutes away in Marshfield, just outside of Plymouth. The Plymouth airport was further away, and it was much larger. Taking flying lessons at a small airport appealed to me.

I drove to the Marshfield airport on my day off. I parked outside the chain link fence and watched the small planes taking off and landing for awhile. The airport was nothing like Logan or JFK. It had one runway, and no more than a dozen small airplanes parked outside. I couldn't even see a hangar from my vantage point.

I was nervous about embarking on this new adventure, and wished I had asked the pediatric nurse to come with me. But I mustered up my courage and entered into the terminal. The front door opened into a long hallway and I could hear laughing coming from the main room at the end of the hall. I headed in that direction, and passed a group of men drinking coffee. One of them asked if I was there to pick up someone. I told him that I wanted information about taking flying lessons. I could see one guy smirk. I debated between leaving or giving the big lug a cuff off his head for being such a sexist pig. The latter option was much more appealing at that particular moment. Fortunately, I did neither. The man behind the counter came around and introduced himself as Ed, the airport manager who also gave flying lessons. He was very polite and soon all the other guys were around me telling me how great it was to fly. Flying was thrilling and provided such a sense of freedom. The guy with the smirk even got up and handed me a cup of coffee. At least I think it was coffee, it smelled and looked like it had been brewed days earlier.

I sat at a little table while Ed explained the rates and the different options to choose from. As he described the different plans available, I couldn't help but watch the planes landing and taking off. He noticed that I was distracted and asked if I wanted to go up then, just to see if I liked it.

"Now!?" I asked, surprised and a little scared. Ed said it would be a twenty minute introductory ride along the ocean and he wouldn't charge me. According to him, people knew instantly if they wanted to pursue lessons once they were airborne. One of the other guys said he'd "man" the phones while the other guys encouraged me to go. What could I do?

Ed went behind the counter, assessed the pegboard that held the keys, and chose a set. We walked outside and he explained the different types of planes that were there. Some had four seats, and the others were the two seat trainer models. Ed chose a blue and white high wing Cessna four seat plane. He showed me the call numbers on the planes' tail, and explained that only the last three were used for identification. This plane was 10T, or *one zero tango*. We walked around the plane, and he kept his explanation very simple. He undid the tie-down ropes, and opened the passenger door for me to climb in. I was surprised at how small the plane was inside, and how lightweight it felt. It was a far cry from the commercial jets I was accustomed to.

We buckled up, and Ed started the engine. The plane jerked forward, reminding me of runner at the starting line of a race when he hears the gun go off. He put on a pair of headphones, and gave me a pair to wear as well. Ed said once we got going, it could get a little noisy, but this would give me an opportunity to listen to the other pilots in the area talk to each other. We taxied down the runway, he boosted up the power, and asked me if I was ready. Hell yeah, I told him, so he pushed in the throttle, and we began to fly down the runway. Literally! When he reached a certain speed, he pulled back on the yoke and the plane began to lift into the sky. That first time was such a thrill!

"Are we talking about flying or getting laid?" Holly cracked.

"Flying Holly. Although getting laid for the first time is a thrill, too.

He banked the plane to the left, and I as I looked out I could see the expanse of Atlantic Ocean and the white caps of the waves. He flew along the beach, and then turned inland so I could see the mansions built along the salt marsh. There was a sharp contrast between the weathered clapboard houses, and the newly built homes. It seemed as if we had just started our ride when he started to head back. I felt disappointed and wanted to keep flying. He asked me if I wanted to fly the plane for awhile, and then he let me take the yoke. Oh God was it fun. I wasn't afraid at all, and I flew it back to the airport. However upon approach, I had to turn it back over to Ed so he could land. I was sold on flying. I told Ed to sign me up for lessons. We went back to his office to complete paperwork and execute waivers.

When we entered in the building, the guys circled around me as if I just came back from a successful bombing mission. They patted me on the back and told me that they heard me on the radio. The general consensus was that I had done a good job. What a great feeling! Their enthusiasm made me feel like I had been admitted to their special little club.

We reviewed Ed's appointment book, and I booked the first available opening for the following Thursday. I wasn't worried because I knew I would be flying with Ed.

I didn't have a lot of time to think about my upcoming flying lesson because we were especially busy at work. When Thursday morning arrived, I didn't know what to wear. Ed and I never discussed it. A long, white scarf around my neck, and maybe a leather helmet on my head? That would give the guys a chuckle. Instead, I chose comfortable sneakers, loose jeans, and a blue blouse. To be on the safe side I took a windbreaker in case I got cold.

Ed and the guys were there when I arrived. I don't think they made a fresh pot of coffee since my last visit. Aside from Ed, most of the men were retired. They advised me to use the bathroom before I left, not because they thought I was going to wet my pants, but because there weren't any bathrooms up there. They suggested that I should get into the habit of using the restroom before my lesson. So I went into the bathroom, but I think I was too nervous to go.

Ed and I walked outside and went to the same plane we had flown previously. This time he explained everything he was doing, but I could tell he was being careful not to inundate me with information. I couldn't decide if this was his usual routine with new students, or he thought I couldn't grasp it because I was a woman. If he only knew the complexity of the medical equipment I used in the Intensive Care Unit. I doubt he could put in a catheter, but I was patient with him and tried to be a good student.

We got into the plane, and this time he let me start it and taxi down the runway myself. When I got it up to speed and pulled back on the yoke, *wow!* We flew around for awhile, practicing different maneuvers, and before I knew it, my lesson was over.

When we landed, Ed asked me if I wanted to go the movies or dinner with him sometime. I hadn't been seeing anyone and hadn't been out on a date for months, so I accepted. Besides, he was cute. We dated for awhile and got along pretty well. We alternated between sleeping at his house and mine. To be honest there wasn't much sleeping going on. We were both young and neither of us was interested in a long term relationship. Our sex life was comfortable, but we both laughed that it was not exactly all that exciting.

One day in late September, Ed and I took a long plane ride to Vermont to view the fall foliage by air. I packed a lunch of fried chicken, potato salad and lemonade for us. The All-American picnic fare. I tried to convince Ed to bring a split of wine, but he insisted that alcohol was forbidden while we were flying. The weather was beautiful when we left Marshfield. It was clear and cool without a cloud in the sky. He explained that planes fly better when there isn't much humidity. We flew to Vermont at a leisurely speed, looking out on the brilliant New England foliage. We could see numerous cars on the roads, especially Route 100 in Vermont, where the leaf peepers can get out and take pictures. After flying around the state a bit, we turned the nose of the plane south and headed back home.

So here we are, flying along, munching on fried chicken and potato salad, when Ed starts to fool around with me. Grabbing my breasts, kissing my face. At first I was slapping his hands away, but then I started laughing along with him. I was getting turned on. At this point, we were back in Massachusetts, flying over Plymouth. I couldn't help but notice that Plymouth Rock wasn't the only thing that was hard. I could see Ed's erection straining against his jeans. I leaned over, unzipped his pants, and his penis sprung out. He gave a sigh of approval so I proceeded to take him in my mouth, which really turned him on. He pulled up on the yoke to take the plane higher so any quick drop in altitude wouldn't put us in the ocean. After sucking and licking him for awhile, I was getting hotter and hotter. I complained to Ed that it wasn't fair that he was having all the fun. Ed asked me if I wanted to join the Mile High Club. I wasn't sure what that meant. So, being the consummate teacher, he explained that it's when you have sex in a plane flying a mile high above the ground. I looked around our four seater Cessna, and asked him if it was possible, and more importantly if it was safe. He smiled and reminded me he *was* the instructor, and would never put our safety in jeopardy. He also reminded me, that we both agreed our sex life was getting quite routine, and this was a perfect opportunity to spice it up.

I pulled down my jeans, then my panties, and helped him take off his pants. His erection was sticking straight up. I climbed on top of him, straddling his thighs, and put his penis inside me, while I was facing him. The energy between us was electric. I was moving up and down on him while he was kissing my breasts. The motion of the plane, the altitude, and the clouds goings by, was driving me crazy. Ed looked over my shoulder from time to time to make sure we still were at a safe altitude, not drifting lower, and then he would get back to business of screwing me.

Everything was fine until I looked out the window to my left and saw a military aircraft. An airman man with a full helmet covering his face with an oxygen mask was looking directly at us! Right there next to us! I screamed and tried to get off Ed, who initially must have thought my I was having a whale of an orgasm. He soon saw the real reason for my yell.

You see, Ed did a good job of maintaining a high altitude, but somehow he drifted into the restricted air space of the Weymouth Air Force base. Let me tell you, Ed lost his hard-on in a hurry! The airman announced on his loud speaker that we had violated air space regulations, and that we had to leave immediately. I couldn't help but notice the grin on his face while he was chastising us.

We were both rattled enough that we immediately returned to the airport and landed the plane. Here's Ed, flying the plane with no pants on, and I'm struggling to pull up my top. What a sight we must have been.

So afterwards, I told Ed that *technically*, we hadn't officially joined the Mile High Club. I think he admired my spunk, and the following week we flew out over the ocean and officially became members. And if you girls ever tell Art, I will *kill* you!"

"Great story Lori!" Priscilla said. "God. I'd love the chance to join the Mile High Club, but I'm not really sure how a couple of lesbians could do it."

"Maybe I can join it when we fly to Vegas." Holly said.

"So when are we going to Sin City?" Anna asked.

"How about going over Labor Day weekend? It's a three day weekend, and it gives us plenty of time to get a SuperSaver fare and book a suite at a fancy hotel."

"A suite! Now you're talking!" Lori said.

"I don't know." Susan said shaking her head. "Tony's not going to like this idea. I'm not sure if he'll let me go."

"Let you go?! What are you, fucking twelve?" Holly wanted to know.

"Let it go Holly." Lori said. "Susan you discuss it with Tony, and let's all figure out our schedules, so we can make reservations the next time we meet. Why don't we meet at the Club for drinks Saturday night while the guys play poker?"

"Good idea." Priscilla said. "Now I do believe we still have Miss Holly's tale to hear."

"Okay ladies." Holly said as she bit into her sandwich. "I think I was about 24. As you can imagine, the aftermath of the childhood rape, and homelessness, left me with a cluster of chronic psychological effects. My confidence in social situations was severely diminished, and I developed an unforgiving attitude toward men. But the irony was that I still craved sex with men, and yet I hated them for it. I always felt that the men I slept with were using me. During sex, an image of my uncle's face would float in front of me. I wished I was attracted to women, like you Priscilla, but I just wasn't. So I carried around this conflict and probably still do. The men I choose to marry are always much older and they don't seem to care much about sexual intimacy. They're happy to have my companionship, and to show me off like a trophy.

"Trophy? Take it easy honey! That doesn't sound like something someone with a poor self image would say" Cat teased.

"So here I am, twenty four, young, but damaged from my relationships with men. I was living in Revere, a city just north of Boston. I would go to Revere Beach almost every day to swim in the ocean. I preferred going on weekday mornings when it wasn't over run with screaming kids and errant beach balls. I avoided the beach on the weekends since it seemed to be a huge pick up place. When I left the house for the beach, I always packed my gym bag with a thermos of black coffee and the *Boston Globe*. After my morning swim, I'd read the newspaper and drink the coffee, while I watched the waves lap against the shore.

One sunny day I decided to linger at the beach a little longer than usual. As I unfurled my blanket on the sand, I noticed that a young guy doing the same not too far from me. I felt like he was intruding on my private beach. I decided to ignore him since he wasn't that close to me, and he appeared to be seeking solitude as well.

As the days went by I noticed he arrived at the same time each morning. We didn't have any interaction aside from a nod or a quick "hi", which suited me just fine. As I was swimming along one morning we collided. Apparently we were swimming toward each other and didn't notice where we were going. We scared ourselves pretty good! I thought a shark had me, and I thrashed around, went under the waves and swallowed a mouthful of salt water. While I'm spitting and gagging, this guy grabbed me from behind, and lugged me back to shore.

I was still spitting out water when we got to shore, so he flipped me on my side and told me to just breathe. I finally caught my breath, and when I turned around to thank him, I noticed that he was just a kid. Well maybe eighteen or nineteen. He was a lifeguard the city hired for the summer. He liked to get to the beach early, take a swim and see if there were any rip tides, or rough waves. He told me once the crowds arrived it was a zoo, so he liked starting his day with a little peace and quiet.

I guess I looked like a fright. He laughed and pulled some seaweed out of my hair. Something about him was disarming. Maybe because of his youth, or that he was a lifeguard, there to help people, not hurt them. Either way, I felt an attraction to him, John, his name was John.

I stood up and he stood up with me. He had the classic long, lean body of a swimmer. I could tell he was shy, and he started to turn around and return to his blanket when I stopped him. I thanked him and asked if I could buy him a beer after work. He laughed and said he wasn't old enough to go into a bar. So I told him just to come to my place. I had a little apartment a few blocks from the beach. He could walk to it. I had to ask him twice before he would agree to come, and then only because I think he'd didn't want to insult me.

After I left the beach I thought about him all day. He said he would come to my place at about eight o'clock. I put a six pack of Blue Moon in the fridge, and ordered a cheese pizza from Frank and Al's. I took a shower before he came, taking extra care to shave my legs and smooth on vanilla scented body lotion. I'd been told that men enjoy that fragrance. I put on a gauzy sun dress, no bra, and some skimpy white thong panties. I felt like a lioness stalking her prey.

John showed up on time and I opened a beer for each of us. We went to sit on the screened in front porch while we waited for the pizza to arrive. It was a warm evening, with a mere hint of a breeze. The night sky was adorned with little points of light as the crescent moon rose to regain its rightful place. We sat on my wicker sofa drinking our beers in silence as we listened to the sweet notes of the night birds. The sofa had three big down-filled cushions that seemed to swallow us up. I sat facing John with my legs tucked under me. He wore a Red Cross white T-shirt, and a pair of cutoff dungaree shorts. I reached down and pulled off his sandals, and placed his feet on my lap. We finished our first beer, and then had another. The pizza finally arrived and I brought napkins out to the porch. We laughed at the morning's calamity as we polished off the pizza.

John was a sweet kid. He was nineteen, and proudly told me he would be turning twenty in less than a month. I said we had to celebrate his almost birthday, and opened the two remaining beers in the six pack. I wasn't paying attention to the story he was telling me because I was fixated on his gorgeous, full lips. When I couldn't stand it any longer, I leaned over and wrapped my arm around his neck and pulled him toward me. I gave him a sweet lingering kiss. He kissed me back tentatively, as if he was afraid to hurt me. His hair looked glossy in the light of the moon and I couldn't help but run my fingers through it I pulled him to his feet and led him into the bedroom. He was reluctant at first, but was overcome with passion as he gently pushed me on the bed and lay on top of me. His lips stayed on my mouth, but now his tongue eagerly sought mine. His hands went to my breast, then lower. His pulled my thong aside and explored me with his fingers. For a man I thought was inexperienced, he deftly caressed me into an orgasm. I unzipped his shorts, and pulled them to the floor. I slipped my hand inside his underwear and rubbed my finger in circles around his hard dick. I pulled his shirt off and rubbed his sinewy shoulder muscles. I kissed his nipples then gave him a playful shove onto his back. I straddled him and began to gently swirl my tongue around the top of his erection, licking off the sweet moisture. He moaned when I took him all the way in my mouth and caressed his balls with my hand. Not being able to take it any longer, he flipped me over onto my back and he opened my legs with his knees. I was so deliciously wet he slid right in. He lowered his body onto mine, his breathing ragged. For a time, he slowly eased himself in and out of me. Then his thrusts became more rapid and intense. We kissed urgently and he held me tightly. After a little while, I could feel him tense and with a deep thrust he came into me. It was exquisite. We both nodded off for a few minutes. When we woke up we started to wrestle. No kidding. We started playing and tickling each other like a couple of kids and then started wrestling on the bed. I would squeal when he would wrap me into a hold, then he'd yell "No fair" when I grabbed his dick. Of course it didn't take long for the wrestling to evolve into lovemaking. This time I told him I wanted to please him. I had him lay down and proceeded to give him a blowjob that he would never forget.

John and I had a great summer together and he'll never know how much his sweet innocent love led to healing my tortured soul. After being with John, my visions of my uncle not longer haunted me. It's as if he cleansed my psyche. We spent the summer swimming each morning, quietly reading the paper, with our legs entwined. We spent our evenings drinking a beer or two, and cooking a simple meal. Sometimes we just made sandwiches. We had far better things to do at night than cook.

"That's my summer story ladies." Holly said.

"And a good one!" Susan said. "Sweet simple love. Like the kind I had with George. Every girl should have at least one great love."

"Ladies, it's getting late, I think we should adjourn The Mahjong Club until next Wednesday night. Susan, I believe it's your turn to be the hostess. But remember, we'll all meet at the Greenbrier on Saturday night to plan our trip to Vegas while the men play poker." Anna said.

"Ok and I'll start checking out the hotels." Holly said. "Any requests?"

"Yes. Try the Venetian. I haven't been lucky enough to make it to Italy yet like our friend Cat here. So this might be my chance to take a gondola ride. You never know, maybe a handsome Italian will ride with me!" Lori said.

"Tony's not going to like this." Susan murmured.

"Just tell him we're going to Vegas, just us girls, to do a little gambling." Anna offered. "After all, he's gone to Vegas and on golf vacations with the guys. Don't ask him, tell him. Since when do you need his permission to spend time with us?

"Jesus! Am I really hearing this?" Holly asked.

"Just tell him Susan. He'll be fine. You're getting worked up over nothing." Anna said.

"I'll see you all at the club Saturday night. Eight o'clock. Don't forget!" Holly said to the group as they all paraded out.

"Jesus Lori. You look like you've been up all night." Anna commented to her friend. Anna was the first to arrive at the club early, so she grabbed the most desirable table located near a big picture window that overlooked the golf course. It was a balmy early evening, and still light outside. Golfers were still on the course, eager to get one last hole in before the sun set completely.

The bar was already crowded. Anna noticed Ashley Big Tits was there, but Roger was nowhere in sight. "Hmm" she thought. Ashley was fawning over a man who everyone knew was recently divorced. If Ashley was fooling around behind Roger's back, she certainly kept it a secret. She just loved the attention she received, but wasn't dumb enough to lose her meal ticket. Roger took very good care of her. It was rumored that he gave her a five thousand dollar monthly allowance. Tony told Anna that he had overheard the guys in the locker room discussing the stringent pre-nuptial agreement that Roger's attorney had drafted. According to one provision, if Ashley was unfaithful she would receive nothing if they divorced. Roger may have been dazzled by her youth and her fake tits, but evidently still had the good sense to protect his assets. He had been married to his first wife for more than twenty years and he had raised three sons, now grown, with her. With children and grandchildren, most people

148

assumed Roger bequeathed most of his property to his kids. His children felt that marrying Ashley was a mistake, but Roger went ahead with it anyway.

The story going around was that Roger met Ashley at a convention. She had been one of the many Verizon sales people attending, and he was the keynote speaker. Knowing he was recently divorced and wealthy, she actively sought him out. One night at the hotel bar, she sat next to him and let him buy her round after round of drinks. Later she invited him up to her room on some pretext, and then let nature take its course. Once she had her hooks into him, she didn't let go. She visited him often at his house, and then took a job near him. Before long, she had moved in with him. Since Roger was older than Ashley and had children of his own, Ashley played on his sense of morality and convinced him that he should do the right thing and marry her. She constantly reminded him that people from his generation didn't live "in sin."

And tonight, Ashley Fake Tits was at the Club alone, if you didn't consider the man she was practically sitting on.

"I was up all night." Lori said to Anna. "You're *not* going to believe *this* story." She whispered. "Art went to New York for six days to play in a golf tournament. In the clubhouse he was telling the boys how he couldn't wait to get home to me, and how he missed, well you know, the sex. One of the guys suggested that perhaps he wouldn't be *up* for sex since he was exhausted from playing golf. So, the guy gave

Art one of those little blue pills. The kind that gives a man an erection. Why Art would take it, is beyond me. As far as I can tell, he has *no* trouble getting hard-ons. In fact, he should take a little yellow pill so he doesn't get so many.

While he was flying home, he popped the pill along with the bottled water and pretzels they gave him on the plane. Well, the pill clearly worked. I met him at the baggage area to pick up his golf clubs, and I could see his hard dick hard straining against his pants.

At first, I was angry. I assumed he was flirting with one of the flight attendants or maybe he had a good looking girl sitting next to him. But when he saw the scowl on my face, he came clean and told me what he did. I had to stifle my laugh. He drove home in record time. We barely get in the door, when he pulled me onto the couch. He couldn't even wait until we got into the bedroom. So there we are, humping away, and having a grand ol' time. He was insatiable. We were bumping and grinding our brains out. It was ferocious. Finally we just sprawled on the couch exhausted. While we're lying there, I noticed Art still has an erection. I asked him if he ejaculated, and he says, oh yeah. I didn't give it a second thought and sure enough after he catches his breath, he wants to go at it again. That's fine by me, because I missed him too, and wasn't really satisfied yet. This time we made it into the bedroom, and even managed to pull down the sheets. So we do it again. A little slower than before. It was nice. I closed my eyes for a moment and must have dozed off. Art woke me up by touching my shoulder and told me he had a problem. Guess what? He still had a hard-on. Somehow the pill he took must have affected him a little too strongly.

There's a medical condition called priapism, where the penis doesn't release the blood after sex, causing the penis to stay erect. Most men think it's funny. At least initially. But then when it turns painful, it's not so funny anymore. So I told him what I thought, and of course he suggested that we should have sex again, and that another orgasm would solve the problem. I told him that wasn't the way we should handle it. We needed to put an ice pack on it, and hope that the swelling would go down. He wasn't too happy to hear that we would have to go to the ER if the ice pack didn't work. He freaked out when I told him a surgical shunt would have to be inserted into his penis to let the blood flow back. He shouted "No God-damn way, but by this point he was in serious pain. He had had an erection for more than four hours which confirmed my suspicion.

 I got an ice pack out of the freezer, and put it against his dick."

"Wait a minute." Anna asked. How do you wrap frozen ice around a dick?"

"I always keep a couple bags of frozen peas in the freezer. They're flexible once you move them around in the bag. Plus they're a cheap fix. I buy a couple bags at Wal-Mart for eighty cents each.

I told him to hold the bag of frozen peas against his dick, but only his balls shrunk. Now I was worried about the ice being on his dick for too long, so I told him we had to go to the ER. God you should have heard him whine like a little boy.

Women go through so much, yet men freak out at the littlest thing. . . no pun intended.

I drove him to the Emergency Unit and we sat there for hours before they took him. They brought him in the back and a doctor I knew was able to put the shunt in, and presto! Down comes the dick. Art was relieved, let me tell you. Once the shunt was in we were out of there in thirty minutes. So yes, Anna, I have been up all night."

"Wow! If the men tell stories during poker like we do at Mahjong that would be a whopper!" Anna said.

"Oh, he won't be telling that tale anytime soon. Hi Priscilla. Nice shoes!" Lori said to Priscilla as she pulled up a chair.

Anna looked down at the white Prada sandals Priscilla was wearing. "Very nice." She said.

"Yeah, I was at the mall and figured it was time to treat myself to something new." Priscilla said.

"Well they're beautiful and I admire your good taste. Is that top new too?" Lori asked.

"Not that new." Priscilla said. She was wearing a low cut, off the shoulder blue and white striped silk blouse. "I just love silk. It's true you should dry clean it, but it gets expensive, so I wash most of mine in cold water and that works just fine. I just love the feel of silk on my naked skin, plus it's so cool in the summer yet warm in the winter."

"Well if I ever turn gay, you're the gal for me. I'd date you just so I could raid your wardrobe!" Anna laughed.

Looking across the room, they could see Cat talking to a man at the bar, but further across the room, it looked like Tony and Susan were in a heated conversation. It was more like Tony doing all the talking and making angry gestures with his hands towards Susan.

Anna looked at Priscilla and Lori and made a face. "Poor Susan. Tony really seems upset about something. He's really giving her hell."

"He's way too hard on her. She's such a sweetheart and she waits on him hand and foot. "Lori said.

"Maybe that's the problem." Holly said joining the group. She gives into his every demand. I honestly think she's afraid of him."

"You don't think he would ever hurt her? Physically, I mean." Anna asked.

"He better not." Holly answered. "My father might have been an asshole, but he taught me how to shoot when I was a little girl. I still have the .30-.30 Marlin lever action my brothers gave me one Christmas, *and* I know how to use it."

"Maybe you can start by practicing on Ashley Fake Tits." Lori said, trying to lighten the moment.

"Her?" Holly answered. "I wouldn't waste the thirty cents on the bullet. Besides, if she moves, I might accidently hit one of her tits and the whole club might explode." she said laughing.

The light moment disappeared when Susan crossed the room and joined the table. "I may not be able to stay long," she said. "It was obvious she had been crying. Her eyes were red and puffy, and her mascara was smeared where she had been rubbing her eyes.

"What's wrong honey?" Lori asked gently.

"I can't go to Vegas. I'm sorry, but Tony won't let me go." Susan said.

Anna, knowing Holly's quick temper, gave her a sharp look to keep her quiet.

"Why not?" Anna asked softly. "Any particular reason?"

"No. He just said I shouldn't be going, that it didn't look right. Me being married and all. Either way, he said no. I'm not going." Susan whimpered.

"That's okay honey. Don't worry. They'll be more trips, okay?" Lori said to Susan.

Holly excused herself from the table. At first, Anna thought her friend was going to go over to Tony and give him a piece of her mind, or kick him in the balls, but instead she headed to the bar to see Cat. Anna could see her lean into Cat's ear, presumably to tell her what just happened at the table.

The women loved each other and had formed a close bond that most men never achieve. They shared Susan's pain, and worse, were powerless to do anything about it. To lighten the mood, they changed the subject to the new Mahjong cards being released, and commented on Roger's noticeable absence.

Susan got up and excused herself saying she was going home. Holly noticed that Tony had jerked his head toward the door, and Susan followed him out. Cat and Holly returned to the table.

"Well that was something." Anna said. "I think Tony's getting worse, but there is nothing we can do about it, so let's get on with planning our trip. Holly, what arrangements have you made for us?"

"Oh you ladies are going to be pleased! Holly said. "I was able to book two adjoining suites at a substantially discounted rate at the Venetian Hotel, and I also was able to get them to throw in six tickets to the *Jersey Boys*, at no extra charge."

"Oh God! I've always wanted to see that show. I hear they sing *exactly* like Frank Valli and the Four Seasons!" Lori said.

"That's great! Good job!" Anna said.

"Of course we have an extra ticket now." Cat said referring to Susan's not being able to go.

"I know." Holly said. We'll find someone to give it to. I've also made reservations for the plane trip out that must be confirmed within twenty-four hours. It's a great rate and we get to sit together! So if it's agreeable to everyone, I'll go ahead and confirm the reservations tomorrow.

"Yea! I'm ready to get away and have some fun." Cat said. "I'm in!"

"Ok. Then it's done. Let's skip our usual Wednesday night Mahjong game and get ready for our big trip. I, for one, am going to the mall to buy myself a new pair of pajamas. Maybe with a leopard print! Grrrr". Anna laughed.

"Oh boy!" Lori said. "We're really doing this! I'm in, too!"

"Four straight women and one lesbian, running wild in Las Vegas! Priscilla said in agreement with everyone else.

"And remember ladies. Holly added, what happens in Vegas...

Stays in Vegas they all yelled together!

Vegas

Holly arranged for a limousine to pick up the ladies. Judging by the amount of luggage he had to load into his trunk, the driver assumed the ladies were going on a month long safari to Africa, rather than a long weekend in Vegas. He evidently didn't travel with women very often.

Once they were all packed in the limo and on their way to the airport, Holly broke out a bottle of Dom Perignon and six fluted crystal glasses. She included one for Susan even though she was missing. She undid the wire stopper, and gently eased out the cork. Despite taking precautions, the cork exploded out of the bottle, struck the roof of the limo and careened off the windows. They all ducked and laughed, while the champagne bubbled out of the bottle. Holly filled each of their glasses and as they were about to take their first sip Anna held her glass up and said, "To Susan. "She should be here with us."

"Here, here! To Susan! She should be with us. She's a founding member of The Mahjong Club! "Cat said.

"I don't like the way Tony treats her" Holly said.

"Really? You could have fooled me." Priscilla said sarcastically.

"I don't like him either. But he is Susan's husband and we should stay out of it." Lori said.

"I'm not sure I agree. I don't think we should shoot him, like Holly wants to do, but I'm not comfortable allowing him dominate her the way he does. How do you know it won't get worse?" Priscilla asked.

"We're there for her if she wants us. She knows that. I'm just afraid we could make it worse by getting involved. Tony can be scary sometimes." Anna said.

"He's only scary to women. I know the type. He wouldn't pull that macho bullshit with a guy. I have a couple of brothers who would be more than willing to come down and throw him in the lake with the alligators if I asked them to." Cat added as she thought of her brawny, football playing, beer drinking brothers.

"Really not a bad idea." Anna said. "We could all pitch in for their airfare."

Before they could discuss it any further, the limo pulled up to the West Palm Beach International Airport. The people waiting curbside turned to see the five attractive ladies pour out of the limo. The driver signaled the curbside porter to take the ladies' luggage. The porter checked their ID's, and ticketed their bags for Las Vegas. Holly paid the driver and added a generous tip for the spilled champagne. In a swirl of color, the ladies went through the door and headed for the gate.

Flying first class has its privileges, Cat thought. When she flew for the Gucci family, she always flew first class. She had accumulated so many frequent flyer miles she upgraded her friends to first class for this trip. Being an executive herself, Holly only flew first class. When she was working, it was a perk of the job. But now she had the money to afford it, and she couldn't see ever going back to coach. She enjoyed getting on the plane first, but never as a slight to the less fortunate passengers. Holly never forgot where she came from, and was always generous to charities. When feeling spontaneous, she would anonymously pick up dinner checks for elderly couples or large families with children who looked like they couldn't afford to eat out. Money was not important to her, and she would have traded it all to have been raised in a loving home. Holly was tough as nails on the outside. Having been beaten both physically and psychologically as a child, she developed her exterior self like a Samurai sword. Hard and sharp. But inside, even though it was a constant struggle, she would not let herself lose the little softness she had remaining. She knew if she did that, she would truly be lost.

Anna sat back, and accepted the glass of white wine that was offered by the flight attendant. Although she was far from poor, she usually did not indulge in first class seats. Sometimes when airlines ran a special promotion, she and Freddy would take a trip and upgrade their seats. As she settled into the wide, soft gray leather seat, she had to admit that she could get spoiled with this. Oh yes, she could. She looked over at Priscilla in the next seat. Priscilla was drop-dead beautiful. Mother Nature definitely had a sense of humor. Men were always hitting on Priscilla and were shocked to find out she was gay. It seemed to Anna that Priscilla was unaware of her stunning good looks. Anna knew Priscilla could be a bare knuckle fighter in the political arena, and that's probably what made her so good at it. Her sharp wit and intellect were the icing on the cake. Anna laughed quietly to herself as she compared Priscilla and AFT. Ashley Fake Tits was marginally attractive, yet so full of herself. As Anna's father would say, 'Ashley was twenty five pounds of bullshit in a five pound bag, and so dumb she couldn't pour sand out of a boot if the instructions were written on the bottom.' Then there was Priscilla, ten times more beautiful, and the most humble down to earth lady one could find. As she finished that thought, the plane took off rumbling down the runway bringing the ladies closer to *Sin City*.

The flight was three hours, but went by very quickly with the help of the complimentary wine. They deplaned and proceeded into the lobby of the airport. There was row after row of slot machines in the lobby. Lights were flashing and people squealing as they won what they considered to be small fortunes.

The ladies walked further to where the cabs were located. Holly had arranged for a limo to pick them up as well, and a handsome man in uniform was holding a placard that said *The Mahjong Club.*

"Oh, that's just *perfect!*" Cat *purred.*

The ladies hopped into the back of the limo, and headed for the hotel. It was a short ride so Holly skipped the champagne. When they approached the Strip, even the blistering Nevada sun couldn't diminish the impact of the flashing neon lights of the many resorts and hotels.

The driver pulled up to the front entrance of the Venetian Hotel, where a doorman opened the limo door. He signaled for the bell hop to get their luggage out of the trunk as the ladies made their way to the front desk.

"Just beautiful!" Anna said, looking around.

"Three whole nights!" Cat said in response.

Holly walked to the reception desk, handed over her credit card and her drivers' license, and received five keys to the two adjoining suites. They walked across the rich inlayed carpet, ignoring for the moment, the beckoning call of the slot machines.

"C'mon girls. They'll be plenty of time for that." Holly said. "Why don't we go up to our rooms, change into our bathing suits, go to the pool and order some lunch."

"And a Bloody Mary." Lori added.

The ladies got off on the 21st floor and headed for their suites. Anna and Cat were staying in the *Tutti Bene* suite while Holly, Lori and Priscilla went into the *Tutti Fresco* suite. Each suite had two bedrooms, each with a king size bed covered in a shimmering white silk bedspread. The rug was a deep pile weave with a red and gold pattern. The curtains were more like giant tapestries, that when closed, kept out the harsh Las Vegas sunlight. Each bedroom had a 46 inch LG HD television, and a small stereo system that doubled as a clock radio. The closet space was big enough to accommodate a large wardrobe. There was an ironing board and steam iron, but most guests took advantage of the complimentary dry cleaning service that was included with the suite. Each bedroom had its own adjoining bathroom that was palatial even by Las Vegas standards. The floor, walls and counter were constructed of white Italian marble with a gold vein running through it. The sinks were made of hand-carved, smoky black granite, and adorned with gold faucets. Thick, rich white with gold trimmed bath sheets hung from the racks as well as four luxurious bath robes, also white with gold trim with the name of the hotel *Venetian* embroidered in gold thread. Beneath the robes, were four pairs of white terry cloth sandals sealed in plastic. The shower had two shower heads, giving the guest, or guests, a rainfall experience while showering. A mahogany cabinet housed complimentary shampoo, razors, toothbrushes and a complete array of toiletries.

The guest living room was situated between the bedrooms. It had sweeping views of both the Strip and the cool, blue water of the pool below. A white Italian leather oversized sofa and matching love seat adjoined each other. On either end of the sofas, were two white leather reclining chairs. They faced a wall-mounted 50" HD television, where if they became tired of regular broadcast, they could order most any movie at no charge. Adult films included. A guest favorite.

To the side of the room, a mini-bar was stocked with the finest of liquors and snacks including brie, smoked salmon and organic whole grain crackers. Bottles of fine wine, both red and white, were stacked above in a black wrought iron wine rack, with crystal glasses beneath. These, however, were not complimentary, and the prices were subtly posted on the door. A room service menu was placed on the table should one not wish to venture out.

There were two doors that connected the suites, and both Holly and Cat opened the doors, allowing all the ladies to go back and forth between suites. When they had put on their bathing suits, and checked and re-checked themselves in the mirror, they headed to the pool to swim and have lunch.

Wolfgang Puck had a small restaurant called "Riva" next to the pool. The restaurant served both lunch and breakfast items around the clock to accommodate the unusual eating and sleeping schedules of the guests.

Cat chose a table with a large hunter green sun shade hovering above it, big enough to cover not only the table, but six chaise lounges next to it. The girls were ravenous, they only had champagne since they left home. When the waiter came over, clad in a pressed white jacket over black khakis, Priscilla ordered the buttermilk pancakes with fresh blueberries and a rasher of maple cured thick-cut bacon. Cat decided on Eggs Benedict, but substituted fresh Maryland crab for the Canadian bacon. She had them with crispy home fries with cooked onions. Lori opted for the Belgian waffle with extra whipped cream and fresh strawberries, and a side of well-done ham. Anna chose bacon and eggs, buttermilk biscuits and fried apples. After changing her mind several times, Holly settled on a Mexican omelet with extra jalapeño peppers and spicy salsa. She also added a pitcher of Bloody Mary's to their order.

The girls sat for a moment, people watching while waiting for their food to arrive.

"If I could sleep with anyone, you know who it would be? " Holly asked.

"Oh, here we go! Anna said. "Ok, who?"

"Jay Leno." Holly answered. I'd like to put my tits right on that big chin. You know, he owns dozens of unique cars and motorcycles, and I hear he does all the work on them himself. I like a man who knows how to use his hands, you know what I mean?"

"Well *my* choice would be Ann Curry. The former host of the Today Show." Priscilla said. She's smart, which is a real turn on for me, plus her Asian eyes and thick black hair are so sexy. I could stay in bed with her all weekend! You know, I think she was my favorite host on the Today Show and I was so pissed when they let her go. Sometimes I wonder if Matt Lauer felt threatened by her. I think she was too smart. She wasn't like the ditzy hosts on other morning talk shows."

Anna waited until the waiter had brought their food and placed their plates in front of them and left before she continued.

"Me? Anna said. "I would go with Mick Jagger. I've been to a couple of his concerts and always splurged so I could sit up close to the stage. He is so fucking sexy! The way he moves his body and dances around with that tight ass. My fantasy is that we are staying in a posh hotel and both of us are dancing naked to one of his songs. Maybe, *I Can't Get No Satisfaction*, then I'd love him to dance on me! If Freddy knew the thoughts that ran through my head when I saw Mick, he wouldn't be going to any more Rolling Stone concerts!"

"But he wouldn't keep you from going, right? Cat asked.

"Of course not. We all have our fantasies. That doesn't mean we would necessarily act on them. I know for a fact, Freddy would love to be with Barbara Streisand." Anna said.

"Barbara Streisand! Freddy wants to screw Barbara Streisand?" Priscilla asked.

"No. I think he would just like to lie in bed and have her sing to him. Naked of course!" Anna said.

"Jesus! Who knows what goes on in men's heads? They say we're the complicated ones, but not to me. I know they think with their dick first, but even still, they can be a mystery. Sometimes there's just no pleasing them." Lori added. "Now for my sexual fantasy? Don't laugh, but I think I would pick Zorro?"

"Sorry. I *am* laughing! Zorro?! Are you kidding us? Do you mean the original actor who played Zorro or Antonio Banderas? Priscilla asked without attempting to conceal her surprise.

"No .No. No. Neither. Let me explain." Lori said to the group. "I first saw Zorro on the big screen when I was a little girl. This dashing man appears, larger than life, riding a black stallion, and he saves the girl from the bandito. I was swept off my feet. I had a huge crush on him. Now, as an adult, I *know* Zorro, isn't real, but the thought of a masked man, handsome and strong, coming into my bed and making love to me makes me hot."

"Ok. I get it." Anna said. "But after, would you unmask him?"

"Oh no!" Lori said. That's part of the sexual fantasy. Being taken by a masked man, not knowing who he is or when he'd return and take me again."

"You could always have Art wear a mask when he comes to bed." Holly added.

"Nah. It wouldn't be the same. No mystery. Besides Art's so clumsy, his mask would probably slip over his eyes, he'd fall down and then I'd be spending the night at the Emergency Room rather than making love to a masked stranger." Lori said.

"Well Cat, you are certainly quiet on this subject." Pricilla noted.

"My fantasy is different than yours." Cat said. "I'm not sure how to begin. Years ago, I went with Jack to a Sunday brunch at a local hot spot in Brooklyn. It wasn't swanky, and was more of a hole in the wall. It was a place that hadn't been discovered yet, which is rare. Today, you probably wouldn't be able to get in the door.

So Jack and I get up one Sunday morning and decide to drive there. I think Jack just was more interested in being seen in his Jaguar than eating out, but away we went. We snagged a table in the back against the wall, and ordered coffee while we looked at the menu. Everything was fresh from local organic farms. I ordered a Swiss cheese and tomato omelet, while Jack had the corned beef hash and eggs. We read some of the paper, waiting for our food to come. At one point, Jack got up to use the men's room. I was looking in the general vicinity of the front door, watching people come and go, when a man walked in. He moved with such confidence, almost a swagger, and took one of the empty seats at the counter. He had jet black hair cut very short, and the coldest, icy blue eyes. I could tell he was muscular by the way his military uniform stretched over his body. He caught me looking at him, and I could feel a shudder go through my body. He neither smiled nor looked away from me. He looked *dangerous.* He had a thin scar which ran from below his right ear almost down to his chin. The scar looked old. God knows how he got that, but it turned me on. I wanted to run my finger down it, kiss it. He was a Green Beret, and I could see that he had it tucked into his pocket, as if he didn't want to call attention to himself.

I wanted to be with him. Not sexually. Well yes, of course sexually, I would have followed that man anywhere. I was mesmerized. This is even hard for me to understand. I didn't care that I didn't know him, hell, didn't even know his name. If he called to me or waved me over to him, I would have gone. I can't explain it, but I would have walked away from Jack, my job, New York, everything to be with this man. He totally captivated me and I never felt that way before with anyone. Not even a little.

Jack came back from the bathroom and I didn't even notice that the waitress had delivered our food. Jack commented about how nice it was that I waited for him before I started to eat, but all I could do was nod. I spent the rest of the time taking small bites of my meal, and watching the back of my mysterious stranger. Jack was too engrossed in the hash and the newspaper to be aware of what was happening. Before long, my soldier finished his food, and he went to the cash register to pay his bill. Before he left, he turned and looked directly into my eyes, then walked out the door onto the street. To this very day, I regret not following him out that door. I *know* it sounds crazy, but it's the truth. I often wonder about that man. Where he is, what he's doing? If I could have one moment to do over again, it would be that morning at the restaurant."

"Jesus, Cat!" Anna said. "I never knew."

"Well, this is our weekend for telling tales, isn't it?" Cat replied.

"You know what's great?" Anna asked. "Here we are in Las Vegas, five somewhat older, mature women, and we still have so much life in us. Ashley Fake Tits thinks we're past our "sell by" date, with no past life or any tickle still left in-between our thighs, but she's so wrong. The only time I know I'm older is when I look in the mirror. Other than that, I'm still in my twenties and as frisky as a farm girl."

"It's true. I actually feel more sexual now than I did in my twenties." Cat said. "I've shed all that guilt and enjoy the pleasure so much more. I don't have to play all the cat and mouse games if I want to sleep with a man. And I enjoy the sex so much more. "

"If someone thinks I'm too old, they should see what I would do to that guy in the speedo over there." Holly laughed. "Okay, let's jump in the pool and make some waves!"

After the members of the Mahjong Club went for a swim, they proceeded up to their rooms. They changed into comfortable clothes and hit the Grande Canal Shoppes for a little retail therapy.

Friday Night / Las Vegas

"Oh God!" Anna said excitedly. "We have *got* to do this more often."

The ladies were at the Palazzo in the Venetian Hotel for the seven o'clock performance of the *Jersey Boys.* All of them were in the aisle, dancing to "Walk Like A Man." They were so rowdy the ushers had to be called to get them back to their seats.

"These young girls today can't rock n' roll like our generation." Priscilla yelled above the music.

"Tell me about it!" Cat said. "I was at Woodstock and these young girls think *they* get wild?! Forget about it!"

"I first saw the *Jersey Boys* seven years ago." Lori said. "Art and I went when the show opened on Broadway in 2005. I swear they're even better today." Lori took a swig of wine she had snuck into the show in a wineskin and then passed it to Holly.

"If I ever got Frankie Valli in bed, he wouldn't be able to walk like a man for a week!" Holly yelled.

The ensemble played their last song, the lights came on and the crowd started to walk to the exit. Some stragglers waited to see if there would be an encore, but the curtain didn't go up again.

"Where do you guys want to eat?" Cat asked.

"Let's go to LAVO's." Holly suggested. "The food's great and there's a DJ that plays all the hottest music and I feel like dancing after hearing that concert."

"Ok. But you have to promise to do your dancing on the dance floor and not on top of our table!" Lori said.

"Don't worry. I plan to find some tall, dark handsome man and rock his world."Holly said.

"Yeah but do it in his room ok? I find it hard to sleep when the bed is bouncing up and down." Priscilla said laughing.

The ladies made their way to the restaurant and sat at the bar until their name was called. The wait staff was very attentive, and their waiter flirted with Priscilla.

"Five of us girls and he picks the lesbian. Go figure." Cat said.

They all laughed and when he returned they ordered the *tuna tartare, baked clams oreganato and the Kobe beef carpaccio* for appetizers for the table. When Holly suggested a dozen oysters on the half-shell, the all yelled in unison "You don't need it!" They added a bottle of Santa Margarita Pinot Grigio.

"I'm still sick over Susan not coming with us." Anna said.

"I know, but there's nothing we can do." Cat said.

"Well the women you gave the ticket to was thrilled. She said that show had been sold out and she was leaving for home tomorrow so it was her last chance to see it. That was very nice of you, but why didn't you sell it to her Holly?" Lori asked.

"Did you see the way she was dressed? I could be wrong, but I don't think she really had any money. Besides, it karma baby! It was my good deed for the night."Holly answered. "Ah see? Karma!" Holly said as the waiters began to put the food in front of them.

"I heard a joke." Anna said, putting a baked clam on her plate. There are these three guys meeting in the clubhouse getting ready to play golf on a Sunday morning. The first guys say "You wouldn't believe what I had to promise my wife to get out of the house. I have to take my wife and her mother to the flower show next weekend."

"That's nothing." The second guy says. "I had to promise my wife I would paint the back porch!"

They look at the third guy and he says "Not me. I woke up my wife in bed and asked if I should play golf today or would you rather me stay home and have sex. She told me to wear a sweater as it might get cold."

"Oh that's too funny Anna. Art will love that," Lori said.

For dinner, the ladies decided to order several different dishes and share them. They ordered the *roasted Chilean sea bass, brick oven salmon oreganato, chicken and mushroom ravioli,* and the *lobster scampi.*

The dinner came, plates were brought and plates were cleared off. They polished off the first bottle of wine and ordered a second. They didn't plan on having dessert, but when Cat ordered the *New York Cheesecake with strawberries,* the will power of the rest of the ladies collapsed and they each ordered their favorite.

After dinner they were stuffed and sleepy. They probably would have called it a night, but Holly dragged them onto the dance floor. Men continuously tried to cut in on their little group, but they were having such a good time singing and dancing together, they ignored their advances. They danced until the wee hours of the morning, then reluctantly gave in to overwhelming fatigue and headed back to their suites.

Saturday Morning/ Las Vegas

Cat awoke to the aroma of fresh coffee wafting through the air. She attempted to sit up in bed, but the pounding in her head felt like a dagger being driven into her brain. She relinquished to the pain and tried to settle deeper into the fluffy, down pillows. In the other room, Anna was snoring like a bear in hibernation. Despite her crushing headache, Cat smiled as she thought about them all dancing the previous night. She was loath to admit at her age she paid a hefty price after a night of heavy drinking. The smell of fresh coffee meant one of her friends was up already.

With a groan, Cat struggled out of bed and brushed her tousled hair back with her fingers. She slipped on the plush *Venetian* bathrobe and cinched the belt around her waist. As she looked around for her slippers, she noticed she hadn't bothered to take off her shoes before going to bed. Cat shuffled to the living room, and without saying a word went directly to the coffee pot. She poured herself a cup and heard someone say "Rough night?"

She turned around and almost dropped her coffee cup on the floor. She was stunned to see Susan sitting on the couch with her legs tucked under her body. "Susan!" Cat let out a high pitched shriek. "Oh my God! What are you doing here? When did you get in?"

"I caught the red-eye last night. Luckily, Holly still had me listed as a guest, so the front desk clerk gave me a key to the room. By the time I got up here, all of you had passed out. So, tough night?" Susan asked again.

"God, I'm so glad you are here. You missed an outstanding concert but to answer your question, yes, we had a great night. As you can see, we all seem to be paying a big price for it."

"Well don't think tonight will be any different! I didn't fly out to Vegas to babysit my hung-over friends!"

Anna straggled into the room, stopped, then walked over to Susan and gave her a big kiss on the cheek and a hug. "Good to see you, honey. So Tony let you come, huh?"

"Not exactly. In fact I'm not even sure he'll be there when I get back."

"Hold that thought." Anna said. "I need some coffee for this."

Anna was pouring her coffee when there was a soft knock at the door. Susan got up to greet the waiter who brought in a tray fresh croissants, assorted muffins, fruit cups, and fresh coffee in a sterling silver pot.

"Just put it down over there, please." Susan said pointing to the sideboard. She signed the check and included a generous tip for the waiter.

Turning to Cat and Anna, she said "Once I heard you stirring, I thought you might need something to soak up all that alcohol," she said smiling. "Besides, it was getting late and *I* was getting hungry! It's eleven o'clock!"

By now, Lori, Priscilla and Holly could smell the coffee and staggered out from the bedroom together. They gathered around Susan, giving her hugs, then immediately went to get coffee hoping that the caffeine would relieve the hammering (throbbing) in their heads. They plopped down on the couches, settling deep into the leather.

"Tell us what happened. But please do it softly." Anna said. "I can't remember tying one on like this in a long, long time."

"Well, I know you all saw Tony and me arguing at the club. We'd been fighting ever since I brought this girls' trip to Las Vegas. He freaked out. At first he gave me some bullshit that we had previous plans, but we didn't. Then he out and out said I couldn't go. He said he wasn't willing to endure the crap his golfing buddies would be giving him about it. Said we would probably all get drunk and get picked up by strange men."

"I should be so lucky." Cat added.

"Shush girl." Anna said.

"So on and on we fought. I accused him of not trusting me, and added that I never did anything to warrant his lack of trust. Unlike him."

"Excuse me. What's that you just said?" Anna asked.

Ignoring the question, Susan went on. "I acquiesced, like I always do. That is, until he made a comment about our group, and how pathetic we were. That did it. I flew into a rage. I told him that I was going on the trip and I didn't give a damn what he thought. He threatened that if I went, he might not be there when I got back. So I told him I really didn't give a sweet shit if he left. I reminded him to take his *pathetic* oil paintings. Elvis on velour, really? I assured him if they were still hanging on the wall when I got home I'd promptly put them out in the trash. "

The ladies were silent. They instinctively knew this was a deep wound that their friend needed to cleanse. So they refilled their cups with coffee and allowed her to continue.

"So I called the airline, and got a red-eye on Jet Blue. I'm not usually awake at that time, but I was so pissed off I could have flown the plane myself. And here I am!"

"Susan, I have to ask. Has Tony ever hit you or been physically abusive in any way? Do we have to worry that he would hurt you? "Holly asked.

No. I don't know how I let things get this bad. I was never co-dependent. I was always self-reliant when I was married to George, and he loved that about me. He nicknamed me his little lioness. He actually encouraged me to be independent. When a man looked at me, he told me he felt proud that I chose him. He taught me how to do little fix-it jobs around the house and on the cars. He used to tease me that he might not be around forever. How prophetic.

But Tony is the opposite. He doesn't want me to do *anything*. He thinks I'm incompetent, and that if I try to fix something I'll screw it up and he will have to redo it. He's destroyed my self- confidence and the very essence of my individuality. Tony has made me a nervous wreck. Then *he* suggested I should talk to Lori about taking medication. I am always on edge, afraid to make a mistake and set off his temper. One time, I didn't buy the right kind of Italian bread for Sunday dinner. I looked *everywhere* but couldn't find it. So I served a different kind of bread. I had made one of his favorite meals: spaghetti and meats balls with sausages and green peppers. God, I'll never forget that day. Tony sat down at the table and seemed to be in a good mood. However, when he noticed I didn't serve his favorite Italian bread, he escalated to being enraged in seconds. He started yelling about how hard he works and why can't he have a goddamn simple meal on a Sunday. I didn't say a word. I was too afraid. The next thing I knew, he grabbed the edge of the table and threw it. Everything went flying. Meatballs, sausages, gravy and of course, the bread. I was covered with food. He stormed off and told me he was going golfing and I had better have the damn mess cleaned up by the time he got home. The mess he made. He said he would eat at the club and he didn't give a shit what I did for dinner. For all he cared, I could eat what was on the floor. After that day, something inside me broke. And I've been broken ever since.

Tears started to well up in her eyes. When she blinked they slowly slid down her cheek. She placed her head in her hands, while Anna wrapped her arms around her. No one said a word. They were too shocked. They knew Tony was mercurial, and that he wore the pants in the family, but none of them suspected that their friend had endured such abuse.

"Susan, what he did *was* abuse." Anna said softly, still rocking her weeping friend in her arms. "Sometimes there is no legitimate reason. Some men can be that way."

"No. I believe I know the reason." Susan whimpered through her sobs. "When we were dating, I told him all about George. Of course I did. There was no reason to hide it. He had been previously married as well. He knew how much I loved George and how much I grieved for him when he died. Christ, I still grieve for him. But life does go on. George was a lovely part of my past. Being with George added a new dimension to my life and made me the person I was when I met Tony. Tony told me repeatedly that I needed to get over George, but I'll always have a special place in my heart for him. He was the love of my life. I truly believe that everyone gets only one great love in life. Tony felt very threatened by my relationship with George. I know it's irrational since George was dead. Tony was the one who couldn't get over it. However, he wasn't like that when I first met him. But slowly things changed. If I mentioned somewhere I had been, he would ask if I went there with George. If I did, I would tell him so, and then he would pout for the remainder of the day. He wanted to know about our sex life. Was George a better lover than him? I should have told him my vibrator was better than him, but I didn't. I began to dread his constant questions. Then he made me get rid of everything that George bought for me. Any gifts, my diamond bracelet, my wedding rings. He said if I loved him, I didn't need to hang onto the past. But the past was part of *me!* Like an idiot, I did everything he asked. This was my second marriage and I didn't want it to fail. But what I didn't know was that it failed the moment I said "I do." at the altar. What an idiot."

"No you're not sweetie." Priscilla said gently. "You just married a very insecure man who has no idea how wonderful his wife is. The truth is honey, he's probably not going to change. So I guess you have some tough decisions ahead of you. Please remember, no matter what, you always have us. Whatever you need and whenever you need it, we'll be there."

"Thanks Priscilla. That means a lot to me and I know you're all here for me. I feel it. I'm sorry I didn't discuss this with you before it got so dire. I was too embarrassed, you know?"

"I know exactly what you mean." Holly assured her. "For some reason, women feel responsible for things we have no control over. We girls carry shame that is not even ours. It's the men who do it to us, but somehow, we end up carrying it."

"But we're the ladies of *The Mahjong Club,* and we're tough!" Lori said, trying to brighten up the moment.

"Well I certainly didn't come to Las Vegas for a cry fest!" Susan said. "Let's put on our bathing suits and show the men at the pool that we're Florida cougars."

"That's our girl!" Cat said. "Let's go show off our *curvaceous bodies*!"

"Let's go!" Holly said enthusiastically. "But first I'm going to eat one of those blueberry muffins!"

"Hey! Leave something for me!" Priscilla cried, as both Anna and Cat raced to the breakfast cart ahead of Holly, scooping up muffins and croissants.

Saturday Afternoon/ Poolside

"Wow! Susan! You look great! Did you just buy that bathing suit?" Anna asked.

"No. Believe it or not, it's *years* old. I'd almost forgotten about it because it was in the back of my closet. Tony thought it was too revealing and didn't want me to wear it."

"Well there are some men over there who seem to appreciate it!" Anna said nodding to a small cluster of men admiring Susan in her bathing suit. "You still got it honey!"

"God. It's been so long, I'm not even sure how to flirt anymore." Susan said.

"You don't have to honey. Just do a few pirouettes in that suit and the men will come running over here drooling like puppies." Anna said laughing.

The ladies met at the TAO cafe beside the infinity pool. Lush velvets and silks hung around the walls of the pool deck. Waterfalls rippled over century old wood beams and ancient stones. The pool was meant to be serene and calming. It was precisely what the ladies needed after a wild first night.

Priscilla was leaning in and speaking in soft tones to an attractive fifty-something woman, who's long auburn hair fell in loose waves over her shoulders. They shared a quiet laugh and discreetly exchanged telephone numbers. Priscilla touched her hand in an intimate fashion and headed over to join the group.

"Doing a little hunting, Priscilla?" Susan asked.

Priscilla blushed ever so slightly and said "She's from Washington D.C. She is here with her boyfriend, and he doesn't have a clue she also likes women as well. So we exchanged numbers and maybe we'll meet for a drink when we're both in D.C."

"Ah." Anna said. "Where's Holly?"

"Not sure." Priscilla said. She said she had to make a call from the room, and then I guess she'll be down. Here's Lori and Cat, and look what they have!"

Lori and Cat walked around the infinity pool each holding a pitcher of margaritas and a tray of shrimp. Anna cleared off a space on the table and groaned. "I'm not even sober from *last* night." She moaned.

"Hair of the dog, honey." Cat replied, as she filled their glasses.

"Here comes Holly now." Lori said looking across the pool. "And does she have a shit-eating grin on her face. I wonder what she's up to."

"Hi ladies! I took the liberty of making dinner reservations for us at the *Canaletto Restaurant*. It serves classic Venetian fare. I checked out the menu already and I know what I'm going to order. I'm sure there's something for everyone on the menu. I requested a table right on the water so we'll have great views of the Grand Canal and can watch the gondolas go by as we eat. Our reservation is for seven o'clock. Then after dinner, I have *quite* the surprise for you."

"Oh God! A Holly surprise! That scares me already!" Cat said. "So what is it?"

"It's a *surprise.* It wouldn't be much of a surprise if I told you now, would it?"

"Should we be afraid?" Lori laughed.

"Oh yeah. Big time." Holly laughed back.

The ladies dug into the platter of shrimp, and completely forgetting their hangovers, finished the two pitchers of margarita's and even ordered another. After all, they were in Vegas.

Saturday Night/ Canaletto Restaurant

The ladies arrived on time for their seven o'clock dinner reservation, and they looked marvelous. Each had gone out of their way to make a fashion statement that said, we may be a little older, but we're still *hot*. Judging by the looks they received from the men, they were right.

 As usual, Holly led the way. They entered the opulent and spacious dining room and were lead to their table by the maître d, not looking too shabby himself. He was handsome, with the olive Italian skin usually found in southern Italy. His jet black hair was streaked with gray and combed straight back over his head. A black tuxedo with a red cummerbund circled his thin waist. His black Ferragamo shoes were so highly polished that they reflected the light.

"He'll do." Cat whispered into Anna's ear.

"Oh yeah. He'll do just fine."

"Ah, he's probably gay." Priscilla said.

"That's the problem with you lesbians. You think everyone is gay, or wants to be."Holly laughed.

"C'mon Holly. I just *know* you're curious!" Priscilla said back.

"And how do you know I haven't tried girl- on- girl?" Holly said over her shoulder, keeping Priscilla quiet and guessing for the moment.

The maitre d' escorted them to a round booth upholstered in luxurious tanned leather. The back of the booth rose high enough to envelope the ladies in privacy. Priscilla slipped in first, while the maitre d' watched Anna and Cat slide in to Priscilla's left and Susan and Lori to her right. The waiter promptly appeared and asked for their drink order. Susan ordered a bottle of Dom Perignon, and asked the waiter to have the second bottle chilled and ready to go. The ladies smiled at their friends' new found assertiveness.

They perused the dinner menu, and again agreed to pick out a variety of appetizers for the table. They decided to be adventurous, and ordered some unusual starters. Priscilla chose the *Sardee in Soar*, which were fresh sardines that were fried and marinated with sweet and sour onions. Cat, having spent so much time in Italy working for Gucci, chose the *Baccala Alla Vincentina*, imported salt cod baked in milk with onions, capers and garlic, and served over creamy yellow polenta. Susan decided on the *Calamaretti Fritti,* baby squid, lightly floured and then deep fried and served with a spicy marina over buttery risotto. Both Lori and Holly decided on one order of the *Carpaccio Con Ruchetta*, thinly sliced raw beef, wild arugula, capers, Grand Padano with lemon olive oil dressing.

The waiter opened the bottle of Dom Perignon, and poured a small amount into Susan's glass. She slowly lifted the crystal champagne flute, swirled it around a few times, then closed her eyes and placed a sip onto her tongue. She smiled, eyes still closed, and exclaimed "Excellent. Thank you." The waiter filled each of their glasses and left to check on their appetizer order and get the second bottle of champagne chilled.

"A toast." Susan proposed. "To The Mahjong Club and the best friends any girl could have!" Holding out her glass, clinking with the other five.

"To The Mahjong Club!" The rest of the ladies joined in the toast.

The truth is, all women need a Mahjong Club. Or a book club, or bridge club or poker club. Women are different from men. We bond differently and need each other more and in different ways than men. Have you ever been to a party where the men don't know one another? They stand around, hands in their pockets with a silly grin on their faces! They can fight wars but have a hard time relating to people of their own sex. They only seem to be comfortable talking about sports." Anna remarked. We open up and share more things than men do. We suffer together, but also have shared happiness. We *talk*. When men get upset, they wash their car, or go to the driving range and hit a bucket of golf balls. Freddy would never call Art and say "I'm feeling depressed about something. Can we talk?"

They just don't do that. Then they want us to be mind readers and get angry with us when we can't figure out what's wrong or how to help. It's a wonder how we get along at all.

"They have a dick." Holly said.

"Don't need that." Priscilla rebutted.

"But your point is well made." Cat said. "I guess I never understood Jack, and maybe that's why I'm living in Florida now."

"That's not fair." Anna said defensively. "Why is it our responsibility to make them happy? Sometimes I think they revert back to being little boys and want us to become their mothers again."

"Well you know what they say. When a woman marries, she either becomes a mother or a nursemaid." Susan said.

The ladies were interrupted in their discussion when three waiters, each young and handsome, evidently you had to be good looking to work here, placed the appetizers on the table. The ladies moved the plates around, each snagged what they wanted to begin with. Anna and Lori speared the same piece of calamari at the same time.

"Tony cheated on me. And not just once." Susan dropped the statement on the table like a bowling ball. I'm sure this plays into how he treats me somehow, but I'm certainly not a psychiatrist. I told him several times that I wanted us to see a marriage counselor, and he flatly refused. He said that he didn't want to go because he was afraid someone would find out.

"Jesus Susan. I had no idea. Freddy certainly never said anything to me." Anna said.

"Nah. He probably doesn't know." Susan said.

"Art never said anything either. These guys play golf together." Lori said.

"He told me no one knew." Susan said. "I told him only the slut he was screwing, the motel clerk, and God knows who else."

"When...how did you find out?" Anna asked.

"When the dumb bitch called my house. She told me they were in love and that he loved me but wasn't *in love* with me. I shouldn't call her a dumb bitch, but she knew Tony was married and she still slept with him."

"Yeah, she's a dumb bitch." Holly said in Susan's defense.

"So what happened?" Cat asked softly.

"Well, at first he was upset. I think he was sorry that he got caught, but not for his indiscretion. When I told him to sleep in the guest room, he said that it was entirely my fault that he had the affair in the first place."

"No way!" Holly said. "What bullshit!"

"What did he give for a reason?" Anna asked.

"A few years ago, he was in the garage and going through some boxes looking for his old passport, and he came across George's and my old wedding photo album. I remember that fight. He really flipped out, and told me to get rid of it. He went on to say that I was married to him now, and it was disrespectful to keep it. We fought for days. So I told him I got rid of it, but instead I sent it to my sister to hold for me. When she downsized and moved, she mailed it back to me. I stuck it in the garage and must have forgotten about it. Anyway he found it again and felt that I had betrayed him so he felt justified in betraying me."

I tried to put myself in his place. I really did. I just couldn't understand it. His reaction seemed so immature to me. For heaven's sake, George had been dead for years! Yes I loved him. Of course I did. Would Tony want me to marry someone I didn't love?

I told him he was using the wedding album as an excuse for being unfaithful. He finally confessed that when he went to Scottsdale to compete in a golf tournament he met a young girl in the hotel lounge. He explained how one drink led to another and since he was still hurt and angry over what he felt was a betrayal, he decided that he deserved this sexual dalliance. Of course, it wasn't just one encounter, he screwed her the entire four days he was in Arizona. To make matters worse, he arranged to meet her in Vermont when he went there to play in a tournament.

After the Vermont trip the little slut called the house. I mean really! Does he think he's friggin' Tiger Woods?"

"Did he stop seeing her?" Anna asked.

"Yes. He did. He probably thought I was with both the CIA and the FBI the way I watched him, but he did stop seeing her. After awhile, I let him back into the big bed, but the betrayal I felt, cut to the bone. I just kept thinking, how many nights did he crawl into my bed after talking to her on the phone? And what did he tell her to make her think he wanted to be with her rather than me? I felt small and inconsequential. I started to look at my body critically. Maybe if I were thinner? I thought. Maybe if I were better in bed? I tormented myself with those and other thoughts constantly. After a long time, the voice of my inner critic settled down, and I went on. That's what we women do, right? Go forward? Of course Tony seemed to get over it much more quickly than I did. I think his only fear was that I was going to boot him out. When he knew I wasn't, he jumped back into his usual routine."

By now, the ladies had eaten their way through the plates of appetizers, and drank the rest of the champagne. Holly signaled the waiter over to the table and requested that he bring out the second bottle of champagne.

The ladies looked at the dinner menu, while still talking about Susan's plight, and reviewed their choices. By the time the waiter returned with the second bottle of bubbly, they knew what they were going to order.

The waiter started at the far right of the table and worked around to the left taking the dinner orders.

Cat ordered the *Ossobuco Con Risotto Allo Zafferano,* which was described on the menu as veal shank braised in a Marsala wine with porcini and shiitake mushrooms, and served with saffron risotto.

Anna chose the *Petto Di Pollo Al Peperoncino.* It was the grilled free-range chicken breast marinated with sage, rosemary, thyme, crushed red pepper, white wine, Dijon mustard and lemon. It was served with sautéed organic spinach.

Priscilla ordered the *Salmone Alla Griglia,* the Chinook salmon filet grilled with lemon-oil and parsley sauce. It was served with roasted Yukon Gold potatoes and sautéed seasonal vegetables.

Susan decided to go with the *Veal Scaloppine Ortolana,* veal scaloppini with fresh mozzarella, eggplant, roasted tomatoes, topped with fresh basil and peperoncino sauce. It was also served with angel hair pasta.

"I don't mean to upset you, Susan, but was that the only time Tony cheated on you? I'm certainly not defending him, but as they say "to err is human, to forgive divine" Anna said.

"No. A few years later, he went to his 25th college reunion at Syracuse University. He asked me to go, but I had the stomach flu, and was in no condition to travel, so he went by himself.

By this time, I had loosened the reins, if you will. I thought he learned his lesson. Sex was good between us. We had it often, and I thought he was satisfied. If he wasn't, he sure didn't tell me.

So he's up in New York at Syracuse, and ran into an old girlfriend. She was divorced, and he *wasn't!"* Susan said forcefully. "When he came home, he instantly confessed. I have no doubt it was because it was so public and we knew some of the same people. He probably assumed it would get back to me. He swears it was because he drank too much and that she was the aggressor."

"Funny how when *we* drink too much, our clothes don't fall off." Cat said.

"So I sent him to sleep on the couch, again. This time I told him either we are going to see a marriage counselor, or he can pick up the Yellow Pages and start looking for a lawyer. He agreed to go, but after three or four sessions Tony said he "got it" and didn't need any more counseling. Again I relented. So we stopped going as a couple, but I continued to go on my own for quite some time. Eventually the counselor told me that in her professional opinion Tony was very immature, and had some underlying issues he didn't want to address. I wanted to say "No shit, Sherlock!", but thought it wouldn't be appropriate.

195

By that time, Tony had just plain worn me down. I was insecure and had a poor self-image. He often reminded me that it was unlikely that I would ever find someone else. I know this is hard for you all to believe, but his psychological assault didn't happen overnight. It was over years."

"You know what really frosts my ass?" Susan asked." I don't understand why he pursued me so ardently? At the beginning of our courtship, he was a totally different man. He was a total sweetheart, very understanding and gentle. He would bring me flowers for absolutely no reason. He'd surprise me with little gifts and soft, sweet words. He even wrote me a poem. If he had such a low opinion of me why did he pursue me?

"So, here I am in Vegas. With my friends *and* here comes my veal scaloppini! See? Things are getting better already!"

"I think you have a rocky road ahead of you, girlfriend, but I'll support whatever decision you make. . .no judgment." Anna said taking the chicken from the waiter.

"All of us are with you. Hey! We're The Mahjong Club!" Lori added.

"I'll drink to that!" Holly said.

"Holly, you'd drink to anything!" Cat said. "Wow, my Ossobuco is delicious! I heard the chef is from Italy."

"So what are you going to do?" Anna asked Susan.

"Well tonight my plans are to drink and raise a little hell here in Vegas. Then I'll go home and buy Tony a more comfortable couch, if he hasn't left already," she said with a grin. "I love the way they put the fresh eggplant with the mozzarella."

The ladies ate in comfortable silence, occasionally moaning how good the food was, and pausing to sample each other's dish. The high-backed booths gave them the privacy they needed to have such an intimate conversation; intimate even amongst close friends.

They watched the tourists and the lovers in the gondolas drifting by, and enjoyed the soft music in the background. They could hear, more than see, the other diners in the restaurant. The maitre' d' came over just once to see if everything was satisfactory, then retreated quietly allowing the women to dine in privacy.

"I suppose I'm not one to throw stones." Lori said.

The ladies stopped eating to look at their friend.

"It was a long time ago, and you need to hear the background story."
"Wait. Wait." Cat said then motioned for the waiter to bring a third bottle of champagne.

"Good idea. I may need it to tell you my tale."Lori said.

"This ought to be good," Holly said.

"Where do I start?" Lori asked herself. "Art and I planned a trip to Antigua. We had booked a lovely suite overlooking the ocean for a week at the *Princess Antigua.* We had to take different flights because Art was leaving from New York, where he was working managing one of his restaurants. We both needed to get away, as both of us had been working long hours and deserved a break. Besides, we hadn't seen each other for a while and needed some alone time.

I had flown from Florida, so I was going to arrive first. I told him I would either be in the room or at the outside bar by the pool. He and I stayed there before, so we knew our way around. I told him I'd leave a note at the front desk if I decided to do anything different, like go shopping.

So I am on the plane, looking out the window, but I'm not seeing anything. I'm holding a letter that I received two days earlier at home. I read the letter so many times that I knew what it said by heart. And I was afraid what it said inside would steer my life in a whole new direction.

I looked down at the signature which said *Miss you, Rick.* I wondered how long it had been since I had either seen or heard from him. It must have been at least five years since we spent that last summer's weekend on Cape Cod. Rick was working as tennis pro on Nantucket, attempting to teach overweight rich women how to play tennis. I was working in Boston at Massachusetts General Hospital. We met one weekend when I took the ferry to Nantucket with some friends from work. I decided to take a tennis lesson, and that's when I met Rick. Let's just say we really hit it off. I didn't want to blow off the girls, so he joined us at night with some of his friends and we would go out as a group. When the weekend was almost over, he said that he wanted to see me again. I agreed and we began dating. Sometimes he would come to Boston, or I would go to Nantucket. We had fun, took long walks holding hands, kissed a lot. It was just easy with Rick. None of that awkwardness you sometimes get when you date someone.

One weekend he rented a small, quaint cottage in Cisco, one of the more rural parts of the island. It overlooked the ocean, and I would go asleep at night listening to the waves break apart on the rocks as they raced to shore, and woke up to the same music. We would leave the windows open to get the fresh sea air, and just snuggle together when it got chilly.

We went for walks along the sea, rarely seeing any other people. Rick would take a backpack and a bottle of red wine, usually a Bollo, that was our favorite at the time, and I would pack some sandwiches, or even just some cheese and bread. We would lie out on the grass, hold hands and not even talk. Rick was a great kisser, and sometimes we would just kiss for hours on end.

On our last day together on the island, I was outside watching the sun come up over the ocean. It was barely light out yet and the only sounds were the sea gulls fishing in the surf. Rick came up behind me and wrapped his arms around me. Being a tennis pro, he had these great muscular arms. Say what you will about the metro-sexual businessman, but give me some strong muscles any day. I remember how he put his face into my neck, setting my whole body shivering. He held me for a moment, and it seemed that we were the only two people on the planet. The sun wasn't the only thing rising, and I could feel Rick's penis, thick and long, getting hard against my backside.

I turned Rick around, and led him inside the cottage. I didn't even bother to close the front door. We spent the morning making love. Hard and passionate at first, then softer, and more gentle.

I always loved the way Rick gazed at my naked body with his smoky gray eyes. Hungrily. Unashamed. I loved the way he would grunt when I took his dick with my hand and placed him inside of me. That weekend was one of the best of my life.

I was in such a deep state of daydreaming, I barely heard the announcement by the pilot to fasten our seatbelts and prepare for landing. I think the jolt of the wheels touching down is what jarred me back to reality.

I placed the letter into my favorite Gucci purse which Art gave me for my last birthday. I felt guilty just by doing that. It was like I was joining the two men together, and they couldn't have been more different. I knew I loved Art, but I had to admit it just wasn't the same. He didn't *excite* me, and with his premature ejaculation, I have difficulty having an orgasm. Often I wait for him to fall asleep, which never takes long, and then I quietly move my hands down between my legs and use my fingers to bring myself to orgasm. Even when I quiver when I climax, he never wakes up.

Art is a kind and decent guy. Yeah, I've heard all his dumb jokes a million times and I cringe when he tells them to people at the club. He tends to be a bit narcissistic, and has to be the life of the party all the time, but we're comfortable together; however getting Rick's letter made me wonder if being comfortable was what I really wanted. In fact, it was Art's need for attention that grabbed Ricks' eye in the first place. Art created a Facebook page for the two of us, even though I asked him not to. So evidently, he posted the fact that we were going to Antigua on vacation. Guess who's the tennis pro at the *Princess Antigua?* Rick. He probably was checking up on me and old friends when he found out we were coming, thus the letter. Rick wrote how much he missed me, and how sorry he was that we drifted apart. We never really broke up. When I took a hospital administrators job at Beth Israel in Boston, he couldn't leave his job as tennis pro on Nantucket. We would get together as often as we could, but my job was demanding, especially during the initial period, and he gave lessons on weekends. We talked on the phone, got together for a couple of hot rendezvous, but gradually drifted apart. We lost touch with each other, as some lovers often do. I met Art shortly afterwards. He was the complete opposite of Rick. Art was always stable and predictable. He was just a *nice* man, my mother would say. So we dated. I didn't really have the time to date anyone else, and the weeks turned into months, and now, I think it had been almost five years when Rick's letter came out of the blue.

Rick told me he dated, had a couple of girlfriends, but that none of them could touch his heart the way I did. He knew I was coming with Art, and certainly did not want to cause any problems or interfere in any way with my relationship, but he did want to see me.

He asked me to meet him for a drink at his place to catch up. He promised he was still a gentleman, and had no ulterior motive. I had to laugh at that because I was always the one attacking his body. God, he was hot! He left me a couple different ways I could contact him discretely at the tennis club.

So, believe it or not, I sent him a quick note saying yes I was coming with Art, but it would be nice to see him again. For one drink. I said I would drop a note for him at the Racquet Club, and let him know what time worked for me.

I was wondering what the hell I was doing. Not only to me, but to Art. This was way too dangerous. What if the passion that burned so hot, ignited again? What would I do then?

Rick was ten years my junior. He had sandy blond hair that was always tousled. At 6'1" he was so much taller than Art. He was also much bigger in other areas, if you know what I mean. I can remember the first time I had seen him fully erect. I just stared at his dick thinking "there is no *way* that thing is ever going to fit inside me. Oh, but I was wrong. I did fit inside me and filled so deeply and more complete than I ever had before. He gave me the most mind-blowing orgasm I ever had, and he wasn't even in all the way. I just held onto his muscular shoulders and rode with it. After that, I couldn't keep my hands off of him. I would reach orgasm just watching his muscular thighs go up and down, slapping on my own."

"God! You're making me hot! Where is that waiter?" Holly asked.

"Easy girl." Anna said.

"So I left the plane and after I got my luggage from the baggage terminal, I caught the first taxi out of the airport. I'm sure the ride to the hotel was beautiful, the road followed along the ocean, but I was too immersed in my dilemma to enjoy it. I knew the smartest thing to do would be to send Rick a note cancelling the drink, but I also knew I wouldn't.

My taxi pulled up in front of the hotel. It was located just across from the ocean with its own private beach and twin pools. A doorman, elegantly dressed in a powder blue jacket with brass buttons and starched white pants, opened the door for me, and called for the porter to take my bags.

I walked into the lobby and peeked around as since I was almost afraid Rick would be standing there. I didn't see him so I made my way to the front counter and checked in. A bellhop escorted me to my room, unlocked the door, and placed my luggage on a rack in the closet. He asked if there was anything else, meaning "Where's my tip?" and I said no and handed him a ten dollar bill. Art always says I tip too much.

Art wasn't due to arrive for a few more hours, so I went to the mini-bar and opened one of the small bottles of scotch and poured it straight into a glass. I felt very on edge and the scotch helped to ease my anxiety. I walked out onto the balcony and sipped my drink. The view of the ocean was spectacular and calming. When I finished my drink I had a nice warm feeling in my stomach. Then, I decided to take a hot shower. I stripped off in front of the large double mirror, and I had to assess my body. I was still in good shape, firm, thanks no doubt to my daily workout at the gym and taking Pilates classes. My breasts were still "perky" as Art would say.

I stepped into the large, luxurious steam shower. It was decorated in earth tones with textured tiles. The effect was very calming. The water flow from the fancy shower head mimicked rainfall. As the cascading streams of hot water sluiced down my back, the world and its worries circled down the drain. I'm embarrassed to continue, but in the spirit of complete disclosure, I started to think of Rick and I placed my soapy hand between my legs. I imagined his rock hard body and his erect penis sticking straight up, and I became very aroused. I fantasized it was his strong hands caressing me, and not my own. I brought myself to such an orgasm, I found myself sitting on the floor of the shower with the water still spilling down on me. At that exact same moment, I became very angry with Art. He never took the time to please me sexually. He didn't like to perform oral sex, but he sure liked it went I went down on him, and he could barely last a minute once he was inside of me.

What a difference from Rick. He would start our love making off by rubbing my shoulders, neck and back with scented oils. While his strong masculine hands rubbed with deep, long strokes, almost too hard, his fingers would knead the big muscles on my back, in between the shoulder blades. By the time he turned me over, I would be so wet and want him so badly, I would pull him down on top of me, and grab his big dick and place it inside of me. Sometimes he would stop me, and first rub oil on my feet, then ankles and work his way up my thighs to my knees. I would be begging him to screw me, but he would caress my vagina with his tongue, while I would be pulling on his soft, silky blond hair, trying to get him up on top of me. Only after I came, would he use his muscular thighs to spread my legs apart, and taking one of my nipples between his teeth, enter me.

Having these thoughts while sitting on the shower floor compelled me to see Rick at least one more time."

"Stop right there! My head is spinning! What a story! Let's have the waiter clear these plates. I want some coffee and would like to take a peek at the dessert menu." Anna said.

"Oh! I hope they have cheesecake!" Cat moaned.

The ladies motioned for their waiter. He arrived promptly and began to clear the dishes. The table looked as if a great feast was eaten, judging by the amount of empty plates. The champagne bottle had one sip left in it, which Holly promptly drained, straight from the bottle.

The waiter handed the ladies the dessert menu, and went to retrieve a carafe of both regular and decaf coffee. The ladies paused for a moment in the telling of their stories, now fully enthralled by the dessert selections.

When the waiter returned, Cat suggested that to fully enjoy their dessert, they should all start with the *Sgroppino.* She explained that this was one of the traditional ways Italians cleanse their palates before dessert. She said it was a mix of vodka, lemon sorbet, prosecco and a dark cream.

"Vodka? I'm in!" Holly chirped.

"Sounds wonderful!" Susan said. Then to the waiter "Please bring us six."

The ladies went over the small but exquisite dessert menu. When the waiter returned with the five *sgroppino's*, they were ready to order dessert. Anna went first, and wanted the *Colombina Al Cioccolato*, which the menu described as a dark chocolate mousse with white and milk chocolate shavings, with fresh raspberry and Kiwi sauces.

Holly followed with the *Crespella Di Mele*, crepes filled with Granny Smith apples and pastry cream, caramelized walnuts, green apple sorbet with caramel and crème anglaise sauce. With a broken smile, she told the girls how she and her brothers would often go to an abandoned farm and pick the green apples from the trees in the orchard, and how inevitably, they would all start throwing the over-ripe ones at each other. The ladies could see Holly struggle with the memory, no doubt trying to keep some of the nice ones from being tainted by the bad. But they all knew, one bad apple could ruin the barrel.

Susan decided she wanted an authentic Italian dessert, so she chose the *Zabaione Alla Gritti*. It was a chilled zabaione with fresh berries, Bellini sorbet, whipped cream, amarena cherries and baicoli cookies. The waiter agreed that it was an excellent choice and one of the more popular desserts.

Priscilla decided to play it safe and get something she knew she would enjoy. She chose the *Tiramisu Al Cucchiaio*. It was the Treviso-style tiramisu, which was her favorite.

Cat wrinkled her nose at the waiter and said "You don't have cheesecake on the menu. That's what I really wanted." The waiter smiled and said here, at the Venetian, we make all the beautiful women's dreams come true, and that he would indeed find her a slice of the most elegant New York cheesecake in Las Vegas. He only needed to know if she would prefer strawberries or cherries on it.

Pushing her luck, she smiled as sexily as she could, and asked if fresh blueberries were available. The waiter bowed and said he would procure the fattest, sweetest blueberries, fresh from Maine to compliment her special dessert. Cat squealed with delight.

Having taken care of ordering desert and sipping both the dark, delicious brew of coffee served in elegant white with silver border coffee cups, and the *Sgroppino,* the ladies urged Lori to continue her story about Rick.

"So here I am, on the floor of the shower, God knows for how long, and Art walked in. Needless to say, he was wondering what the hell I was doing down there. In an instant, his curiosity turned to panic, and he asked me if I had slipped and fell. I told him I was just relaxing in the spray. The perfect water temperature and the gentle spray was the ideal antidote to my knotted muscles and jangled nerves. He helped me to my feet, and handed me a huge white bath sheet, and started to dry my back. Of course I couldn't help but think that had Rick found me on the shower floor he would have had his hands on my breasts squeezing and rubbing, then he would have placed his fingers inside me to get me going. Then he would probably have picked me up and carried me to the bed where he would have ravished me. For some reason, wet hair really drove him crazy. I swear it gave him a harder erection than usual, and let me tell you, you could hang a five pound bucket of cement off of one of Rick's hard-ons. But sadly, Art just helped me dry off, and went on and on about going down to the Tiki bar to start our holiday off with some fruity "umbrella drinks." So I dried off, donned a pair of silk thongs, again no reaction from Art, and a short floral skirt bursting with color. My sleeveless raspberry colored silk blouse matched it perfectly. I slide into a pair of strappy Vince Camuto sandals with a kitten heel, put on a little make-up and we are out the door.

Downstairs at the Tiki bar, Art was right at home, renewing old acquaintances with the waiters and bartenders. I always wanted to tell Art, *you know, they do work on tips.* But I didn't because he loves the way they laugh at all of his jokes. Me? I was looking around as nervous as a whore in church. I was afraid Rick was going to show up, and I didn't want that to happen. I wasn't ready to see him yet, especially with Art there. I'm not sure how Art would have taken it. He knew about Rick. We talked freely about past relationships, and he used to say that's why they call it the past. Certainly not like Tony handled it, Susan.

We stayed there for a while, and then decided to walk on the beach a little before dinner. That was very nice. We held hands and Art carried my sandals so I could walk in the surf. He glanced at his watch and realized it was 7:45 pm. We had to turn back since we had made dinner reservations for 8:00 pm.

I'll be honest with you, I was a nervous wreck. I just didn't know what to do."

"Well, I have the perfect solution to your dilemma. You screw Rick in the morning while Art's playing golf, and Art in the afternoon when Rick is teaching tennis." Holly offered.

"Great help Holly." Susan said.

"You know, it really wasn't a bad suggestion. Then you can have side-by-side comparisons and pick the winner at the end of the week." Cat offered.

"Oh you guys are a great help!" Lori laughed. "Now may I continue? So while we're having dinner, of course which I can't enjoy, despite the fact everything is beautiful, the moon hanging over us, shining on the blue-green ocean. The steel guitars in the background, the salmon I ordered, cooked to perfection, with the crispy skin on the outside, and the pink tender meat on the inside, surrounded by fresh vegetables and wild rice with slices of almonds. They might as well have brought me a cheeseburger from McDonald's.

I got up after eating, and told Art I wasn't that hungry after all, but I was going to the Ladies Room, and asked him to order me some decaf coffee. As a rule I never drink decaf, but the *last* thing I needed was caffeine! He was still eating his steak. Here we are in Antigua and he orders a New York sirloin. When I asked him why he just said "But honey. I like New York sirloins!" Men!

I got up from the table, folded the pale blue linen cloth napkin, and headed in the direction of the Ladies Room. But instead, I went to the Front Desk, and left a note for Rick saying that I would meet him the following night at his place at seven o'clock. I implored him to ignore me if we crossed paths. Now, I go to the Ladies Room to wash my face as I'm sure the perspiration on my forehead is noticeable. When I got back to the table, the waiter had cleared the dinner plates and brought Art and me our coffee. Art asked if I would like dessert, and I said I just couldn't, but I did want to stay at the table, looking at the moon and the evening's stars, and enjoy my coffee.

I think Art sensed something was wrong, but he didn't pry or ask me what it was. He sat quietly with me, listening to the sound of the waves coming to shore, and watching the moon, a pale white orb in the sky.

When I had enough, it was actually getting a little chilly, I told Art I was ready to turn in for the night. We went back to the room, and he surprised me by having flowers delivered while we were at dinner. There were a dozen beautiful orchids, my favorite, arranged in a crystal red vase, surrounded by green ferns. Next to the flowers, was a little card that read "I love you Babe. Always, Art" God! I felt like such an ass. Here I am, making plans to sneak off like some wanton, lustful teenager at night after her parents have gone to bed, and this wonderful man is considerate enough to have flowers sent to the room. But you know what? It didn't matter. Even then, something inside of me knew I had to see Rick."

"Yeah that something inside of you is called a pussy." Holly added.

"Maybe." Lori said. But whatever it was, I had to see him.

Art went into the bathroom first, and did his usual routine of flossing and brushing his teeth, then went to bed while I used the bathroom. I put on a new silk, *very short*, black teddy with red embroidery, and walked out of the bathroom and walked *slowly* in front of Art, gently swaying my hips."

"Did you have any underwear on underneath?" Priscilla asked.

"Naked as a country girl running through the fields." Lori answered. "So Art is just staring, and I could see his dick starting to get hard and acting like a tent pole. So I slip into bed and he starts to turn off the light but I stop him. No, I tell him. Then I proceed to yank off the covers and the sheets, leaving us fully exposed. I *slowly*, slip off his boxers, down over his erect dick, and stop to take him in my mouth. I was afraid he would come then and there, *but,* I had learned a little trick from a nurse that worked under my supervision."

"I wish she worked under *me.*" Priscilla said.

"That might be arranged."Lori said to Priscilla. "I hear she likes men and women."

"Oh boy!" Priscilla said. "I'll remind you later, but please continue. And what's that trick? Not that I'm ever likely going to need it."

"Well this nurse told me she had been sleeping with a doctor and he had the same problem. You know, he came too soon. So she would hold him tightly by the base of his dick and squeeze until he was ready to come. Somehow, that diminished his hard-on slightly and they could continue screwing. Every time he got close, he'd tell her to squeeze his dick until he said ok. Then, when he was ready to let go, he just did. Evidently, it's a proven way to deal with premature ejaculation.

So my head is in-between Arts knees, and I'm kissing and sucking his dick, and I can feel him start to tremble. Before I get a mouth full, I grab him by the dick and hold it tight. He was looking down at me, wondering what the hell I was doing, but as soon as I felt him start to get a little soft, I took him in my mouth again. Believe me ladies, when you have a guy's dick in your mouth, their whole need to communicate ceases.

I did this for a few times, then I slipped up on him, and holding his dick, still hard now, I placed him inside me. By now he would have come ten times, so I tell him that I read about this in a medical journal, he doesn't need to know his dick is being discussed in the nurse's lounge, and to let me know when he's ready to blow.

I moved slowly up and down on him, I prefer being on top far better than the missionary position. I can feel him better inside me that way, and it's easier for me to reach orgasm. Anyway, I'm sliding up and down and he tells me he's ready. This time I didn't want to stop him. I figured he's good and ready to come, so I reach down, and cup his balls in my hands and give them a little squeeze, at the same time I lean down and slip my tongue in his mouth. He came *so* hard, it was like a small explosion!

I fell on top of him, and he held me tight. I think he knew that something was amiss, but we also improved our sex life by one hundred fold. I have a feeling Art was always a little insecure about his performance. He would always ask me if I was okay and if I was satisfied, and of course I'd tell him yes."

"So now how are you feeling about seeing Rick?" Anna asked.

"It didn't change anything. I still had to see him and the memory of him still excited me. I hoped and hoped he had gotten bald and fat, but somehow I doubted that.

Art and I fell asleep, but not before I pulled up the covers. I don't know what it is, but no matter how hot it is, I still like to be covered."

"Me too." Holly said. "But I usually like to be covered with a man."

"God, Holly." Cat responded. "Me too, but not *every* night!"

"Yeah yeah. I can't wait to hear some of *your* stories, Cat."

"We'll see." Cat winked at Holly.

"OK. Back to Lori's story." Anna said.

"Alright." Lori continued. "I woke up the next day feeling good about my decision to see Rick. I knew if I didn't, I would probably regret it. I recognized I was taking a chance in ruining my relationship with Art, but that was a chance I was going to take. I mean, I wasn't some silly little girl who couldn't control herself anymore."

"True. But it is amazing how many stories there are about girls going to their high school reunions and hooking up with old boyfriends." Susan said.

"I guess. But I think I knew if I ended up sleeping with Rick, it meant that I would leave Art completely. Rick was unfinished business for me. We never really ended the relationship. It was like it was frozen in place.

Art and I went down and had breakfast in the hotel restaurant. I think the salt air stimulated Art's appetite. He had the full order of French toast with a side of bacon. I just had a small fruit cup and coffee. Art joked that I was staying slim for my bathing suit. Of course, I agreed with him. Certainly better than telling him I wanted to look good for my past lover that I was going to meet on the sly that night.

He actually thanked me, for the great sex we had the night before. He wasn't threatened at all by my taking charge, or if he was, he never admitted it. He thoroughly enjoyed it and said he wanted to try new things with me, *and,* wanted to try to please me orally. Wow! I was blown away. We never talked about why he didn't like to perform oral sex on me. I just assumed he had some kind of hang-up. Maybe he thought it was not sanitary. But his reason was probably the simplest one of all. He felt he wasn't good at it. Maybe another woman put that thought in his head. Either way, helping him keep his erection, made him want to please me more.

We left breakfast. Art headed off to be the fourth playing 18 holes of golf, and I decided to do some window shopping and get a spa treatment. I signed up for an hour long Swedish massage, a pedicure and a manicure, then some sort of weird hot mud bath."

"All this for Rick?" Anna asked."

"Nah, Rick only wanted something else." Holly said.

"No. I actually booked the spa treatments weeks in advance. Once we flew down for a long weekend and I couldn't even get in, so I didn't want that to happen again. I took the hotel's shuttle to the quaint little downtown, with a few other ladies from the hotel. We stuck together as a little group and shopped for souvenirs for people back home. I bought myself a cute little rattan beach bag with wooden handles, which had sea shells woven right into it. I bought my sister a pretty little beach frock, in a swirl of different pastel colors. I even bought Art a tie I knew he'd probably never wear, but I knew he would appreciate. The backdrop was the ocean and was bright blue, and it had all these fish swimming around on it. Really tacky! When I gave it to him he says "Oh no! You shouldn't have. No really! You shouldn't have!" I laughed and told him if he didn't want to wear it, he could always use it to tie me up.

Knowing Art would be playing golf through the afternoon, I stayed with the ladies and had lunch in town. We had the fish fry at a little shack with tables outside. I had a nice cold bottle of local beer. The food was so fresh. We sat around and chatted about our families, our jobs, some of them talked about their kids or grandkids, but through it all, I had Rick on my mind. I still hadn't come up with an excuse for Art, and didn't know what I would say if I was late."

"Or never came back!" Holly said.

"Yeah. That too. We finally finished our late lunch and most of us were eager to get back. It was getting hot by now, and most of us wanted to either hit the beach or the pool. We called the hotel and they sent their van for us. In no time, we were being dropped off back at the hotel.

I checked my messages at the front desk. Rick left me a very cryptic, innocuous message saying that my tennis lesson was still scheduled for seven and left his address. I asked the clerk for some paper, and wrote back that I would be there, but couldn't promise I could stay for the whole lesson. Now I needed an excuse for Art.

Art came back after playing golf and met me in the bar. I could tell he had a few at the 19th hole, and was feeling no pain. He was laughing and telling me how well he played and even made a few dollars off the other guys. He asked me about my day, although I could plainly see he wasn't interested in hearing about women shopping. I told him I wanted to bring him back to the little fish shack. Then, out of the blue, I told him some of the ladies were going to have a Mahjong game that night, and would it be okay if I played, or did he have other plans. If he did I said, I'd gladly cancel mine. I held my breath when he said hell no, go play. I know how much you love that game. Go kick ass and have a great time. Then I find out, the guys he was playing golf with were going to play poker and smoke cigars and drink brandy. He was thrilled that I had plans. There was nothing stopping me from meeting Rick now.

Neither Art nor I were hungry, so we agreed we would just grab a snack on our own later. A few minutes to seven, we both left the room with a hug and a kiss. He joked he was ready to see how the tie I bought him worked as handcuffs. I'm sure I weakly smiled at that remark. We walked outside, then he headed left taking the path to some outside cabanas, and I went right, following the marked pathway to the tennis courts.

Rick lived right behind the tennis courts and when I passed by, some people were playing, hitting the green ball back and forth in their fashionable tennis whites. I walked behind the courts and came to a row of smaller, simpler cottages in the back. They were white framed cottages, with pink plantation shutters. Rick lived in Unit #10, at the very end of the row.

I was wearing black pants and a white cotton pullover top. I should have been wearing a chastity belt, but I didn't see one for sale in the gift shops. A little late for saving my chastity anyway. I raised my hand to knock on his door, when it opened in front of me. There stood Rick, a little older, but still had the same shaggy blond hair and looked to be in great shape. He had on a pair of cut-off denim jeans, slouched over his hip, with no belt. A loose, well worn white t-shirt advertising the local beer, showed his rock hard abs. I caught myself looking too long at those.

He grabbed me by my shoulders and whisked me into his arms. God he was so strong. He planted a big kiss on my cheek, and then held me aside to look at me. I nervously walked in, and shut the door behind me. He asked me if I wanted a beer, and when I said yes, he went into the small kitchen off the living room and grabbed two from the fridge.

I looked around his apartment. It was classic Rick, meaning it was sparse. He had a small couch, and across from it a well-worn brown leather reclining chair, with a lamp behind it. He had built in bookshelves, no doubt built by Rick as he was handy with his hands."

"Yeah. I bet he was." Holly sneered.

"I'm ignoring you Holly. On the bookshelves, he mostly had history books and biographies. When he wasn't playing tennis, Rick preferred to be outdoors. He had a small television that I bet hadn't been turned on in weeks. He wasn't a couch potato. What caught my attention the most was a 4x6 framed photo of Rick and me from Nantucket. We had been sailing that day, and he set the timer on the camera. We had been sitting in the front of the boat with our legs dangling over the side. He had his arm around me and we each looked so happy. I went closer and picked it up. Seeing it brought back a rush of warm memories.

Rick came in the room and said "Hey! You remember that day?" I told him of course and asked him if he dusted it off from his box of old girlfriends and just put it out. He laughed and told me I hadn't changed. I watched him grab my beer and twist off the top with his masculine, rugged hands. Cheers he said as he did the same to his bottle and clinked it to mine. I put the photo back, looking at our smiling faces and my wind-swept hair and took a seat on the recliner. Rick sat opposite from me on the couch. "You look great, Lori," he said. I told him he still looked in shape, and he said playing tennis everyday will do that to you. He could now start to feel the aches and pains he never really felt before, and knew his career as a tennis pro was nearing an end. He said he could switch to golf, as he'd become a pretty decent player, good enough to teach, but he did not want to do that.

"Remember what I always said I wanted to do?" he asked me.

"The farm in Vermont. Of course. You would build a small barn, raise organic vegetables, and swim in your own pond. I remember."

"And you said you would paint. And write, by a little window that captured the morning sunshine. And we would have picnics every day. Take bike rides and hike. Remember?"

"Yes. Of course I do. That was a long time ago Rick. I guess life got in the way."

"Did it, Lori?'

He got up and walked to the bookshelves, and reaching to the very top, pulled out an old, silver tin box. He plucked it down, and sat back on the couch. He took the lid off the box and opened up a piece of folded paper. He straightened out the paper and looked down at it. He leaned over and handed me the page. It was an old listing of a farm in Peacham, Vermont. It had a small white, one story cape house on it, with a green metal roof, front porch and looked to have an ell that connected it to a large red barn. A three rail fence with a metal gate circled the barn. The ad indicated that the house sat on 52 acres and there was a small stream on the property. The asking price was $115,000, and the owner would consider throwing in his 1958 Ford tractor.

"I bought it Lori. I bought it for us. I've been renting it out ever since, thinking when we finally figured out how to make our schedules work, we could spend weekends there, until we decided to pack it all in and live there."

I was dumbfounded. She expected Rick to want to have sex with her, to...she didn't know what. But this...? She stared at the real estate listing, almost afraid to lift her eyes to his.

"Rick. I had no idea. But now, after all this time?"

"Lori I love you. I always have. There may have been other people in our lives and I know you are with Art now. But Lori, we were always meant to be together. We were magic, honey. I know you feel the same way."

He put his hand in the box and came out with a ring.

"Oh no. Don't" Lori said.

"It was my mother's. My father gave it to her before he went to war. It was always yours honey. Your finger was the only one it could possibly be on."

I knew that Rick's father gave his mother that ring, and he didn't survive the war. His lasting present to his child bride was Rick. She didn't even know she was pregnant before Rick's dad was killed in Germany. She named Rick after his father and always told him that her ring, her special ring, was to be worn by her son's wife.

"Rick I'm flattered and shocked. It's been years. I don't know what to say. We're not even the same people anymore."

"Of course we are. Why, have you turned into Queen Elizabeth? Am I now the Duke of Earl? We're older, that's all. You're here. You came. Marry me, Lori. Marry me and let's start our life together in Vermont. I have saved enough money that we would be comfortable. Please."

The tears started to run down my face, onto the picture of the house and barn, with the three rail fence. My mind was a jumble and I felt shaky. I stood up, but needed Rick's help getting to my feet. He stood in front of me, with his arms around me, and pulled me into his chest. He closed his eyes and pressed his forehead against mine. I leaned up, and put my arm around his neck and kissed him. I kissed him deeply. I kissed him goodbye.

"I can't Rick. I'm sorry. I have a life now with someone else, and I'll admit, he's not you. But he's a good man, and I love him. If I went to Vermont with you I would be miserable, not because of you, but because of what I did to Art. Because I would be betraying not just him, but myself. I love you Rick. I do. I always will. But we just can't be together. I'm so sorry"

I walked out trembling, and wondering if I was the biggest fool on the planet. But I made my choice and I'm happy with it."

"I think you should have boffed him one last time before you left."Holly said.

"Boffed? Holly, where do you come up with these words?" Priscilla asked.

"You wouldn't understand. You're a lesbo." Holly answered.

"Oh yeah, right. We lesbo's can do some damn good boffing of our own, I'll have you know!"

"So did you ever see or hear from him again? Anna asked.

"No. I never did." Lori answered.

"What about Art? Did he ever find out you went to see him?" Cat asked.

"No. I never told him. I was conflicted between getting on the next plane out of there, as I was afraid that Rick would seek me out, but I decided that it would not be fair to Art. He had so been looking forward to this vacation. So I sweated out the remaining days, and I breathed a big sigh of relief when we finally went to the airport to leave." Lori said.

"Wow! What a story! So do you think this gorgeous man with the big dick, is up in his Vermont farm? Holly asked. "Do you still have the address by any chance?"

"Holly!" Susan said exasperated

"He all yours, honey." Lori said laughing. "You can drive up to Peacham, Vermont and ask for the good looking guy with the big dick. I'm sure you'll find him." The ladies all shared in that laugh.

The waiter arrived. "Ah. I see you lovely ladies are having a wonderful time! Marvelous! And now for the dessert."

Cat anxiously looked over Anna's shoulder, and spied a gigantic piece of cheesecake, golden yellow with a brown sweet edge crust, adorned with large Maine blueberries.

"You did it!" She said with great approval to the waiter.

"But of course, madam. At the Venetian, we make all your dreams come true!" He replied. "In that case...." Holly started to say but got shouted down by the group.

"I think he means food honey." Priscilla said.

The waiter passed out the plates of dessert, and with a flourish, refilled their coffee cups. When he asked if there was anything else, and received the polite "No, thank you." he left the ladies alone to enjoy their after dinner treat.

"This is *so* good!" Cat said. "I don't know where the waiter got this cheesecake, but here, try some." She offered tiny forkfuls to her friends, and everyone accepted.

"Ok Anna. You've been quiet. Everyone's been spilling out the intimate details of past loves and sexual adventures and you have been noticeably silent. Let's hear one from you while we're finishing up our desserts" she prodded.

Anna looked down at her plate pensively. She scooped a small spoonful of dark chocolate mousse in her mouth, pausing to savor the flavor spreading through her taste buds. She looked up to see the rest of the table, smiling and waiting patiently.

"Ok." she said. "But if this gets out..."

"We're The Mahjong Club, remember?" Susan said. "It stays here. Now spill the beans!"

"Ah Jesus. I thought I would take this one to the grave." Anna said.

"Really? Wow, this must be really good. Miss Lily White playing under the sheets, are we?" Holly teased.

"Okay okay. Remember the trip we took to Jamaica?" Anna asked Cat.

"For the wedding? Years ago?"

"Yeah. That one." Turning to the other ladies, Anna said "Years ago, I'm not sure how many, *but,* let me state *emphatically*, I was single at the time."

"Oh God! It's good already!" Holly said.

"*As I was saying,* I wasn't married, nor did I have a steady boyfriend. Cat and I were invited to Jamaica to attend a friend's daughter's destination wedding. Destination weddings were quite trendy at the time.

I had never been to Jamaica, and I remember when we landed, it was if we landed on a different planet. You see, I travelled mostly to Europe for vacations. I was drawn to the museums, shopping, and culture. Sophisticated, cultural venues always appealed to me. So when we land in Jamaica, well, it was different from anything I ever experienced. I was never a beach bum, so I never did the islands like most people.

The atmosphere and concept of time on the island was so different from other places I had been. Everyone and everything was laid back and casual. Cat and I took a cab to the hotel where we were staying. I forgot the name."

"The *Coyaba* on Montego Bay. Lovely place." Cat said.

"Right. The Coyaba. It was a lovely, small boutique hotel with only 50 rooms. But it was situated on four acres with its own pearly white sand beach. It was also all-inclusive, which was nice because you didn't need to worry about getting hit with a big bar bill at the end of your stay.

It had a British colonial atmosphere, and the wait staff was very proper and polite. It even had a nanny service, which I think was a big reason the family chose it as there would be young kids attending the wedding as well. So the nannies would feed the kids and organize games for them to play, which would allow the parents to have time alone.

Cat and I played several sets of tennis, which I usually won."

"You cheated!" Cat reminded her.

"Poor loser. Any way we played some golf, and even went horseback riding. Cat promised me I would probably have an orgasm on the horse, but the only thing I got out of it was a sore ass.

The wedding was very nice. Small and quick. My favorite kind. No long winded speeches of undying love. Afterwards, they had a seafood buffet set out on tables overlooking the ocean. They did do some of the usual things, like cutting the cake and dancing with the parents. But all in all, it was really charming. We drank and nibbled on the food until the wee hours of the morning. The wedding was held on Saturday, and just about everyone left the next day.

Cat and I decided to stay on for a few extra days, and make a mini-vacation out of it. She was busy flying back and forth for Gucci, and I was busy covering the fashion beat. It worked out well.

Sunday was a down day, with everyone leaving and all. There were lots of good-byes, and vows to keep in touch. It was the usual display of disingenuous promises.

"So romantic Anna." Priscilla laughed.

"Yeah. I want to visit the happy bride and groom after she's gained 15 pounds and he's leaving the toilet seat up and his dirty socks on the floor.

Sunday, Cat and I had a quiet night, especially since we overindulged the previous night. The next morning, Cat was snoring..."

"I *don't* snore!" Cat protested.

"Yes you do. Like a grizzly bear in hibernation! I got up and walked out to the balcony. We were staying in a lovely little suite painted in shades of pink and white. I stood on the balcony, and watched the azure blue ocean come ashore on the crystal white sand.

Times like these are particularly conducive to reflecting on the path your life is taking. Your inner critic accosts you with a barrage of questions: Where are you going? What do you want? I remember thinking how I always played it safe. With men, with traveling, with everything. I think new experiences were out of my comfort zone.

It was still fairly early in the morning, maybe 6:30, so I decided to go down to the lobby and get a cup of coffee. I walked down the two flights of stairs, and went outside where carafes were set up on a breakfast bar along with assorted muffins and freshly squeezed orange juice. The small sign said breakfast didn't start until 7am, so I decided to get the coffee in a paper cup and take a walk. I stepped out of the red brick terrace onto the sand and looked down at my feet. I still had on my socks and sneakers. That's me. Playing it safe. So spontaneously, I reached down and pulled off my sneakers, without even undoing the laces, and then peeled off my socks and put them by the wall. I had to laugh at myself, because my first reaction was to run back up to the room and put them in the bedroom in case someone stole them. Imagine.

So off I went, toes wiggling in the sand. I walked down to the ocean and turned right, walking along the beach with my feet splashing in the water. It brought back a memory of a boy in college, who liked to nibble on my toes."

"Yeah. I bet that wasn't the only thing he nibbled on." Holly laughed.

Anyway, it was so quiet and serene. No one was out yet. I could see some small local fishing boats, painted different bright colors, small white sails unfurled to catch the morning breeze.

I continued walking down the beach. Once I checked my watch to see what time it was. I don't know why. It wasn't as if I had to be somewhere. Just habit I guess. Of course, I left it in the room. So here I am shoeless, no socks and no watch. Pretty wild for a city gal like me.

I don't know how long I had been walking or how far I had gone, but evidently I was deep in thought, because I ran smack into the side of a small ocean front conch stand. There was a large black man inside He was loading cases of conch into white metal ice chests. I was so startled, I didn't say anything at first. He was *so black*, like a deep shade of ebony. I could see the sweat rolling down his muscular arms as he hoisted the heavy metal chest up onto an old wooden counter. Ziggy Marley was playing on his radio.

He was naked except for a small, skimpy pair of shorts and a pair of rope sandals on his feet. He had a tiny diamond stud in his left nostril. His chest was wide and hard, with black, tight curls sprouting out of it. His dreadlocks fell past his shoulders and he had a tattoo of a mermaid on his left bicep.

I don't know how to explain this, but I immediately felt a deep primal lust arising in my loins. It was if my sexual desire was a beach ball that had been held under water for too long, and was now trying to push itself to the surface.

The man approached me smiling. His teeth were brilliant white and looked like perfectly aligned chicklets. In his mellifluous Jamaican accent, he asked if I wanted to buy some conch. He assured me that it was the best on the island and would make delicious chowder.

I was momentarily mesmerized by his imposing presence. I was certain he could both sense my desire and read my mind. He took me by the hand, and smiling with an understanding known only to him, he cupped my face in his big, rough, calloused hands, and kissed me on the mouth, slipping his pink, sweet tongue between my lips."

"You did all this while I was sleeping?!" Cat exclaimed!

"I know. I can barely believe it myself. But it was more like I let it happen. I was frozen. I let him do what he wanted."

"What happened next?" Susan asked.

"He led me into his little conch shack..."

"You mean *cock* shack, don't you Anna?" Holly teased.

"I was a limp rag doll." Anna continued. "Quite honestly, I wanted it to happen, but he had complete control. He kissed me for awhile. I never kissed a black man before. His mouth was warm and soft. His tongue was *sweet.* I can't describe it except to tell you it was unlike any other tongue I've tasted. His outer lips were so black, but the inside of his lips were pink.

He put my arms around his neck, and I held the back of his head while he kissed my cheek, the base of my neck, and took my ear in his teeth, biting down softly. I know I was groaning, but it sounded like it was coming from someone else.

I kissed his neck, and ran my tongue up into his mouth. The whole time he was squeezing my breasts with one hand, while the other was unbuttoning my shorts. I could feel his dick, which felt like a *log*, rubbing up against me. He unbuttoned my pants, and slid them down to the floor. Then he put his hands under my ass, and giving them a hard squeeze, lifted me up and put me on his bench.

By now, I was trying to pull his shorts down. He kept his mouth on mine, his tongue playing with mine, and yanked his shorts off. I pushed him back a foot, and told him I wanted to see him. I had never seen such a big dick, black or white.

His fingers were inside me, caressing, stroking. He took a finger that had just been inside my wetness, and placed it in my mouth. I sucked on his finger, and drew him close to me, so I could feel his dick with my hands. It was throbbing, as if it was an independent, living being of its own.

He pushed me back, so that my head was against the wall, and he placed his hands on my knees and forced them apart. He kneeled down in front of me and began to nuzzle me between my legs. First he just licked me up and down, up and down, and then I could feel his tongue inside of me, swirling around. I tried to pull back as I could feel an orgasm coming like a strong wave over me, but he held me tight, his fingers buried in my ass, and kept his mouth on me and his tongue in me until I came. Twice. He then, got to his feet, and keeping my legs spread wide apart, placed his dick where his tongue had previously been. He rubbed it up and down, both wetting it with my juices and making me arch forward to take it in.

He felt immense. It felt like it was penetrating my stomach and coming out my back at the same time. He slowly slid it in and out, but then held me tight, and started to really bang it in me. I held onto his neck, my teeth biting. He moaned in my ear, as he screwed me roughly. My head and back were banging against the back wall of his shack, but all I could feel was that immense dick inside me. He rammed me harder and harder until he grabbed my mouth and jammed his tongue inside. I sucked on his tongue when I could feel his dick throb and pulse, releasing deep into me.

He leaned into me, and I now began to feel the aftermath of all that pounding. My vagina ached, and my back hurt from the strain of being pushed up repeatedly against the wall while he was screwing me. He placed a hand on my face and kissed me softly a few times on my lips. He then pulled back, and allowed his dick to slip out from inside me. Even flaccid, he was huge. I could feel him dripping out of me.

He helped me to my feet, and for a moment held me in his arms. He asked me where I was staying and if I would like to do that again. I told him I was leaving that day, but the truth was I don't think my body could take that kind of a pounding again. It felt like he stretched me inside out.

I walked back, or I should say, waddled back to the hotel, the whole time, still feeling his semen oozing out of me into my shorts.

I went up to our room, and gratefully, Cat was still snoring. I stripped off my clothes, throwing my shorts into the trash, and took a scolding hot shower. He was still dripping out of me. I was sore, but I'm sure I had a smile on my face."

"You little slut." Cat laughed. "You never told me!"

"What was I going to say? Wow Cat! I had the shit fucked out of me by this big black guy with dreadlocks and I didn't even know his name?! Don't think so!"

"So, did you ever have sex with a black guy again?" Priscilla wanted to know.

"No, he was my first and last. But wow, what a humping I got."

"I never screwed a black guy." Priscilla said. "But I did have some pretty wild sex with a pretty young black girl. Want to hear about it?"

"You go girl!" Holly said. "It might even turn *me* on!"

"Breathing *air,* turns you on lady!" Anna laughed.

"Okay then. Let me tell you my story. By the way, I'm taking off my shoes. I hope no one minds."

"Mine have been off for an hour now." Susan said.

"My black girl sex story. Where do I begin? I had taken a consulting job in Boston, to work on some legislative issues for a Congressman, who will remain anonymous, of course. The work was pretty tedious. Mainly researching the law, first to see if it was constitutional, then to do some polling to see how popular it would be with his constituents. Let me tell you, these politicians don't wipe their ass without checking to see what the public favors in toilet paper.

I'm in Boston, its winter time and I love it. Boston is one of my favorite places in the world. When I'm there, I always find time to go to this little pizzeria in East Boston called *Santarpio's.* It's on Chelsea Street as you get out of the tunnel on the way to the airport. It's one of the little neighborhood bars, that serves not only the best pizza, but lamb and Italian sausage roasted over a wood grill. The bread is made there, and if I ask nicely, they give me a small glass of pepper juice, to dunk it in."

"There is some sex in this story right?" Holly said. "Or are we just going to talk about pizza?"

"Hold your horses. I'll stop talking about *Santarpio's*, but oh, the Italian men who work there! If I wasn't gay... especially this waiter named Tony. God"

"Yeah, but you are, so let's get back to the pussy." Holly said.

"Alright already. I did get side-tracked. One of the nice perks of my job was that I had an apartment on Beacon Hill. This worked nicely, because it was right near the State House, and I could walk to work. Most days, I was in the office by seven, and apart from taking a lunch break, which basically meant eating a sandwich at my desk, I often didn't leave until well after dinner. Some nights I just made it home in time to fall into my bed.

Boston is a rather conservative city. While I never hid my sexual orientation, neither did I post it on any bulletin boards. Some guys would routinely ask me out, but I fluffed them off with some well worn excuses. If a guy was especially bothersome, I might tell him my boyfriend was in prison for murder and due to be released soon, and would probably kill us both if he found out we went on a date. That usually was enough to put ice down their pants.

There were a few discreet bars and lounges that catered to gays and lesbians. Now you may or may not know, but gay men usually don't hang with lesbians and vice-versa."

"Well, yeah. What do gay men want with a pussy?" Holly said.

"Touché. When I did finish early and wanted to go out, there was this quiet little lounge hidden not far behind the State House. It was dark, always had soft jazz playing, and in addition to chairs by the bar, it had little sofas and large arm chairs scattered around the room. Sometimes I would see a woman from work there, but the unspoken rule was you didn't approach someone unless you did the little flirtatious dance first. Some winks, some nods. You get the picture. So one Saturday night, I finished work early, went home and actually cooked dinner for myself. I had a piece of wild, Alaskan salmon, one of the senators gave me, and so I fried it in some lemon butter, with a little salt and pepper. I threw together a small salad, made twice- baked potatoes and opened a bottle of white wine.

After dinner, I wasn't feeling particularly tired, so I decided to go out to that lounge. When I arrived, it was not overly crowded with all different kinds and types of women. There were hard core dykes that looked like they could beat up most men. The "lipstick lesbians" who were feminine and fashionable formed their own clique. The shy ones, hiding behind their glasses of wine, were probably out taking a walk on the wild side before they went home to hubby and the kids. You always could count on some lesbian tourists, checking out the local scene, and then of course, there was me.

I took a seat in one of the large upholstered arm chairs, and ordered a Pinot Grigio when the waitress came around. I scoped out the place, seeing if there was anyone interesting I might want to take home. There were a couple that caught my eye, but I decided that I would just sip my wine, and see how the evening unfurled.

Before long, the waitress came over and set another glass of wine in front of me. I started to tell her that I didn't order it, but she waved me off, and said someone sent it over. Wow! A secret admirer! I looked around. Was it that pretty red-haired girl over there? Maybe it was the girl with the short blond bob hair style. She was cute. Or still, was it that older lady, dressed kind of matronly. It could be her.

While I'm looking around, trying to figure out which luscious lady wanted me, I look up. In front of me, is the ultimate butch dyke. She had her hair gelled straight up, numerous piercings through her lips and eyebrows, and God only knows where else. She had a large tattoo on her arm, which resembled a dick with a spike or a nail going through it. She was about 5' tall, and must have weighed 200 pounds. Best of all, she was wearing a studded dog collar around her neck.

 I just looked at her. I was speechless. This was a first for me, and quite frankly, I had no idea how to handle it. I certainly didn't want to piss her off and have her beat the shit out of me.

So she gave me the once over and said "I sent the drink over. So, you come here often?" At least she didn't ask me for my sign. Just when my tongue is tripping over itself, trying to come up with some answer, this *beautiful*, young tall black girl shows up, and sits on the arm of my chair and says "Sorry I'm late honey!"

The dyke looks at her, then looks at me, makes a face like she just swallowed a lemon, and marches off.

My hero I tell the girl! She says she could see I looked uncomfortable, and thought she would walk over and save me. I laughed and thanked her, and handed her the extra glass of white wine that was sitting on the table.

She pulled up a chair, took her off shoes, and tucked them under her legs. She had the biggest, darkest, pool of eyes. Although she was black, her hair was straight, and fell in gently around her cheeks. She had a soft pretty face, and had put a subtle shade of red on her lips, accentuating their fullness. She had an easy way about her. Quick to smile, and obviously very intelligent.

I thought she was young, maybe too young, but she told me she was in Boston working on a legal matter. When I inquired further, she said she was a prosecution attorney handling a criminal case. The District Attorney brought her in from Providence, Rhode Island because she had extensive experience working on organized crime cases. You know, the Mafia, the Mob. La Cosa Nostra. . .Tony Soprano? Any of this sound familiar to you.

"I know what the mob is, smart ass! It's what appears every time I shake my ass!" Cat said.

We spent the night talking, and when it started to get late, I asked her if she would like to come home with me. She smiled and said she had planned on it. We walked along Beacon Street, along the Public Garden, and Janet, that was her name, explained to me how back in Revolutionary times, the colonists put their cows on the park, hence the name Public Gardens. It also was the reason Boston had maddening, twisty, turning streets, as at one time, they were the original cow paths.

We walked to my apartment, and I let us in. Now the rest of the night's story is kind of vanilla pudding, but wait, there's more.

So we walk in, undress each other, and make love. Now I know ladies, you love the dick, but women know how to make love better, and are better at pleasing their partner. Lesbians tend to spend a lot of time caressing and kissing. We take our time and usually can reach orgasm together.

Janet was an excellent lover. She took control, and just knew what buttons to push. We fell asleep in each other's arms. In the morning, we went to the Paramount Restaurant on Charles Street for brunch. We had to wait in line for awhile, but it was well worth it. We lingered over breakfast and read the Boston Globe. Then we went back to my place and made love again. She said she couldn't spend another night as she had to prepare for trial, but asked if I would like to meet her next weekend. She said it would be a surprise, but assured me, it'd be a wild time I wouldn't soon forget. Of course I said yes, and we planned to meet Saturday night.

The week went by, and I didn't think too much about it as I was pretty busy myself. I had a few nights that I could have gone out, but I was afraid I would run into the dyke and that thought kept me home watching TV.

Friday came, then Saturday. I planned to meet Janet outside my apartment building at seven o'clock. She never told me what to wear, so I chose a pretty, frilly pink blouse with pearl buttons, and a short, white linen skirt. For shoes, I wore a pair of white slip-ons with a low heel. I knew at some point in the evening, I would want to slip out of my clothes.

Janet pulled up in a Mercedes SLK AMG in Midnight Black, with a rich, light tan leather interior. I was impressed. She had the passenger side window open and said to hop in, which I did. I leaned over and gave her a small kiss, one that any two straight ladies might exchange.

I ask her where she would like to go, and she gave me a wickedly sly smile, and told me it was going to be a surprise, but that I would like it. She drove out of Boston down Route 3 heading for Cape Cod, but when she turned onto I- 195 heading to Providence, Rhode Island, my curiosity peaked. I figured maybe she didn't want to go to a lesbian bar in Boston, with both of us being professionals working there at the time.

She drove expertly down the highway, keeping her hand on my thigh. I covered her hand with mine and slid it upward.

"No panties! You naughty girl!" she said. "But you'll have to wait." She made no effort to remove her hand, in fact, ever so softly caressed me with her fingers. She expertly passed car after car, evidently not worrying about any police stopping her. Working for the District Attorney had its privileges.

We crossed over into Rhode Island, took the second exit, and turned into what looked like a warehouse district. I was confused as I assumed we were going out to dinner, then maybe a club for some dancing. She kept passing row after row of run down, non-descript metal warehouses. I held my questions and we soon came to a chain link fence covered with razor wire, and an armed guard manning a security post.

Janet slid down her window, and flashed some sort of ID to the guard. Upon seeing the ID, he opened the chain gate, allowing us to pass through, closing and chaining it behind us.

She drove a little further, then pulled behind a larger metal building, where I noticed an assortment of high end cars already parked in the lot. I opened my car door, and as I got out, noticed the security lights on top of the building. There were two security guards patrolling the property, one on foot, the other one driving a 6X4 John Deere Gator.

Janet grabbed my hand and said "Come on." and led me into the building. The transformation from the façade outside to the inside interior was immediate. We walked into a lobby, through a heavy steel door, and Janet produced her identification once again to a lady sitting at a small wooden desk. There was a spacious lounge inside decorated in a way which made it appear small and intimate.

Small low voltage lights that resembled torches, hung on the walls, and Persian rugs adorned the floor. There were enormous oil paintings of ladies in various state of undress in Victorian style displayed throughout the area. Some of the ladies in the paintings were in various positions of lovemaking with other women. There were no pictures of men anywhere.

Janet led me over to bar that was upholstered in rich, white leather, and pulled out two chairs. A young girl, no more than 20, came to take our drink order. She was thin, with a black satin vest, open, with nothing on underneath it. She wore a matching mini skirt that didn't hide much. Her breasts were as round and firm as two freshly plucked Georgia peaches. Her legs could rival those of any high fashion model. If she knew Janet, she did not acknowledge her.

Janet ordered champagne, Cristal. There were other women at the bar, some laughing and talking, some in a passionate embrace and kissing. A young bartender, almost a twin to the one who took our order, came with the Cristal and two Waterford champagne flutes. After she poured the correct amount, Janet clinked her glass with mine and took a long sip. She then pulled me close and kissed me full on the lips. She laughed as I had asked no questions, but by the look on my face, she could tell I had many.

"Come." She said and we slid off the bar stools and taking the bottle of champagne with us, walked into an adjoining room. In it, were two large banquet tables. A carving station stood at one end, with a young lady, also in a vest and nothing else under it, who was carving a massive prime roast and a roasted goose. To her left stood an array of fresh lobster tails, Alaskan King Crab legs, oysters on the half-shell, jumbo shrimp and salmon. Further down still, was a tureen of hot soup, fresh rolls and a spread of every kind of cold cut you could imagine. Various salads and cheeses filled the rest of the table.

Next to the first table stood a smaller one. This one held the desserts. Fresh strawberries with whipped cream, blueberry and apple pies, cheesecake, and sliced apples, pears and oranges.

Janet and I filled our plates, and went into the lounge to eat. Other groups were also eating and some nodded to Janet, or gave a slight wave. One woman was completely naked, being fed chocolate covered strawberries by another lady. Soft music was being piped in from an unseen source, and a few ladies were dancing, holding each other close.

"OK." I asked Janet. "What is this place?"

"It's a *very* private club for lesbians. It was originally set up years ago by a couple of prominent ladies as a place to get away from prying eyes. You need to be referred by another member to join, and pass a committee's approval. It's costly. Five thousand to join, and another five hundred a month. Then you pay every time you use the facilities. It's not cheap, but for professional women, you can't beat it. As you can see by the security, your little friend with the dog collar wouldn't get in this place. You must sign a non-disclosure agreement, and no picture taking allowed. Money alone doesn't buy membership.

"Well, I'm impressed." Priscilla said.

"Honey, eat up. You haven't seen anything yet." Janet said.

We sat and ate, while watching the other ladies in the room. There was an assortment of women, some older and some middle aged. Not all beauty queens, but it was obvious they hired only, young beautiful lesbians to work as the wait staff. Their uniforms all consisted of a very short black skirt and a black satin vest. Always unbuttoned.

"Want to see the rest of the club?" Janet asked.

I did, so she led the way. We went past the lounge area, and the dance floor, and turned down a dimly lit corridor. There were small doors on either side. Some had a painted eye on the door, while some had no door at all, but a blue silk tapestry as a covering.

"If the door had an eye on it, it meant you were welcome to watch the people make love, but not to join in. If there was no door on a room, it was an invitation to join the couples inside.

We walked further down the corridor and came to a large room that held an immense hot tub. It was almost as large as a small pool. There were a number of women in the tub, some locked in passionate kisses, another had her head back, her legs wide open with a young, black haired girl performing oral sex on her. We walked past the hot tub room, and came into a room decorated as an eighteen century castle. In it were benches with silk ties, a beam cemented into the floor, cloth handcuffs hanging from it. To the side, was a table with a cushion upon it, with soft cotton ropes dangling. An array of rubber whips hung from the wall.

"Want to try?"Janet asked me.

"I had never done anything like this, but it certainly sounds sexy, so sure! I'm game."

Janet sat me down on the table, and proceeded to unbutton my blouse, stroking my breasts and squeezing my nipples harder than I was used to. She had me lie down on the table and made sure I was comfortable. She then produced a black silk handkerchief, and tied it around my eyes."

"*That* would freak me out." Holly said.

Janet then tied my hands down next to my side, and taking one leg, stretched it across the table and tied that down. Then she did the same with the other leg. I was completely immobilized. But I really wasn't scared. I couldn't see a thing, but could hear various voices softly in the background, mixing with the soft music that was piped in. I felt a soft, like a feather duster touch my shins and dance around my feet. It then jumped up to my face and neck, then lower to my breasts. I felt Janet's tongue swirl around my breasts, nibbling and licking, before taking my nipple in her mouth. I was getting so wet, I felt I would leak on the table. She then moved the feathers down in between my legs and brushed the feathers back and forth, really making me moan.

I felt her tongue replace the feathers, and tried to reach across and stoke her hair, but was unable to because of the restraints. I twisted first towards her probing tongue, then away from it. I could feel myself lift my hips, trying to get her tongue to go deeper inside me. Fingers began to stroke me at the same time and I felt an unbridled orgasm wash over me. Then another. Even more powerful than the first. I felt lips on mine, and a mouth I knew wasn't Janet's' began to kiss me. Gently at first, then feminine hands held my face and her tongue probed my mouth aggressively. My pussy was on fire, still receiving direct attention. I felt other hands caress my breast, and someone began kissing my feet, and then taking my toes in her mouth, nibbling on them. Janet whispered in my ear asking if I was alright. I moaned yes, yes. She kissed me again and again, while someone else's mouth explored the sweetness between my legs. Time and time again, I strained against the restraints holding me down.

"Jesus." One of the girls at the table whispered.

"After many orgasms, almost too many to count, I lay exhausted. I felt a hand loosen the ties around my leg, then the other one. By reflex, I pushed my quivering legs together, as the binds that held my hands slipped off. Soft fingers removed my blindfold, revealing Janet's smiling face.

"Did you enjoy that?" she asked.

"Oh yes. Yes I did." I peered around the room to find it empty of anyone other than Janet and me.

"The others…?" I asked?

"Others?" She said smiling. "How about a drink?"

"Only if you can carry me there! I'm not sure my legs will hold me."

We walked out by the same rooms we passed on the way in. They all appeared to be occupied, and the ladies within, in various throes of excitement. One room was a mass of writhing bodies, twisting and turning as if it were one. We walked into the lounge, now filled with women dancing with each other. In another room women were quietly sitting in chairs watching a young Asian woman pleasuring a much older lady. The music now was mixed. Some slow and some faster.

We walked to the bar and sat down. The same, I think she was the same, waitress came over, and this time I ordered a Johnny Walker Blue, a double please, straight up. I needed it. Janet ordered a split of champagne. We swiveled in our chairs to watch the rest of the room. We finished our drinks, and Janet signed the check. No cash or credit cards were allowed. All charges went directly onto the member's monthly statement. We then decided to drive back to Boston.

Janet drove more slowly on the return trip, and we held hands not speaking. She pulled up in front of my building, and I asked her if she would like to come up, but she declined, begging off as she had a grueling week ahead of her.

I saw her a few more times while I was in Boston, but her trial ended, as did my project.

"End of story? Did you see her again?" Cat asked.

"No. I suspected she had someone else in her life. We exchanged numbers, but nothing ever came of it."

"Hell of a story, lady." Holly said.

"Okay Cat. No ducking your turn." Anna said.

"Right. Well, unlike my good friend here." Cat said looking at Anna. "I didn't sneak out in the middle of the night to get laid by some big, black stud!"

"Hey! I didn't sneak out! You were snoring and dead to the world! You can't blame a lady for getting a little morning *exercise*, now can you? Besides, it was the first thing in the morning."

"Sure beats going to yoga class!" Holly laughed.

"Cat?" Anna reminded her.

"Okay okay. My story, at least the one that I want to share with you, happened in Italy. I had just spent the week in Rome wrapping up an ad campaign which introduced Gucci's latest fashion line. Gucci had expanded from purses and handbags into shoes, watches, jewelry and other accessories.

My last meeting was on a Friday, and I had an open ended ticket to return to New York, but decided to do a little exploring. As often as I was in Rome, I never really visited much of the rest of the country.

I had been seeing a local baker..."

"A baker? Are you shitting me?" Holly asked.

"Yeah. A baker. And let me tell you he was half my age and had the most incredible hands!"

"Did he try to sprinkle you with flour?" Susan said joining in the fun.

"No, but he did roll me around a lot and stuffed me with an Italian sausage! Now, may I continue?"

"Yes dear, of course." Priscilla said.

"So I'm in Rome. I decided not to see Mario, the baker. I had the use of a company car and decided to drive to Palermo and spend a few days looking around. Italy is a fabulous country to explore by car. Everyone drives fast and Gucci was good enough to let me take a silver BMW M5. It had 555 horse power and twin turbo."

"Listen to Miss Motor Trend, over here!" Lori said.

"Yeah, well I drove the *shit* out of that car. It handled so well, and it was incredibly fast. Anyway, I was in no hurry, but I did get to Palermo in record time. I didn't make hotel reservations, so I just drove into the center of town and came across an old, ornate hotel, on one of the side streets off the main square.

I handed the keys to the parking attendant, and went inside. The hotel was beautiful. It had an old world charm, with oil paintings on the walls and a deep red wall to wall carpet on the floor. The front desk was painted in some sort of a fresco. The hotel had seen better days, but was still intimate and charming.

I went to the front desk and inquired about a room. The man behind the desk said he did have one available, but it was on the second floor and the elevator did not always work the way it should. I told him that would be fine, so he called for the bell hop to bring my bag to my room.

The bell hop was no more than a boy…"

"That didn't stop you, now did it? Holly asked. "Or is it just bakers you like young?"

"So, as I was *saying*, I walked up to the second floor, and opened the window. The window opened up on to a small courtyard that was adjacent to a small, stone church. I tipped the bell hop and sprawled out on the bed."

"With the bell hop?" Holly persisted.

"No, wise guy! By my lonesome. I must have fallen asleep, because when I woke up, the sun had set and the moon had just begun to rise. I stepped into the shower and thank God, the water pressure was good. I washed my hair and slowly turned the hot water, cooler to wake myself up."

"Did the bell hop soap up your back?" Holly smirked.

"I'm ignoring you! So I dried off, and put on a simple dress and walked downstairs. I wasn't even sure if this hotel had a restaurant. I asked at the front desk, and the receptionist said they did, but it wasn't open yet. In Italy they tend to eat much later than we do in the States."

"After 5 o'clock?" Anna asked.

"Yes. After 5 o'clock. They had a small lounge with a couple of chairs grouped around small dark round oak tables, so I sat down. I waited for a while but no one came to take my order. That can be one of the maddening things about Italy. I was about to get up, when I noticed an older handsome man, sitting a few tables over from me. Catching my eye, he walked over and asked me what I would like to drink. I asked him if he was the waiter, and he just smiled and shook his head. I asked him for a glass of house red, and with a nod, he left. He seemed to have left the bar, but returned with a bottle and two glasses. At first I was put off, but I did not wish to be rude. He asked if he could sit down, and I said yes. He opened the bottle and said it was from a private reserve in the basement. Chianti, a specialty of the region. He expertly opened the bottle, and poured out two glasses. We clinked our glasses and toasted to "buona salute", good health. I couldn't help but notice he was wearing a wide gold ring with a ruby in the center of it on his right hand. He had a solid gold *Presidential Rolex* on his wrist. He was elegantly dressed in expensive tailored clothes, and had a dignified demeanor.

He sipped his wine, told me his name was Domenic, and as quickly as he sat down, wished me a good evening and left my table. That was different. Italian men are notorious for their aggressive behavior with women.

I sipped my wine, poured myself another glass, and noticed that the restaurant was now open. I picked up my glass and bottle, and walked over to where they were seating. It was still early by Italian standards, but I was hungry and wanted to turn in early. They seated me at a small table, underneath an oil painting depicting a small Italian village, as it must have looked like a century ago.

The waiter brought a bowl of olives sitting in a green olive oil, and some fresh baked bread and golden butter. While enjoying my wine, I ordered grilled calamari as an appetizer and a simple dish of pasta cooked with pomodoro sauce. The food in Italy is not what you get here in the States. Some of the best dishes are simple ones, the food is so fresh.

I was sipping my wine and biting small pieces of my calamari, when I noticed that the gentleman who had so graciously brought me my wine in the bar was sitting at a small table by himself, all the way across the room. While I ate, I noticed different men, not of his ilk, talking to him for a moment, and then leaving when he dismissed them with a wave of his hand."

"I'm not sure I know what you mean." Susan asked.

"Domenic was an older, well dressed, refined gentleman. He had an air of sophistication. You could compare him to a Southern gentleman from Louisiana. The men who came up to him, looked rough. Violent looking. They were dressed well, but not like him. They obviously treated him with great respect, and I even detected with a bit of fear. It only took a wave of his hand to get them to leave the table hastily. I can't quite describe it.

My waiter came with my bowl of pasta, which by the way, most Italians call macaroni, and while he was setting it down, I pointed out Domenic and asked the waiter if he knew who he was. The waiters' reaction was immediate. He looked across the room and when he became aware of the man I was inquiring about, he quickly mumbled that he did not know him and abruptly left my table.

I was confused to say the least, but was more interested in enjoying my pasta, which smelled divine. I was almost finished with my meal when I looked up to see Domenic at my table. He asked if he could sit down. I smiled and said of course. He motioned to the waiter, the same one who claimed he didn't know him, and ordered two espressos and a bottle of Anisette.

He asked if I was from the United States and that led into a conversation of my working for Gucci, living in New York, and why I decided to take a side trip to Palermo. I asked Domenic what he did and he replied he was a businessman, and he owned a variety of different companies in Italy. I asked him for more details about his life. After all, he knew my last name and my story. He said his last name was Barone, and he was born in Sicily but spent most of his time here in Palermo. In fact, he replied he owned this very hotel.

Ah, I figured. That's why everyone was deferential to him. He was the boss.

He stayed and we sipped our espresso and he regaled me with stories from his boyhood. His father was an olive grower before he died, and his brother still ran the groves and used the same stone press to produce, deep rich, green olive oil. We shared an after dinner drink of brandy, again from some fine vintage from deep within his cellar. When he got up to leave, he asked me if I would like to take a tour of Palermo with him the next day, and have dinner with him after that. I was charmed and readily accepted.

The next morning I awakened to the sound of church bells. I could observe from my window the townspeople walking into the old, stone church across the courtyard for daily mass. There was an old priest at the entrance, dressed in a long flowing black robe, greeting the parishioners as they arrived. Most of the women had their heads covered, and I could see that it was an older crowd. The men were dressed up, many wearing well worn sports coats and jackets, and there wasn't a pair of blue jeans or sneakers to be seen.

I went downstairs and decided to take a walk. I turned onto the street and joined the multitude of people who where most likely heading to work. I walked along the street until I came to another square that had black, wrought iron tables and chairs outside a small bakery. I went in the bakery and my hunger was instantly aroused by the smell of the dark, rich coffee, and the freshly baked pastries. I ordered a cup of cappuccino and some almond biscotti, and went outside to enjoy them. I sat for a bit people watching. Old men were sitting and speaking excitedly about the recent soccer games, women were holding small children's hands on their way to shop. An occasional student, poured over his books in front of him, while his coffee got cold. I sat enjoying the morning.

When I finished my breakfast, I walked back to the hotel. I had not set a time to meet Domenic, but when I arrived at the hotel, there was a handwritten note, telling me he would pick me up outside at ten. That gave me enough time to go up to my room, shower, and put on a pair of casual slacks and a light sweater, as the weather had gotten chilly.

I looked at myself in the mirror, and wondered if I was attracted to this man. He had a certain way about him. Something mysterious. Sometimes, there is something very sexy about an older man, as if he has hidden knowledge about how to please a woman in bed. I smiled at the contrast between my baker boy and Domenic.

I was happy with my reflection. I made a last minute adjustment to my makeup, applying a bit more blush, brushed my hair one last time with my fingers, and went downstairs.

Domenic was parked outside. For a moment, I had to stop and look at his car. He was sitting in a black Aston Martin V12 Vantage. The only time I had ever seen this type of car was in a James Bond movie. He smiled at me, with a wide broad grin. He had perfect, large white teeth, and was wearing blue dress pants with a salmon colored dress shirt and a white cashmere sports jacket.

"Ready for your tour?" he asked as the valet opened my door for me.

"Nice car." I said as I slid in. I figured it must have cost him a cool quarter of a million dollars, but who's counting. He shifted the car into gear and took a side street to avoid the pedestrian traffic from the square. We drove to the outskirts of town, and took a twisting, winding road up the mountain. I now could appreciate the way the car easily handled the sharp curves of the road. A few times, Domenic would have to accelerate to pass another vehicle or person walking. The raw power of the car was impressive.

We pulled up to the top of the hill overlooking Palermo. The city spread out before us, and Domenic got out of his side of the car, and opened my door for me. Walking to an overlook, he pointed out the different landmarks, old churches, marketplaces and museums. My shoulders shook from the chilly mountain air. Domenic took off his sports jacket and placed it around my shoulders. His cell phone rang, and he excused himself and took the call. He wasn't on the phone but for a few minutes, and then hung up and asked me if I wanted to take a little trip with him. Having absolutely nothing planned for the day, hell for the week, this all seemed like one big adventure so I said yes.

We got back into the car, and figured we would be driving somewhere. I was partially right. Domenic drove to the outskirts of Palermo, and pulled his car into a restricted parking area of a small local airport. A man immediately arrived from inside the building, and greeting Domenic, took his car keys.

Domenic and I walked through the fence and across the tarmac where a small, twin engine jet was parked. When I stopped suddenly he asked me if I was afraid of flying. I said no, just surprised by the change of mode of transportation.

He assured me that I was completely safe, that the pilot was his employee and he owned the plane. This man became more mysterious by the moment. As we approached the plane, I still was not sure if I was ready for this kind of a high adrenaline rush. Then the door to the plane opened, and a steward, I guess you would call him, beckoned us in. Not wanting to appear childish, I entered the plane.

I had never been in a small jet before, but was surprised by the spacious interior and the level of personal comfort.

There were four captain's chairs that swiveled, each having the required seat restraint. We had just barely sat down when the pilot engaged the engine. The steward handed Domenic a glass of white wine and I nodded when he asked me if I would like the same. In a moment's time, we were taxing down the runway and pulling up into the cloudless, blue sky.

"Should I ask where we are going, or am I your hostage?"

"And what a lovely hostage you would make. We are heading down to Sicily, to my family's farm. I am needed there. This is so much quicker than driving, plus you did say you wanted to see some of Italy."

"Ah that I did."

Almost at the same time Domenic and I were finishing our wine, the steward came back in the cabin to inform us that we would be landing shortly, and suggested, we fasten our seat belts. I looked over at Domenic. He had a grim look on his face that evaporated when he looked at me.

"You must be famished. When we land, I've arranged for us to eat at the farm. At least you'll know the food will be fresh."

I looked out the window at the island that was getting closer and closer. Some small boats were in the harbor, but overall it appeared quiet. It was not as lush as Tuscany, but instead appeared to be covered in hard, grey rock.

As if reading my mind, Domenic said "The ground is difficult to grow crops. We manage to produce a small crop, but the fruits and vegetables are the sweetest to the taste, as you'll find out. The plane touched down on a small runway, and the first thing I noticed was that we had the only plane there. You really couldn't even call it an airport. It consisted of a hard packed dirt runway, with a small tin shed that mostly housed this plane. To the side sat a small structure, more like a guard house.

The plane taxied to the end of the runway, and the pilot killed the engines. The steward opened the plane's main door and helped me down the stairs. The hot air that blasted us was mixed with the salt air from the sea. A large man in a dark colored pin striped suit, helped me from the plane, and whispered something in Domenic's ear.

A long, black limousine approached and then stopped in front of us. The driver exited to open the back door for Domenic and me. A song from *La Traviata* was playing on the sound system, and before we left, the sound proof divider was raised.

"This has been quite some day." I remarked.

"I know. But after I attend to some personal business, we'll dine at the farm and I'll show you Sicily. It's very old and has quite a history."

I was going to mention that its history ran to the notorious, but I didn't want to offend my host, so I remained quite. "Has your family been on the island long?"

"We can trace our roots back to the days of the Roman Emperors. There were five founding families, and mine was one of them."

We approached a very high, old stone wall, and built into it, a heavy black iron gate. It was closed, but when the guard saw us approaching, motioned to someone unseen, and it swung open. The limo proceeded in over a driveway of paved stones and pulled up to a long rectangular building. The building, which appeared to be very old, was constructed from large grey stones seamed together with gray mortar. A few older women came out of the front door to greet Domenic. At first I could not tell if they were wait staff or family. We left the car without Domenic introducing me to anyone. We walked into the expansive kitchen that looked to have been built in the 1800's, with a large built in stone oven. In it, was a roast of lamb, fresh vegetables, and loaves of crusty bread. Two pewter plates were set out with course white linen napkins. One of the women filled the two pewter mugs with red wine and put a glass pitcher of water with sliced, yellow lemons on the table.

"Let's eat first. Afterwards I'll take care of my business while I have Maria show you my farm, then I'll take you on a tour of my island. Maria has been with me since I was a child. You ride, don't you?"

"Horses?!" I asked.

"Of course. Horses. They are very well trained, and it's the best way to see the island. We can go where it's inaccessible by car. But now please eat."

Maria passed the platter of lamb to Domenic first, and then I selected two pieces, cooked perfectly rare with the red juices flowing warm from it. I put two medium sized roasted potatoes on my plate along with fresh asparagus. Domenic took the loaf of bread, still hot from the brick oven, and tore off a piece and put it on his plate. Then he tore off another piece for me.

"Here when we say we break bread, we mean it." he said with a smile.

The food was delicious, and the red wine was a perfect accompaniment with the roasted lamb. I was famished, and Domenic laughed as I put two more slices of lamb on my plate with some roasted onions. When we finished, Maria brought us a small plate of fruits and nuts, and some torrone, candied nougat. I was told that pasta was available should I desire it, but unlike most Italians who preferred to eat a large heavy meal for lunch, Domenic felt it slowed him down, so he had his pasta at night. I agreed and told him often when I was working I usually had only a small garden salad. Maria brought out just one cup of espresso, as Domenic rose from the table. Taking my hand, and giving it a soft kiss, he told me he had to leave for a short time, but would return soon. He invited me to walk around the grounds and make myself at home. However, he cautioned me to stay within the compound as there had been some daylight robberies, and he did not wish any harm to come to me.

He left instructions to Maria in a dialect I did not understand, and left for his appointment. It was still early in the day, and after such a large meal, I decided to go for a walk. Leaving the front door, I could see that the stone wall we came through actually extended all around the farm. I could noticed some open farm land, so I walked that way. I passed the stone stables, and letting myself get sidetracked, went inside. There were at least a dozen stone horse pens with a few men cleaning out the stalls and putting in fresh water and hay. The horses were smaller than I had imagined, but one of the men said that they were specially chosen for their gentle temperament and their sure-footedness, as most of the trails were covered with rock. He encouraged me to pat them, and gave me some carrot pieces to feed them.

I left the stables, and continued walking to the fields. I noticed that despite being close to the ocean, the air was drier than in Rome or Palermo. I assumed it must have been due to its southern exposure.

There were a few people working in the fields. There weren't any mechanical farm implements, and it looked as if the farm workers did most of the work by hand or horse drawn plows. Some women were picking corn in one field, taking their time to peel off the green husks and exposing the white whispers over the deep yellow color of the corn. It appeared that they were saving the hulks, perhaps to feed to the other livestock.

In another smaller field, some men were using hoes to pull up the weeds that were growing in-between the rows of beans. They would occasionally stretch their backs in the hot afternoon sun, before bending back to their work.

Children were kicking a soccer ball around a dusty patch of ground, and a stray cat looked to be hunting for mice. I continued my walk until I had completely walked around the perimeter of the farm, which was more like a compound. When I got back to the front entrance, the iron gate was indeed closed, and heeding Domenic's warning of the risk of my being robbed outside, I turned and went back into the kitchen.

Maria was busy turning flour and water and other ingredients into homemade pasta. I offered to help, not being a stranger in the kitchen, but she indicated that I was a guest and shouldn't. But when I took off my jacket, and rolled up my sleeves, she laughed and pushed a large heavy board in front of me, to help her mix the ingredients. When the raw pasta firmed up, we took small knives and cut them into strips and hung them on a rack with numerous wooden dowels to dry. Everything was done by hand, as it had been for years. I looked up, my arms covered in flour and paste to Domenic's laughter.

"Well, if you ever decide to quit Gucci, I certainly could use another cook here!"

I laughed and went to the deep soapstone sink and ran the cold water over my hands and arms then dried myself off with a clean red and white checkered towel. He came around to the sink and kissed me on the cheek.

"Are you done in the kitchen, or is there something else you plan to prepare? I thought we might go for our ride."

"I'd love to, but I really don't have the right clothes for it."

"Well I took the liberty of putting out some riding clothes for you. We often have guests, and keep extra clothes and boots available. They are laid out in the bedroom up the stairs to the right. It is getting late, so if it's possible, perhaps you may spend the night *in your own bedroom,* and we can fly back tomorrow morning. I have some business back at the hotel that I must attend to"

"Of course. That would be lovely. I will go up and change, and be right down. I walked up the wide granite steps, and peeked into the first door on the right. It had a single double bed and a solitary wooden dresser, and little else. A simple wooden cross hung over the bed. It looked more like a room a monk might stay in. On the bed, was a pair of woolen riding pants, boots, and a loose comfortable cotton jersey. I went into the room, and shut the door. The room did not have a bathroom of its own, so I stripped off my clothes and put on the ones left for me. Without even a mirror in the room, I was unable to check my appearance."

"I assume, sooner or later, probably much later, you'll get around to telling us about his dick." Holly asked exasperated.

"Sorry Holly, but you want to hear the whole story, don't you?"

"Yes. Pay her no mind. Now please continue." Anna said.

"Ok. I'll try to speed it up. Domenic and I walked to the stables, where two of the horses had already been saddled and were waiting for us. I was used to a western saddle, so the small flat saddle was different for me. The stable hand helped me up on my horse, and Domenic, already mounted..."

"Is this when he mounts you?" Holly asked, with a giggle.

"No. It isn't. Now stop interrupting me." So we rode out the gate, and turned up a path that meandered up a hill. The houses below fell away as we climbed higher and higher. The ocean appeared before us, but rather than stop, we rode on for almost two hours. We never encountered another person, and it felt like the island was deserted. My horse was very sure-footed and never stumbled. We circled the village from that height, and hardly spoke, just enjoying the solitude and scenery.

We made our way back to the stables, handed the reins to the stable hand, and dismounted. We walked back to the kitchen, and Domenic said he was sure I wanted to freshen up before dinner. He instructed me that if I went past my room, a bathroom with an ample supply of hot water awaited me, and he took the liberty of putting out some casual clothes for me to change in to. *That,* sounded like heaven.

I went to my room, and there on the bed, were indeed fresh clothes that appeared to be my size. In addition, there was a thick brown bathrobe with two monogrammed towels and a facecloth. I stripped off my riding clothes, which carried the sweat and scent of the horses, and wrapped myself in the robe.

The shower was very large, but simple. It, too, was made of stone, but so very wide there wasn't a need for any shower door. The shower head was set high up, over my head. While the bathroom was comprised of old granite stone, the plumbing was new. I let the hot, steaming water wash over me, barely moving, letting it scald my sore muscles from the days ride. There was a small stone shelf that held a bar of unused soap and a bottle of shampoo. I washed my hair, then let the hot water rinse away the shampoo, then washed it again. The soap had a grainy texture and smelled like lavender. It felt so good I scrubbed every inch of my body.

I shut off the water after what seemed to be a long time, put on my robe and returned to my room. The clothes Domenic chose for me appeared to be of a local vintage. There was a simple white peasant-style blouse that hung off the shoulders and was adored with tiny, blue flowers. The pants were a plain brown cotton, pull-up, and cinched at the waist with a small corded rope. The sandals that I had worn earlier in the day were at the foot of the bed. It was clear that someone had cleaned them.

I finished dressing and left the room, closing the heavy wooden door behind me. I noticed there wasn't a lock on my door, or any other door for that matter.

Entering the kitchen, a small, simple wooden table, that looked like it was hand-hewn by a local craftsman, sat in the corner near the fireplace where a small fire had been started. Domenic was sitting at the table, but stood up when I entered.

"Ah. The clothes fit. Bene! Allow me to say you look lovely."

"Thank you. And thank you for the clean clothes. I'm afraid the other clothes I was wearing while riding will be carrying my body odor and should be burned!"

He smiled at that. "Please." He said, pulling out a simple wooden chair for me to sit on. "Wine?"

"Yes please." Maria appeared with two red, ceramic goblets, and poured red wine into each of them.

"I had Maria cook us a meal. One common to the area. I hope you'll like it."

"I'm sure I will."

Maria brought out a platter of fresh pasta, with simple tomato gravy, as the Italian's like to call it. Another platter held fresh meatballs with oregano, and sweet Italian sausages.

"Don't fill up as there's more."

"You may have to have someone help me to my bed, if I eat all this."

"Maria is stronger than she looks, so she can put you to bed."

I looked at Domenic. He was older than me, but hard to say by how much. Very handsome, with mostly wavy gray hair brushed straight back on his head. He was definitely Italian looking, and had a prominent chin and nose. I was very aware that he had always acted as a complete gentleman around me. He never did or said anything inappropriate. I felt relaxed around him. If he was interested in me sexually, he sure wasn't indicating it. Maybe he had a wife, although I didn't see a wedding ring on his right hand. Or perhaps he had a lover. I pondered this while Maria cleared away the first course, and put a platter of sliced pork, rich in natural juices, surrounded by small baked potatoes, onions and roasted apples. She stopped before leaving to refill our wine goblets.

I put a smaller piece of pork on my plate, along with a single potato and a spoonful of both the onions and apples. The cinnamon from the apple, perfectly complimented the roast pork, and despite my getting full, I eagerly ate my food.

Domenic asked me about my job, how I liked Italy, about my family. He was soft spoken and a good conversationalist. He asked questions, but never probed. His questions never strayed into my personal life, or mine into his. It was just pleasant dinnertime conversation between a man and a woman getting to know each other.

Maria came once again, and I held my hand over my wine glass. "Please, no more." I begged.

Maria laughed and cleared the plates, and then ignoring my pleas for respite, came back with more platters covered with sliced prosciutto, mortadella, sopreassata, and a variety of cheeses. There were bowls filled with freshly washed cherries and apricots, as well as a dish with an assortment of nuts. She replaced my wine goblet with an espresso cup which she filled with the hot, black liquid. She placed a small plate of dark chocolates with nuts next to me, and patted me on the hand.

"It's a wonder you don't weigh five hundred pounds." I said to Domenic.

"I guess we're used to eating like this, but I must admit, I don't eat this much as often as I did as a young man. Time catches up to you, I guess."

I laughed and told him about my brothers back in Ohio, and how the last time I checked, they still enjoyed going to the all-you-can-eat buffets and doing as much damage as they could.

I had to admit that Americans did not eat the fresh foods that most Europeans do, and that fast food has taken its' toll on both our waistline and our health.

"It's getting that way here in Italy as well. If you look, you will see your McDonalds and Kentucky Fried Chicken in our cities."

After sipping my espresso, nibbling on some nuts, and demolishing the chocolate, Domenic suggested we retire early as we had an early return flight back to Palermo. He motioned to Maria that we had finished, and he walked me up the steps to my room. He gave me the slightest kiss on my cheek, and said good-night. He turned and walked down to his quarters.

I went into my room, and walked to the bathroom to comb my hair and brush my teeth. Before I crawled into bed, I went to the window to admire the night sky. The moon was luminous and the stars looked like tiny diamonds scattered on a canvas of black velvet. I lay in bed for awhile and decided I wasn't done with the night.

I slipped out of bed, and put my robe over my nakedness. I opened my door quietly, and softly walked down the hall to the room I saw Domenic enter. Without knocking, I opened the door to his room, and spied him in bed, sitting up and reading by the light of a single candle.

"Would you like some company?" I asked as I dropped the robe to the floor, exposing my naked body to him.

"Afraid of the dark, Catherine?" he laughed.

"That must be it." I said as I slipped into his king-sized bed. I stroked his chest and let my hand slip down to hold his penis while my mouth found his. He rolled toward me and kissed me back hard. I felt his member swell in my hand and felt my own wetness begin. I ran my hands through his thick, grey hair, pulled his mouth hard into mine, and hungrily slipped my tongue into his mouth."

"I must ask Maria, whatever did she put in the potatoes?" He asked in a husky tone.

"I think it was the dark chocolate." I said as I lowered my mouth to first nibble on his breast then lower. His dick was thick, barely fitting into my mouth. I ran my tongue up and down its shaft, caressing his massive hairy balls with my other hand.

He grabbed me by the hair and yanked me roughly up to kiss him. He put his hands around my body, picked me up, and put me down under him hard. His passion was inflamed and so was his dick. I could feel it bang against me searching for the way into me. I spread my legs wider, and grabbing the shaft, I began to guide him into me, when he thrust in deeply. I gasped with the sudden pain and pleasure. He forced my mouth open and licked and kissed my mouth. I could taste the remnants of the espresso on his tongue, on his breath. The bed shook every time he withdrew his penis from my wet vagina, and then plunged in again and again. I had my hands on his ass, and could feel it rise and fall as he continued to pound me. He was moaning something in my ear that I couldn't understand, but the urgency in his words matched the thrusts of his thighs, slapping time and time again on my own. His former gentlemanly behavior turned lusty.

When I felt I could take no more, his weight crushing me, his hands rough on my body. His tongue deep in my mouth, he shuddered, and with a great gush, came inside me. I could feel him immediately leak out of me, dripping onto the sheets. I was completely immobilized, my muscles sore and paralyzed.
He collapsed on me. And I barely could slide out from beneath him. I could feel his body shudder, trying to regain his normal breathing. One hand caressed my leg. We lay there for a moment, and I must have drifted off to sleep as I awoke to him gently shaking my shoulder.

"Catherine. Time to get up. You're certainly not a kitty cat, but more like a wild tiger!"

I got up from the bed, straggled more like it, still feeling sore between my legs. I went into his bathroom and looked in the mirror.

"Oh God! I have the JBF'd look!" I said to Domenic as he wrapped his arms around me.

"JBF'd look?" He asked.

"Just been fucked! Look at my hair!"

"You look great. But you felt even better. I hope I wasn't too rough last night."

"Not at all. Now I know what it's like to have sex with a Grizzly bear."

"Ok Cat. You have just enough time to take a shower and grab some breakfast Maria is making for you. I'll call and tell the pilot to get the plane ready. An hour, okay?"

"Perfect, although I think just coffee for me please. Tell Maria I can't start the day off eating fifty pounds of food!"

Domenic laughed and kissed me on the cheek, and was about to leave and said "With your permission, I'll call my hotel in Palermo, and make a suite available to you as my guest, should you like to remain in Palermo for a few days."

"That'd be great." I said with a smile, but not sure if my pussy could take that kind of pounding two days in a row.

I was about to get into the shower when I heard my cell phone ring from the other room. Afraid it could be important, I closed the robe around my body, and hurried down to my room. I grabbed it just as it was going to voicemail.

"Hello?" I answered.

"Cat! I'm glad I got you" It was Antonio from Gucci. I had been working with him on the new line of Gucci watches. "Are you still in Rome?"

"No. Actually I'm in Sicily, but I'll be back in Palermo this afternoon. Why?"

"Well, I wondered if you would call your friend Anna in New York to see if she would like to fly to Rome to cover the unveiling of our new line of watches. Of course, we'll pay her airfare and hotel accommodations. By the way, if you don't mind my asking, Palermo? Sicily? In a day?"

"Anna would love it. I'll call her when I'm off the phone with you and make arrangements. As far as my travels... I told Antonio about my trip to Palermo, meeting the owner of the hotel, and the tour of the city that turned into an unscheduled flight to Sicily in a private jet."

"Jesus Christ." Antonio whispered. "Does this man have a name?"

"Sure. What kind of a girl do you think I am? Going to run off with a guy without even knowing his name?!" I teased. "It's Domenic Barone."

"Jesus Christ!" Antonio yelled. "What the fuck are you doing with him?! Do you even know who he is?!" His voice rose even louder.

"Antonio, with all due respect, please don't yell at me. I will see whomever I wish!" I barked back.

"For Christ's sake, Cat. He's the head of La Cosa Nostra! The fuckin' mob! Is he there now?"

"No, he's showering."

"Showering?!" Antonio sounded like he was coming apart. "Can you get out of there?"

"Well seeing as I am in a guarded compound with no car, probably not. I do know where a horse is though. Listen, slow down Antonio. Are you sure it's the same guy? I mean Domenic Barone *could* be a common name."

"Big guy. Owns a small, luxury hotel in Palermo, a compound in Sicily, and you go back and forth with a private jet, I think it's safe to assume you are with *the* Domenic Barone."

"Ok Listen to me. I have to hang up. We're leaving within the hour and I'll be back in Palermo later this morning. Once I get there, I'll sort things out. But I have to go back with him. He won't hurt me." She said remembering her tender and sore vagina. Antonio doesn't need to know that, she thought. "I'll call you when I land. Ciao."

I raced back to the shower, and this time hurriedly washed my hair and body. I changed into the clothes that I had worn on the flight to Sicily, and walked down the stairs to find Domenic and Maria waiting for me.

"Everything alright?" Domenic asked, sipping his cappuccino, evidently hearing my end of the phone call.

"Oh yeah. That was my sister. She's always getting involved with the wrong guy." I said, regretting the words as soon as they came out of my mouth.

"Your brothers will take care of it. That's how it would work in Sicily."

"Maybe she should move here." I said kissing his cheek and sipping my cup of cappuccino."I know she'd love the food. She can eat as much as my brothers."

"It would be an honor to have her. Are you ready to leave? The car will take us to the airport."

"Of course." I hugged Maria and thanked her profusely for the wonderful meals she made for me. I promised to send her a Gucci watch as a gift, but judging from her attire, a new housecoat might be more appropriate. I walked outside, and Domenic opened the door to the limo for me. I slid in making room for him to slide in and sit beside me.

I can't say what I was feeling. Domenic pulled out his cell phone and was speaking to someone, while I watched him. It was undeniable that he was a rich and powerful man. What was the likelihood that there were two Domenic Barone's? The man beside me had been nothing but a complete gentleman to me, not counting his animal passion, and that I had to admit, I aroused and invited.

We reached his private airport, and the plane was waiting for us, as promised. We boarded the plane, and took our seats. This time, instead of wine, the steward gave us American coffee. We declined food, and while Domenic made his phone calls, we made the short flight from Sicily to Palermo. The pilot taxied to the gate, as Domenic wrapped up his last call.

"I'm sorry I kidnapped you for the day, but I hope you enjoyed yourself. At least I was able to show you my lovely island."

"I had a wonderful time, but I think I put on five pounds." I blushed.

"You could use it." Domenic laughed. "My driver will take you to the hotel, and my assistant there has been instructed to give you every hospitality."

"And that's my story Mahjong Club. I only went back to the hotel to retrieve my belongings, and drove back to Rome."

"Why didn't you stay the night? It seemed like you enjoyed his company?" Susan asked.

"Work. I had a very high profile job with Gucci, and they couldn't have me seen with a mobster who was under investigation by the federal government. My career could have been ruined if Domenic was indicted and I was linked with him. Besides, I *was* attracted to him. What kind of a future could I have with him?"

"Whatever happened to him?" Priscilla asked.

"He disappeared. Completely. About two years after I met him. The Gucci family said either he disappeared to avoid prosecution, or someone made him disappear permanently, so he could never testify against them. I did send Maria that watch and a lovely Gucci scarf, but that was the last I ever heard from them."

"Our Cat having an affair with an Italian mob boss! Wow!" Anna said. "I had no idea. So that was the time I flew over to cover that story?"

"That's right." Cat answered.

I had some rough sex once." Susan said, as she dipped her finger into the cloud of whipped cream topping her zabaione, while smiling at the wide eyes of her friends.

"Whoa, girl! What's this?" Holly asked. "Rough sex? How rough?"

"Well hearing Cat's stories of her tumble in bed, brought to mind an experience I had once."

"Do *tell!*" Lori asked. "You *are* full of surprises Susan. I think you've had *way* more sexual escapades than Ashley-Fake-Tits!"

"Ok. Let me think about it for a moment." Once again Susan scooped up a tiny bit whipped cream from the top of her dessert with her fingers and slowly began to lick it off. She smiled like a Cheshire cat while keeping her friends in suspense.

"It was years ago. I wanted a solitary, lazy vacation up in Maine. I intended to eat, sleep, read and enjoy nature. I wasn't even going to bring a wrist watch. I didn't want to stay in a motel because they had little charm. Besides, it was winter and most motels were closed for the season. I checked a Maine Tourism Guide book, and found a rustic, little cabin for rent north of Camden. It was more inland than I have hoped for, but the price was right.

It had two bedrooms, a small living room, with, and get this, a bearskin rug that was made from a bear the owner shot, a screened in porch complete with rocking chairs, and a tiny kitchen. It wasn't heated, but it did have both a fireplace and a wood-burning stove. The owner had supplied a couple of cords of seasoned chopped wood for my use. It was small and perfect for my planned retreat.

I packed a couple of silly romance novels, stopped at a small local store and bought the food I thought I would need for the week, and, loaded up on Lay's potato chips and Hershey's dark chocolate. I only packed some warm, flannel L.L. Bean pajamas, some old heavy sweatshirts, and thermal socks since my feet were always cold. I wasn't planning to go dancing or eating at any upscale restaurants, if there even was such a thing north of Camden.

I drove up Interstate-93, only stopping at a Dunkin' Donuts for a coffee and a pound of ground coffee. I did enjoy my DD in the morning. The "siren song" of the honey-dipped donuts called to me, but with herculean effort I conjured up enough restraint to resist, and you know how much I love honey-dipped donuts!

The drive up was scenic and relaxing since there was little traffic on the road. When I arrived in Camden I stopped at the Camden Real Estate office and spoke to a realtor named Annie, who gave me the final directions to the cabin. She warned me that cell phone coverage was spotty in this area, but I shouldn't be concerned because there was a landline in the cabin. I drove the remaining hour and found the dirt road leading to the cabin. It was in the woods a little further than I imagined, and I did feel a twinge of nervousness. John, the owner, was there to greet me. He helped me bring in my groceries, and showed me how to operate the stove. He was thoughtful enough to leave me his friend's telephone number, should I need anything. He was heading up North to go bear hunting for the week, so I wouldn't be able to reach him.

We walked outside and startled a deer that was grazing in his yard. John told me I was apt to see deer come and go, and that they were harmless. He showed me the wood pile and on the screen porch, where he kept a stack of newspapers and kindling to start the wood stove. I assured him that while I wasn't skilled enough to shoot and skin a bear, I could easily manage making a fire.

The cabin had an abundant supply of candles and oil lamps in case there was a power outage. He mentioned that often times in the winter power lines would come down after a heavy snow. I remarked that being marooned here in a blizzard might be fun. He looked askance at me and I assumed my comment sounded ignorant to a native of Maine. With that, he took the rental fee, and walked out the door to his rusted and dented Ford pickup truck.

I watched him drive off then went back inside the cabin, and put on a pot of coffee. It was getting chilly in the cabin so I put some kindling and newspaper into the woodstove. Lighting that, I waited until the small wood caught, then put two larger pieces into the flames. I poured myself a cup of coffee, and went into the bedroom. The twin size bed has a suspicious crease in the center. When I sat on the edge of the bed, it threatened to swallow me up. I decided to check out the other bedroom. The mattress in the second bedroom looked even softer than the first. So I went back into the original bedroom, and pulled the mattress directly onto the floor. That appeared to solve the problem.

I went back into the kitchen, refilled my coffee cup and peeled back the wrapper on a Hershey's dark chocolate candy bar. I felt better already. Fetching a book out of my duffle bag, I walked out to the screen porch and sat on one of the rocking chairs with a pretty red and white quilt that was old but looked handmade, and pulled it up over my legs.

The doe that had been grazing in the yard, instinctively lifted her head, alerted by my presence. Apparently, she decided that a woman reading a book and eating a candy bar was not a threat. She wagged her white tail, and resumed foraging for vegetation.

I leaned back in my chair, and thought I really needed to do this more often. No radio, no TV, no neighbors. Just the towering evergreen pine trees and the mesmerizing silence of the woods. I snoozed a little in the chair, and when I woke up, the deer was gone. The sun was setting and I was getting hungry. I went into the kitchen to start dinner. The fresh air must have done wonders for my appetite because I was famished. I put a pot of water on the stove and turned up the burner. I added a pinch of salt, and when it began to boil, placed a large handful of wheat angel hair pasta into the bubbling water. I opened up a jar of store bought tomato sauce, gravy to you Cat, and opened a bottle of red wine."

"Why didn't you just shoot and eat the deer?" Holly asked.

"Oh, if you looked into those big brown eyes, you just couldn't!"

"Oh yeah, I could have. But continue. The fucking pasta cooking story is fascinating!"

"Screw you honey. It was. I'll see how *your* story is. So I cooked my spaghetti, mixed in the sauce, and almost ate the whole bowl."

"Well that figures. I mean with all that exercise! Opening the wrapper on a candy bar, taking a nap in the chair. Who wouldn't be hungry?" Holly teased.

"Yeah yeah. You should know better than anyone else, being from Maine. But I finished my dinner, just about finished the whole bottle of wine, and by then it was dark outside. I loaded up the wood stove, closed the damper a bit, and crawled into my bed on the floor. I read my cheesy novel with the help of my book light, but not for long. I was serenaded into a deep sleep by the wind whistling through the trees and an owl asking "Who? Who?" When I woke up in the morning, everything was covered in white. The fire had gone out..."

"Rookie." Holly added.

"I'm ignoring you Holly. The fire went out, so I went outside, shook the snow off a couple pieces of wood, getting the dry pieces in the middle, and started the fire again. I then put on a pot of coffee, and took a large, black cast iron frying pan from the pantry, put in a little tab of butter, and added six thick strips of bacon. When the bacon was cooked, I picked each piece out of the pan and put them on some paper towels to soak up some of the grease, then cracked open two eggs and added then into the already hot grease. I added a couple of pieces of wheat toast and sat at the little kitchen table to eat my breakfast and drink a cup of my Dunkin Donuts coffee.

After all that food, I decided I should take a walk and do a little exploring. I pulled on my boots and headed outside. There was more snow than I thought, maybe five inches and it was still coming down."

"If a guy had five inch cock, I'd throw him back and ask if he had a big brother." Cat said.

"Cat, you're getting as bad as Holly." Anna said.

So, I took a path that was easy to follow, and went for a walk in the woods. The thing I remember the most was how *quiet* it was. There weren't any sounds from cars or people talking. No flashing neon lights. I wasn't sure exactly how far I was from civilization, but I stuck close to the path. I sure as hell didn't want to get lost in the woods. So when I thought I had gone in deep enough, I turned around to head back. By now, the snow starting falling more heavily, and began to cover my tracks. By the time I made it back to the cabin, seven or eight inches of snow had accumulated.

"Ok. Eight inches. Now we're talking." Holly said.

My car was completely covered and I started to get concerned that I wouldn't be able to get out. I removed the snow brush I had in my trunk and began clearing the snow off my car. My hands were frozen after cleaning off my car, so I went inside and reheated the coffee, and wrapped my hands around the steaming mug.

John left some names to call if I got into trouble, so I found the name of a man that plowed driveways. I called his number and was lucky to catch him home. I told him I was staying at John's cabin, and he knew exactly where it was. Good thing, since I'm terrible at giving directions. I kept a vigil at the window, drinking my coffee, until he arrived. I was on my third cup when a pickup truck with ridiculously large tires and a bright yellow snow plow came up the driveway. He rolled down the window and asked "Are you the lady who needs to get plowed out?"

Looking inside the truck I saw this mountain of a man. A hairy beast. He had big meaty hands, and a full face with a mop of brown, unruly hair falling everywhere. His big, bushy brown beard covered half of his face. He was wearing a black and red plaid jacket with a matching hat, but no gloves. His eyes were deep-set and black. His hair was wet as if had just gotten out of the shower. Pieces of wood chips hung from his clothes, and split logs were in the back of his truck, covering a tarp.

"I have NO idea, why I responded this way, I'll never know, but I'm sure I could have qualified as a contestant in the "Ms. Slut of the Month" pageant. But I said "Yes. And when you're done plowing me, can you clean the snow off the driveway?"

"*You didn't!*" Priscilla said.

"Oh I did. I don't know why, but I did. It just slipped out. I think the cold weather may have short circuited some of my brain synapses.

"What happened?" Anna asked breathlessly.

At first he just looked at me, a little stunned, trying to understand if he heard me correctly. When I didn't clarify or deny, he leaned over and turned the key to shut off his truck. He got out of the driver's side door, and walked around to the side of the truck where I was standing. He was even bigger than I thought. Maybe 6 foot 6 inches? I could see a roll of fat hanging over his belt. His pants had pieces of wood chips stuck to them. He had on high, black rubber boots, with a green sole. He walked up to me, squinting at me with his beady eyes, and took me by my arm the way you might handle an unruly child. He marched me into the kitchen, and looking around and not letting go of my arm, walked me into the bedroom. He sat down on the mattress, which was now on the floor, taking me down with him. He pawed at my breasts while pushing me down on my back. I remember thinking "Just let him take control. Just let him take you." I felt an animal response to his gruffness. While he was pulling at my clothes, I had a vision of a caveman just taking a woman for his sexual pleasure, and it turned me on. He smelled wonderful. Like the Maine woods. He had the scent of pine trees and fresh cut grass. He managed to pull off my sweatshirt, and I helped him undo the buttons on my pants, but he wanted to pull them down himself. He first reached down and pulled my shoes off, tossing them into the bedroom wall. I felt myself getting aroused. He then pulled my pants off, and threw those over his shoulder. He pulled his own pants down, not even bothering to unbutton them or lower his zipper. His legs were a mass of brown curly hair. He started to mount me, but I squirmed away and pulled at his coat, which he was still wearing, and his dirty flannel shirt. He quickly yanked them off revealing a chest completely covered with hair. He had a roll of fat around his belly, and beneath that, an immense cock, straining upward. He pushed me down, but again I squirmed and licked his ear whispering, I want to taste you first. I sucked on his nipples, through his matted chest hair, and could taste his sweet salty sweat and outdoor pine body musk. I moved lower, nipping at his belly button with my teeth. I guess he couldn't take it much longer because he grabbed me by the side of my head with his two meaty hands and pushed me roughly down to his cock. I could barely wrap my hand around it. I began by licking his shaft, but he grabbed his dick and brought it to my lips. I opened my mouth, and swirling my tongue around its' enormous head, went down on him. He moaned and bucked, still holding my head tightly in his hands. He began to violently thrust himself my mouth, wrapping his fingers in my hair, helping me to go up and down on him. Before long, he filled my mouth with an enormous load of his sweet seed.

I fell down on his belly, my hair now being caressed by hands that first were so rough, now turned gentle.

All he could say was "Wow."

"And all I can say is wow!" Cat said. "Please tell me there is more."

"There is. So I'm lying on the floor, feeling kind of slutty ,I mean think about it, I didn't even know his *name,* but I was sated. It was an incredible experience. Just basic, raw sex between two, very horny people."

"Yeah, that Maine air will do that to you." Holly said.

So I finally ask this guy his name. He tells me it's Brownie, or at least that's what people call him, because he's as big as a brown bear. I don't know how big a brown bear is, but I bet it's just as hairy as this guy.

We lie there for awhile, then struggle to find our clothes, which have been scattered to the four walls, and managed to get dressed. At this point Brownie asks me if I'm hungry. By the look of his gut, this guy is always hungry. So I tell him that, yes I am. So here I am picturing getting into Brownie's truck and maybe going into Camden and sitting by a little ocean front table eating lobster and drinking white wine. Well, beer at least. Brownie doesn't look like the white wine kind of guy.

So I pick myself off the floor, dust myself off, and head for the bathroom. While I'm trying to run my fingers through my very messy and tangled hair. I crawl in the shower, not waiting for the hot water tank to do its job, and shower off in quite chilly water. It came out of the downspout in little more than a trickle. When I step out of the shower, I hear all kinds of commotion coming from the kitchen.

I walk all of the ten steps into the kitchen to find Brownie in front of the stove with the cast iron frying pan bellowing black smoke, filled with some kind of flour-covered meat cooking in grease. Next to it, was a pot bubbling with onions, carrots and potatoes. He turns towards me with a big grin and tells me he's cooking. No shit Tarzan, of the Maine woods. I see my lobster and white wine evaporate into thin air.

"Looks good Brownie. What is it?"

"Venison!" he proclaims excitedly. "I was going to save the loin for a special occasion, but I thought, Brownie, this is about the biggest special occasion *you'll* ever have! And you know it's the most tender cut of the deer!"

"Oh boy." I said trying to sound excited, and wondering how long this meat's been sitting in his truck.

He was done frying the venison, so he chose some of the smaller pieces and put it in with the vegetables, after he strained the water from them. He took down two metal camping plates from the shelf, and spooned the deer meat and vegetables on them. He handed one to me, then he sat down, and without a napkin on his knee or waiting for me, dug into the plate of food. He grunted as much eating as he did during sex. I watched him thinking underneath all that hair and muscle, he was really a charming little boy. With a big cock.

I speared one of the chunks of deer meat and put it into my mouth. It was delicious! I began to eat as enthusiastically as Brownie, until my plate was empty. Brownie gave a belch, and rubbed his stomach. I felt a belch coming myself, and rather than stifle it, as I would always do, I let it out loud and long. Brownie and I shared a long laugh, as I got up and opened two beers.
We walked outside and sat down on the porch to drink it. Brownie wasn't big on small talk, so we just drank in silence watching it slowly get dark. The deer that previously had been dining in the yard, evidently didn't want to end up on Brownie's dinner plate, and so was noticeably absent.

I asked Brownie if he would like to spend the night. He grinned and said that he would, but he had to hang his deer first. But he could do it here. I was puzzled, and asked him what the hell he was talking about.

"My deer! The one you've been eating. He's in the back of my truck."

"No way." I said, and got up to look for myself. Sure enough, the deer was under the tarp.

"I'll hang him from that tree over there. He'll be alright. I already gutted him you know."

"Of course you did Brownie. I took you for the kind of man who would *gut* his deer. Why don't you hang him up, and then come on in. I'll make a fire, and find something sweet for dessert."

"That sounds great!" I figured it would.

So Brownie hung his deer and spent the night. He was gentler than the last time, but he wanted to be on top of me. I had it in my mind, with him so big, it'd probably be better if I were on top. But he wasn't having any of that. He wasn't big into foreplay, just wanted to get inside and bang away, like I was going to disappear on him, or something. It was erotic in a different way. There were no untruths being said. No "I have to get up early in the morning." It was all about the sex, and I enjoy that *he* enjoyed being on top of me, completely taking me.

He stayed around for a few days, coming and going. I told him the door was open for him, and a few nights I went to bed only to wake up to his hairy body and erect cock. I got to like his Maine woodsy odor, and straight forward way. I did finally get my lobster and wine, but I shared it with a good book.

"And that's my Maine vacation story." Susan said.

"Shit. They should put your story in the tour books. More interesting than "Come up and eat Maine clams!" Holly said.

"Your right. It could read more like, "Women, come on up to Maine and feel a real log!" Cat laughed.

"Did Brownie ever, well you know, eat your clam?" Priscilla asked.

"Are you kidding? No! I think he'd skin and eat a woodchuck, but a pussy? No way!"

"Maybe you should have covered it in fur and told him you just shot it. He might munch on it then." Cat still laughing, said.

"Thanks Cat. I'll keep that in mind. But let me tell you girls, if I ever decided that I wanted to live deep in the Maine woods, Brownie would be my guy."

"I hear that, girlfriend."

"What do you girls want to do tonight?" Anna asked.

"Oh, I made reservations for us. But it's early yet." Holly answered.

"Who or what are we going to see?" Priscilla asked.

"It's a surprise." Holly said.

"Holly, I cannot believe you've haven't shared a *secret* story with us tonight. What gives? Are you holding out on us?" Cat wanted to know.

"No. I have a story for you guys. But it's b-o-r-i-n-g!"

"Holly. Nothing you do is boring" Cat pressed.

"I don't know. After hearing about the *Slut of Maine* story, most stories couldn't compare." Holly said.

"Ha! I surprised *you*? Isn't *that* something! This ol' gal really knew how to rock that lumberjack's world. They're probably still singing songs and writing poetry using me as their inspiration." Susan laughed. "Enough about me. Let's go Miss Holly. Time for your tale."

When I turned 30, I was in Chicago on business. I was alone, and feeling a tad blue about not having a significant other in my life. My meetings ended on Friday, and my birthday was the next day. I spent Friday afternoon walking down Michigan Avenue, otherwise known as the Magnificent Mile, daydreaming. I finally stopped in Celtic Crossings, an Irish Pub for dinner. I had lamb stew with soda bread. The Irish really know how to make a great lamb stew. It came in a bowl big enough for two, rich brown gravy, loaded with chunks of lamb and carrots, onions and potatoes with three thick slices of homemade soda bread on the side. I ordered a Guinness to complete my meal. I sat at the bar, not wanting to sit alone at a table that night. Normally it wouldn't bother me, but with the big 3-0 looming, I wanted to be surrounded by people.

There was a lively group of people at the bar. It seemed like some were friends and others were just getting acquainted. .

"Strangers are just friends you haven't met." Susan said.

"Oh Christ! Where did we get this girl?" Holly teased. So I'm at the bar, thinking that I might even come back the next evening. You never know. Pick up some red-headed Irishman, see where it goes. When the bartender came over to re-fill my glass, I asked him if there was anything special going on in town that weekend. He walked to the end of the bar, and took down a poster that had been hanging on the wall. He brought it to me, and said the annual American Cancer Fund charity event was going to be held the next evening at the swanky Drake Hotel. He said the event typically included dinner and an auction. The price of the ticket was two hundred and fifty dollars, which included a dinner buffet. Probably rubber chicken, but what do you want for two-fifty? Some of the most eligible bachelors in the Windy City were going to be auctioned off. There were a few sports figures, a television personality, a few socialites, you get the picture. The auction was called *Slave for a Night.* If you successfully won the bid, the men could take you out for dinner, or perhaps if they cooked, prepare a meal for you and a few friends at your home. I thought it would be the perfect way to spend my birthday. I asked the bartender if I could still get a ticket at this late date, and to my surprise, he had a few unsold tickets at the pub. So now, at least, I had my birthday plans arranged. I polished off my stew, had one more beer and fought off the unwanted advances from some very drunk men.

On Saturday morning, I went for a run along Lake Shore Drive. Lake Michigan looked pristine and calm. The air feels cool along the lake during every season, but it's so invigorating.. . . well maybe not in January. I ran thinking about my plans for the night and decided that I should buy something new to wear. After my run, I went shopping at Marshall Fields and picked out a pretty, but conservative, navy blue dress with white piping, that fell just above my knees. Of course, I had to buy get a new pair of shoes to go with my dress. After trying on several pairs of pumps, I settled on a pair of Christian Louboutin midnight blue suede stilettos. At first I thought the heels might be too high if I was going to be spending time mingling in the crowd, but then I thought 'what the hell'. After all, this was a high-end event that was likely to attract some very influential people, and I couldn't look shabby now, could I?

"As if we need a reason to buy more shoes." Priscilla said.

Satisfied with my selections, I left the store and headed back to the hotel. I stopped at a little French bistro on the way back to my hotel and had a Cobb salad. Even though it was a Saturday and technically not a work day, it was very crowded and I had to share a table with a lovely older woman. I told her that I was planning to attend the charity auction that evening, but neglected to tell her that it was my birthday. Since she appeared to be in her fifties, I didn't think she would have much sympathy if I were to whine about turning thirty. Instead I dragged out my shopping bags and showed her my new purchases. One thing about women, we *all* like to shop, no matter how old we are!

Chatting with her, I got the surprise of my life. Guess what this sweet older lady did for work?"

"She was a hooker!" Lori yelled out, as if it was a game show contest.

"An exotic dancer! Like on poles?" Cat followed.

"No, no, no." I said. "She was a fish and game warden. Here's this sweet lady, in her fifties, and she's a game warden! I mean, she does it all. Hunts, fishes, traps. She's been doing it all her life. It just goes to show you, that you can't judge a book by its cover."

"Isn't that the truth?" Anna said. "Looking at us, I think most people, especially men, would be shocked to hear *our* stories. They look over at us, and see six, older women, dressed well, no tattoos, at least I don't think we have any tattoos. But we have Cat here making love to the Black Knight on a grassy field, and screwing a mob boss, our little Susan here, playing Mrs. Robinson, and Priscilla sleeping with the rich and powerful in our nation's capital."

"So true." Cat reflected.

"So," Holly said continuing," We ended up having a lot in common, with my growing up in Maine. We talked about guns, best fishing lures, whether or not deer were really colorblind. It was a fascinating lunch. We of course, exchanged cards, and even talked about going hunting together someday.

When lunch was over, I went back to my hotel, and made some last minute business calls. I managed to arrange a few meetings for the following week and returned some voice mail messages. I showered and relaxed. I lounged in my fluffy robe, polished my fingernails in OPI Big Apple red, and read a magazine while I waited for them to dry.

I was excited about this gala. It sounded like a lot of fun and I believed it was a worthwhile cause. At six o'clock, I decided to just get dressed. I thought I looked understated, but elegant in my new ensemble.

The doorman hailed a cab for me. Traffic was light and the driver chatty, before I knew it, he was pulling up to the

Drake Hotel. I certainly wasn't the first one to arrive. There were cabs and private cars lined up, waiting to drop off their occupants. As I watched the crowd enter the hotel, I thought I may have been underdressed. Some of the men were wearing tuxedos, but most were wearing dark suits. The women out-numbered the men by ten to one. It was a mixed crowd, age wise, but financially, I'd guess most of the people were pretty well off. The older women wore heavily beaded gowns, but the women in my age group were wearing cocktail dresses. I was glad I wore my double strand of Tahitian pearls with the gold clasp and matching 9mm stud earrings. They always made me feel sophisticated and unforgettable.

My taxi finally made it to the entrance, and a doorman gallantly opened my door with a flourish. I disembarked and made my way inside. The atmosphere was charged with excitement, and unlike me, most people knew one another.

I made my way to the bar, which had a line six people deep. Everyone was trying to get the bartenders attention to order a drink. The bachelors who were being auctioned off were also in the bar. They sported bright name tags that identified them by name and provided a short bio. The women surrounded them, grabbing their arms. When one of the guys lurched forward, I assumed someone in the crowd had pinched his butt. All the men were attractive, some more so than others, but all had a unique quality.

There were black men, white guys, some Asians and some of indeterminate ethnic backgrounds.

I walked around, peeking over shoulders, making mental notes on which one I might like to place a bid. The men were obviously enjoying the attention lavished upon them, and someone said they had a private betting pool to see which guy would command the highest price.

I managed to slide into the bar and ordered a double of Johnnie Walker Blue Label, gave the bartender a generous tip and a wink, hoping he'd take my next drink order promptly. Holding my scotch, I entered the ballroom and handed my ticket to the women at the door.

The ballroom had the ambience of a high school dance. The organizers must have thought that happy, drunk people would give more than sober, serious ones. Members of the Cancer Society were distributing pamphlets and posters hung from the wall, but there was no question, that the women were there for the "beef cake" auction.

There wasn't any assigned seating, so I chose a seat midway from the stage and against the wall where I had a good view of both the men and the crowd. A woman took the stage and gave a speech about the importance of cancer research, and urged the audience to be generous in their bids. The crowd was getting restless, making it clear that they wanted the auction to begin, so she turned the microphone over to the voluptuous auctioneer. She got the crowd yelling and hooting, as if they weren't in a hotel ballroom, but a strip club in Western Kentucky. There were programs on each table listing the names and a short bio of the men being auctioned, and with that she invited the men to come out from behind the heavy velvet curtains on the stage.

Some of the men were dressed in suits, some casual, and a couple of them wore nothing but Speedos. Evidently, they had the most money wagered on the betting pool, thinking being half naked would fetch the highest price.

The auctioneer introduced the first man, a light skinned black guy, who wore a blue pinstriped suit, which he filled out very nicely.

"Who'll start the bidding off at five hundred dollars?' She bellowed.

"Five hundred!" Came the response from four different tables.

"Okay then ladies, who'll give me a thousand?" She now asked.

Two women yelled "I will!"

When the bidding stopped, a rather large woman in a bright yellow dress waved her numbered card excitedly. The man, whom she successfully won, at a price of twelve hundred dollars, looked a little chagrined. They wasted no time in bringing out the second man. He was a stark contrast to the first. He looked like a banker, pale, with horn-rimmed glass, and thinning hair. He stood nervously as he was introduced, and probably wanted to die, when no one bid the first five hundred. The auctioneer cajoled the crowd and lowered the bid to get it started at two hundred and fifty. With that, a few women entered the bidding, and when it was all done, he fetched a respectable thousand dollars. He definitely breathed a sigh of relief.

The next man was wearing a Speedo. I had to admit he had a nice body, tall and lean, like a swimmer. He had hypnotic brown eyes, and a full head of wavy brown hair. He smiled for the crowd and pranced around, blowing kisses to the ladies in the front row. He obviously thought he was the night's grand prize..

I yelled out "Ten dollars!" and his prancing stopped. The ladies laughing just increased the red crawling up his neck onto his face.

"Now now," the auctioneer said, "this fine specimen should surely bring more than ten dollars?"

Another woman joining in with my humor yelled out "Twelve dollars!"

The auctioneer looked over to me as if to say "Now look what you started." When I yelled out "Two thousand dollars!" The audience gasped, trying to figure out if I was still joking, or had indeed placed the largest bid of the night. A woman at a nearby table, scowled at me, and probably assumed that I had reached my bidding limit.

Smirking at me, she yelled out her bid. "Twenty-Five hundred dollars!"

The room quieted at the unexpected drama. I looked over at my competitor. She was older, hair done perfectly, and no doubt went to a salon that day. She was wearing a formal gown and was draped in antique gold jewelry. She was sitting with a man I presumed to be her husband. He was small and wiry, bespectacled in large glasses that were too big for his face, and had the look of a man emasculated by his wife. He shrunk lower in his seat as unwanted stares were directed at them.

"Three Thousand Dollars", I said in an even voice, looking at the other woman bidding against me and not the auctioneer.

"Five Thousand Dollars!" the other woman countered. The man on the stage wasn't sure what to think. At first, he looked happy at the record sum, but then uncomfortable at what had become a hostile bidding war.

Calmly, I looked over at the woman and smiled. The room was fixated on me. Was I going to bid higher, or accept defeat from this woman who was clearly out to win this young man. I brought my scotch to my lips, enjoying the moment. The crowd was dead silent, waiting in anticipation for my response.

In a clear voice, but in an even tone I said, "Ten Thousand Dollars."

Now, the crowd erupted. The man onstage fist-bumped and slapped hands with the other men on the stage. The crowd whistled and cheered.

"I have ten thousand dollars. Do I have any other bids? The crowd turned to the other bidder who appeared to be in utter shock. Her husband was slowly turning his head back and forth at being thrust into this drama. The woman flipped her hand, dismissing any other bids, but her humiliation was obvious.

"Sold to the lady in blue for ten thousand dollars. I sure hope he's a good cook." she said.

"Oh, he doesn't have to be. That's why there's room service." I replied. I motioned for the man to join me at the table. He had a wide, questioning smile as he sat down. I wrote out a check for ten thousand dollars, and beginning his training, I said "Now be a good boy and bring this to that lady sitting over there. Then go the bar and please get me another drink."

The auction continued, but when I looked over trying to find the woman with whom I had competed, she had left the ballroom. Greg, that was his name, brought my drink and asked me if I wanted him to cook for me, or would I prefer to have him take me to dinner.

"For ten thousand dollars, do you think I want to waste time watching you cook me a steak? You're the steak, Greg."

I looked him up and down as men often to do women, with the same result. I don't think he liked my appraising stare.

"Oh no, Greg. This is my last night in Chicago, and I plan to enjoy the rest of my evening being a little more adventurous. Let's go, big guy."

I led Greg by the hand, which stopped the bidding on the next man, as the crowd watched us walk out of the ballroom. I started to walk toward the front door, to where the cabs where parked, then realized that Greg was only wearing a Speedo.

"That was your choice, buddy. You can come back later, and pick your clothes up when I'm done with you."

We walked outside and took the first cab in line to my hotel. I walked my birthday present to the front desk, and had them send up a bottle of champagne and two glasses, not bothering to ask Greg what he wanted to drink. Needless to say, we captured quite a few stares on the way while we walked through the lobby. By now, Greg was feeling very uncomfortable in his Speedo, and evidently his manhood was as well, diminishing greatly in size.

"You should have put a sock down there to account for shrinkage, Greg." I said laughing. "I'm beginning to think I overpaid for you."

"I can't believe this is happening." He replied weakly.

"What? You're a high priced hooker. Men do it to women all the time. Now hush up. I didn't pay for conversation."

We got off the elevator and walked down the hall to my room. We passed a middle aged couple. The woman grinned at me, like I bagged a lion while on an African safari. The man just shook his head at Greg.

"Bought him off the street." I couldn't help saying in jest.

I had Greg open the door for me, and we walked into my room. Luckily, I chose a room with a large Jacuzzi tub. The room service arrived at the same time with my champagne.

"Greg, please be a dear and open the champagne then draw me a bath. And lose the Speedo."

He just stared at me, wondering if was having a nightmare and couldn't wake up.

"You want me naked?"

"Ah you're a bright boy. Strip off. I just want to see you wait on me naked. For now, that is."

Greg slowly stripped off his Speedo, obviously uncomfortable. His manhood retreated inside of his pubic hair.

"Hmm. Not a lot for ten thousand."

Greg turned, shaking his head, and opened the champagne with a loud pop. He then poured me a glass, and as instructed went into the bathroom to draw my tub. I could hear the water running, so I took the opportunity to put on an oversized men's t-shirt that I liked to wear when I wanted to be comfortable. And I was comfortable.

I went back out into the living room and called for Greg to sit down beside me.

"Pour yourself a glass of champagne honey. Don't be shy. Think of the stories you can tell your children. That is," as I looked down at his privates, "if you can have any."

"You're really enjoying teasing me, aren't you?" Greg said, finally relaxing a bit.

"Well you guys have no problem teasing us ladies. How about a joke that's popular with men, I'm sure you heard it.

How do you cure a nymphomaniac?

You marry her!

"So the shoes on the other foot here, my friend. Let this be a teachable moment. Now grab the champagne and let's go in the jacuzzi. Greg was definitely relaxing now judging by the growth of his manhood. We slipped into the hot bubbly water.

"Greg, soap and wash my back."

"With pleasure boss." He soaped up my back and shoulders, and began to rub the muscles in my back and neck. When I moaned, he slid his hands down lower to my breasts.

"Excuse me? I'll let you know when I want you. *If* I want you." With my back facing him, I know he couldn't see the grin on my face. Perhaps he heard it in my voice. I turned and splashed soapy water in his face, then pulling his head to mine, kissed him hard on the mouth, then just as quickly, pushed him away.

"Now get back to work." I commanded. Ah yes, I could get used to having a man servant! By the time the water in the Jacuzzi cooled, I'd had enough playing scrubba-dub-dub, and stepped out of the bath. Greg just looked at my naked body, not knowing what the hell to do.

"You may get out of the tub, and get a bath towel and dry me off."

Greg jumped up, sloshing water on the floor. He pulled a bath towel off the rack and very slowly began to pat me dry.

"Harder." I said.

He began to rub the towel harder, over my shoulders, back and arms, and then hesitated when he came to my breasts, not wanting to be chastised again.

"Don't forget my breasts and private parts."

He carefully began to dry my breasts, and both my nipples and his cock began to get hard. I spread my legs, giving him access to my womanhood, and I must say, he was gentle with the towel. When he was done, I said "Now you may pick me up and carry me to bed. No wait. I want a piggyback ride instead!"

Greg laughed and bent over so I could clamor up on his back.

"Good horsy!" I yelled. "To the bed! To the bed!"

He twirled me around, and I nuzzled my face in his neck. His soft brown hair was in my face. I nipped at his neck and ran my tongue along his ear. He made it to the bed in record time, and when I began to lean over and dismount, I pulled him down on me.

"You don't need to know the details, but let me just say I had him please me in every way I wanted before I freed him from his servitude the next morning. It was ten thousand well spent." Holly concluded. At that moment, Holly's cell phone rang and she answered it, thanking the person on the other end of the line.

"Okay ladies, our ride is here." Holly said.

"Where are we going?" Susan asked.

"It's a surprise, remember? Anna reminded her.

"Oh God. Here we go again." Lori muttered.

"I love Holly surprises!" Cat said.

Anna summoned the waiter over and signed the check for the party, billing it to the room. She left a generous tip and thanked the wait staff profusely for the great service they received. With that, the ladies got up from the table and followed Holly out to the lobby. A chauffeur, dressed elegantly in black, was waiting for them, holding up the all too familiar placard saying *The Mahjong Club.*

"Oh boy! I love surprises!" Cat said.

"I don't know." Anna said looking suspiciously at Holly.

Holly, giving nothing away, said "C'mon ladies. It's Saturday in Vegas! Let's have some fun!"

So the six ladies piled into the limo. Holly popped open the bottle of champagne awaiting them, and with a lurch, the driver drove off. They drove down the strip, still bustling with party goers and gamblers, sightseers and tourists. They continued well beyond the dazzling lights of Vegas and onto a smaller road heading into the desert.

"Are we going to see the Hoover Dam? I hear it's pretty at night." Susan said.

"Could be." Holly answered.

"Yeah right. The Hoover Dam. Holly's big surprise is to rent a limo and take us to the Hoover Dam at *night.*" Priscilla wasn't buying it.

Cat turned up the stereo in the limo and got everyone dancing in their seats. The limo driver looked back and just shook his head, smiling. Another group of wild women in Vegas. While the ladies danced, the driver proceeded to the surprise destination.

The windows of the limo were so heavily tinted that when he arrived, the ladies could not see out clearly. Holly pushed the button to roll down the window.

"No way! No way! No way!" Anna said.

"Oh my GOD!" Cat shrieked.

"You have GOT to be kidding me!" Lori said.

"I'm not sure I'm getting out of the limo!" Susan said.

"I'm not sure this works for me." Priscilla said.

The driver opened the door to the limo. He had pulled into an old, wooden corral. There was a large area off to the side with fenced in horses, braying and kicking their heels. A smaller shed housed bales of hay, stacked high, one upon another. Some other cars and limos where parked inside the fence as well.

The ladies looked up at the sign that was hung from the building, with awe and shock.

The ladies looked at one another, and then walked through the gate.

WELCOME TO THE STALLION RANCH

THE PREMIER MALE STUD FARM FOR WOMEN.

The End

for now.

www.ingramcontent.com/pod-product-compliance
Lightning Source LLC
Chambersburg PA
CBHW071247170626
46809CB00001B/103